NO DEALS, MR. BOND

Other James Bond Books by John Gardner

Nobody Lives Forever
Role of Honor
Icebreaker
For Special Services
License Renewed

Also by John Gardner

The Secret Generations

NO DEALS, MR. BOND

John Gardner

G. P. Putnam's Sons
New York

G. P. Putnam's Sons
Publishers Since 1838
200 Madison Avenue
New York, NY 10016

Library of Congress Cataloging-in-Publication Data

Gardner, John E.
No deals, Mr. Bond.

I. Title. II. Title: No deals, Mister Bond.
PR6057.A63N58 1987 823'.914 86-25271
ISBN 0-399-13254-6

Printed in the United States of America
3 4 5 6 7 8 9 10

To my good friend Tony Adamus, with thanks.

Contents

1

Seahawk

The navigation officer, like so many of his Royal Navy counterparts, was known affectionately as Vasco. In the red glow of the submarine's control room he now quietly leaned over and touched the captain's arm.

"Coming up to RV, sir."

Lieutenant Commander Alec Stewart nodded. "Stop all. Planes midships."

"All stopped," came back from the watchkeeper.

"Planes midships," answered the senior of the pair of planesmen, who sat strapped into their seats, like pilots, in front of depth and turn indicators, their hands on the yokes which operated the hydroplanes that controlled the submarine's depth.

"Sonar?" the captain asked quietly.

"Distant activity around Bornholm Island, usual heavy stuff in and out of Rostock, two targets that sound like small patrol boats distant, up the coast at around fifty miles, bearing Zero-Two-Zero. No submarine signatures."

Lieutenant Commander Alec Stewart raised an eyebrow.

He was not a happy man. For one thing, he did not like operating his Trafalgar Class nuclear submarine in forbidden waters. For another he did not like "funnies."

He only knew they were called funnies because he had read it in a novel. In other jargon he would have called them "spooks," or maybe simply spies. Whatever they were, he did not like having them aboard, even though the leader held a Naval rank.

During wargames, Stewart had performed facsimile covert ops, but the real thing, and in peacetime, stuck in his throat.

To begin with, when the funnies had come aboard, he thought the Naval rank was simply part of a cover, but within a few hours he realized that Seahawk, as their leader was cryptonymed, knew a great deal about the sea—as did his two companions.

That fact did not reduce Stewart's annoyance. It was all too cloak-and-dagger for his liking. It was also far from easy work. The orders had been explicit and precise: *You will afford Seahawk and his companions every assistance. You will run silent and submerged, making all possible speed, to the following RV.* This was a latitude and longitude that, after a quick glance at the charts, confirmed Stewart's worst fears—a point some fifty miles along the small strip of East German coast, sandwiched between West Germany and Poland, and around five miles offshore. *At the RV, you will stand by, remaining submerged, under the direct orders of Seahawk. On no account will you disclose your presence to any other shipping, especially DDR or Russian naval units that operate out of nearby ports. On reaching the RV, it is probable that Seahawk will wish to leave the boat, together with the two officers accompanying him. They will use the inflatable they have brought with them, and after their departure you will submerge to periscope depth and await their return. Should they not return after three hours, you will make your way back to base, still running silent and submerged. If Seahawk's mission is successful he will probably return with two extra people. You will afford them every possible comfort, returning to base as instructed above. Note, this operation is covered by the Official Secrets Act. You will impress upon all members of your crew that they will not talk about the operation—either among themselves, or to others. An Admiralty team will debrief you, personally, upon your return.*

Damn Seahawk! Stewart thought. The submarine's destination was not the easiest place to reach undetected: under the North Sea, up the Skagerrak, down the Kattegat, skirting the Danish and Swedish coasts, through the narrow straits—always a tricky navigational exercise—and out into the Baltic for a final fifty-odd miles. Then inland into waters that undeniably belonged to the DDR—East Germany—crawling with Eastern Bloc shipping, not to mention Russian submarines from bases at Rostok and Stralsund.

"Periscope depth." Stewart muttered the order, observing the quiet atmosphere of the silent-running mode of the boat.

The planesmen caressed their aircraftlike yokes, bringing the submarine up slowly from its 250 feet below the water, then gently eased off.

"Periscope depth, sir."

"Up periscope."

The solid tubular structure hissed upward, and Stewart slammed the handles down, flicking on the night-vision switch and doing one complete circuit of 360 degrees. He could just pick up the coastline—bleak and flat. Nothing else. No lights or ships. Not even a fishing boat.

"Down periscope."

He knocked the handles up, took two steps across the control room to the radio array, and picked up the internal broadcast microphone, switching it on with his thumb and speaking in almost a whisper: "Seahawk to the control room, please."

Up in the fore-ends, surrounded by red-marked safety equipment, just behind a bank of torpedo tubes in the only space available for passengers, Seahawk and his two companions heard the captain's voice as they lay on makeshift bunks, four feet above the deck.

Already, having had plenty of warning prior to the approach to the RV, they were kitted out in black rubber diving suits, each with waterproof holsters attached to his belt, while the cumbersome folded inflatable had been unstowed and now lay within reach.

Seahawk swung his feet onto the metal deck and, without undue haste, made his way abaft to the control room.

Only those inside that magic, confined, inner circle of specialists that is the global intelligence community would have recognized Seahawk as Commander James Bond. His companions were members of the elite Naval Special Boat Squadron—officers known for their discretion and often used by the Service to which Bond owed his allegiance.

Stewart looked up as Bond stooped to enter the control room.

"We've got you here on time."

His manner showed no particular deference, merely a taut professionalism.

Bond nodded. "Good. In fact, we're about an hour early, which gives us a little leeway." He glanced at the stainless-steel Rolex on his left wrist. "Can you let us go in about twenty minutes?"

"Yes. How long will it take you?"

"I presume you'll surface only partially, so just enough time to get the inflatable blown and paddle out of your downdraught. Ten, fifteen minutes?"

"And we use only the radio signals, as instructed?"

"Three Bravos from you for danger. Two Deltas from us when we need you to resurface and take us aboard again. We'll use the exit hatch for'ard of the sail, as arranged. No problem there, I trust?"

"It'll be slippery on the casing, particularly on return. I'll have a couple of ratings out to assist."

"And a rope. A ladder for preference. As far as I know, our guests haven't had any experience boarding submarines at night."

"Whenever you're ready."

"Right, we'll get shipshape, then." Bond turned and made his way back toward the pair of Special Boat Squadron officers—Captain Dave Andrews, Royal Marines, and Lieutenant Joe Preedy, Royal Marines.

Quickly, they went over the drill again. They

lugged the inflatable paddles and the small lightweight engine back toward the metal ladder that would take them to the forward hatch, and from there to the casing and the cold wetness of the Baltic.

Two ratings in oilskins already waited for them, and the entire party stood at the foot of the ladder—one of the ratings ready to scramble up as soon as the order came.

In the control room, Lieutenant Commander Stewart had taken another quick look around through the periscope, and, as it was lowered, gave the order to surface to casing and black light. As the second command was obeyed, the interior of the boat became completely dark but for the glow of instruments in the control room, and the occasional flicker of a heavily shaded red torch. One such was carried by the rating at the foot of the ladder. He began to move quickly up the rungs until the soft voice came from the communications speakers: "Casing surfaced!"

There was a slight clang as the man turned the wheel unlocking the forward hatch; then fresh air poured in, like cold water, from the small open circle above them.

Joe Preedy was first up the ladder, assisted by the dimmed red glow of the torch held by the rating below. Dave Andrews—partway up the ladder—took one end of the inflatable from Bond, hauling it up to Preedy, and together the two men heaved the bulky thick rubber lozenge up onto the casing.

Bond followed them, the rating below him passing up the paddles and the heavily classified lightweight engine. Easy to handle, with small propeller blades, the IPI, as the engine is known, can run effectively, with little noise, on a fuel supply contained in a self-sealing tank that is a standard part of the rear section of the inflatable.

Finally Bond ran the air tube up to Preedy, and, by the time he reached the dark slippery metal of the casing, the inflatable had become its true self—a long, slim, low cutter, complete with bucket seats and hand grabs.

Bond checked that the two-way radio was firmly attached to his wet suit and balanced himself on the casing while the two SBS men launched the inflatable, the rating holding a line from the shallow rounded bow until the paddles and IPI were transferred. Bond then slid from the casing, taking his place in the stern. The rating let go of the line for'ard, and the inflatable was jerked away from the submarine.

They allowed the little craft to drift clear while Bond took a quick compass reading. Then he set the luminous compass—still attached to a lanyard around his neck—onto the plastic well in front of him, and, using his paddle as rudder, he gave the order to make way.

They paddled with long steady strokes, fighting the choppy sea but moving the little boat with speed through the inky blackness. After two minutes, Bond checked their course and, as he did so, heard the hiss of water as the submarine submerged again.

Around them the night merged with the sea, and it took almost half an hour of strong paddling, combined with a constant checking of the compass, before they could distinguish the coastline of the DDR. It was going to be a long pull to the shore, but if all went well they would use the engine for a quick sprint back to the sub's position.

An hour and a quarter later they were within striking distance of the coast, right on course, for Bond could see the inlet, free of rocks with a tiny spit of sand, light against the surrounding darkness. They allowed the craft to drift in, alert and ready, for they were now at their most vulnerable.

Andrews, in the stern, raised his unshaded torch and flashed two fast Morse code Vs toward the small stretch of sand. The answer was returned immediately, four long flashes.

"They're here," Bond muttered.

"I only hope they're on their bloody own," grumbled Preedy, and they allowed the inflatable to drift inland, grinding onto the beach—Andrews leaping into the water and holding the bow rope to steady the craft as two dark shapes came running to the foaming water's edge.

"Meine Ruh' ist hin." Bond felt a shade stupid quoting Goethe—a poet of whom he had little knowledge—in the middle of the night on a deserted, dangerous East German beach: "My peace is gone."

"Mein Herz ist schwer." The answer came back from one of the figures on the beach, completing the couplet—"My heart is heavy."

The three men helped the pair on board and had them quickly seated amidships, while Andrews hauled on the for'ard rope to bring the inflatable around as Bond set the reciprocal course on the compass. Within seconds they were paddling out again. In thirty minutes they would start the engine and give the first signal to the waiting submarine.

Back in the control room of the sub, the sonar operator had been monitoring their progress via a small short-distance signaling device installed in the inflatable. At the same time he swept the surrounding area, while his partner did the same on a wider scale.

"Looks as though they're coming back, sir," the senior sonar operator muttered.

"Let me know when they start their engine." Stewart had no idea what the funny business was about, and he really did not want to know. All he hoped for was the safe return of his passengers—and whomever they brought with them—followed by an even safer, undetected run home to base.

"Aye-aye sir, I think . . . Oh, Christ . . ." The sonar operator stopped short as the signal came loud into his headphones and the blip appeared on his screen. "They've got company." His voice resumed its professional tone. "Bearing Zero-Seven-Four. He's coming from behind the headland on their starboard side. Fast and light, I think it's a Pchela."

Stewart swore aloud, something he rarely did in front of his crew. A Pchela was a Russian-built patrol hydrofoil, and though now elderly, carrying two pairs of 13mm machine guns and the old Pot Drum search radar, these craft were formidable in both inshore water and choppy seas—fast, and using a shallow depth foil.

"It's a Pchela signature, sir, and he's locked on to them, closing rapidly," from the sonar operator.

In the inflatable they heard the heavy thrum of the patrol boat's engines almost as they left the shore, pulling away with the paddles.

"Use the engine? Make a run for it?" Dave Andrews shouted the questions back at Bond.

"Never make it." Bond knew what would have to be done, and didn't like to contemplate the consequences. He was spared making any decision by Andrews, who leaned back and shouted, "Let him come abreast and be ready for the bang. Don't wait up for me. I'll make my way back overland providing the limpet doesn't get me!" He was quickly over the side, disappearing into the sea.

Bond knew that Andrews carried two small limpet charges that, if placed properly, would blow holes directly into the fuel tanks of the hydrofoil. He also knew they would probably blow the SBS man to pieces as well.

At that moment the searchlight hit them, and the patrol craft appeared to bleed off speed, settling on her bows, off the long foils—a skilike structure—that ran under her hull.

The strong pool of light hit the inflatable, dazzling them, and a voice came loud over the closing gap of water, carried by a loudhailer and speaking in German— "Halt! Halt! We are taking you on board so that you can state your business. This is a military order. If you do not stop we will open fire on you. Heave to!"

"Raise your arms above your heads," Bond commanded. "Show yourselves to be unarmed, and do as you're told. There will be an explosion. When it happens drop your heads between your knees . . ."

"And kiss your arse goodbye," Preedy muttered.

". . . and cover your heads with your arms."

The patrol boat was low in the water now, engines

at idle as she drifted in toward the inflatable, the searchlight unwavering.

The gap closed to almost fifty yards before Andrews' mines did their work.

The bows of the patrol boat suddenly disappeared in a blinding white flame turning to crimson. The explosion came a second after the flash—a great ripping crump, followed by a deeper roar.

Bond, who had ducked his head at the first flash, now raised it to see that Andrews had set the mines in perfect position. He would, Bond thought. Any good SBS man would have known the exact position for maximum effect on all Russian or Eastern Bloc craft, but this had been exceptionally well done. The boat had already tipped back by the stern. Fire ran its entire length, and the bows with their distinctive foils rose well out of the water as down she went—all in less than a minute.

The inflatable had been affected by the blast, blown sideways to skid over the water and spin like a child's toy. Bond reached down for the lightweight engine, which they had already attached to its fuel line. He lifted it over the stern, pressing the ignition button. The little IPI buzzed into life, the propeller blades whirling. Holding its grab handle, Bond pushed the engine down into the water, then leaned back and manipulated the machine so that it acted as propellant and rudder alike.

The whole area was now illuminated by the flames from the doomed patrol boat. Half a dozen queries went through Bond's mind—had the patrol already alerted other vessels along this closely guarded stretch of coast? Was the inflatable even now locked on to a land-based radar system, or another fast ship? Had Dave Andrews got clear after setting the limpets? Doubtful. Would their submarine have gone deep, preparing to crawl out to avoid detection? That was certainly a possibility, for a nuclear sub was more precious to its captain than Operation Seahawk. He thought on these things as Preedy shouted back corrections, using his own compass to guide them. "Starboard two points. Port a point. No. Port. Keep turning port. Midships. Hold it there . . ."

Bond struggled to control the inflatable's progress by heaving on the engine, which seemed to be trying to pull itself free from his grip. It took all his strength to keep the little craft moving on course, amid constant demands from Preedy to alter to port, then starboard, as they bounced heavily on the water, crashing down, then up again, with the stern low and bows lifting.

He felt spray and wind in his face, and in the final dying light of the patrol boat's last seconds he saw their two passengers, hunched together, huddled in anoraks and tight woolen caps. You could tell by the set of their shoulders that they were terrified. Then, as suddenly as the hydrofoil had ignited and lit the deep black waters, the darkness descended again.

"Half a mile. Cut the engine!" Preedy shouted from the bow.

Now they would know. Any minute they would discover if their mother ship had deserted them or not.

Back in the submarine's control room, Stewart

had witnessed the death of the hydrofoil. He wondered if Seahawk and his companions had perished in the explosion, and decided to give them four minutes. If sonar did not pick them up by then, he had to go deep and silent, preparing to edge his way out of the forbidden waters.

Three minutes and twenty seconds later, sonar said he had them. "Heading back, sir. Going fast. Using their engine."

"Prepare to surface low. Receiving party to for'ard hatch."

The order was acknowledged. Then, "Half a mile, sir," from the sonar operator.

Stewart wondered at his own folly. All his instincts told him to get out while they remained undetected. Damn Seahawk, he thought. Seahawk? Bloody silly. Wasn't it the title of an old Errol Flynn movie?

The radio operator heard the two Morse code Ds, clear in his headphones, just as Bond transmitted them from the now almost stationary inflatable. "Two Deltas, sir."

"Two Deltas," replied Stewart with little enthusiasm. "Surface to casing. Black light. Recovery party clear for'ard hatch."

When the Seahawk party had been pulled on board and slithered down the ladder—Preedy last, after ripping the sides of the inflatable and setting the charge that would destroy the craft underwater leaving no trace—Stewart submerged, going deep and changing course. Only then did he move through the boat, toward the fore-ends, to the Seahawk party.

He raised his eyebrows at Bond when he saw they were one short.

"He won't be coming back," Bond said, without waiting for the question.

Then Lieutenant Commander Stewart caught sight of the two new members of the Seahawk team. Women, he thought. Women! Nothing good about having women aboard. Submarine drivers are a superstitious breed.

2

Seahawk Plus Five

It was the best time of the year, spring, and London was at its most seductive—the golden carpets of crocuses in the parks; the girls unwrapped from a particularly hard winter; and the sense of summer just around the corner. James Bond felt at peace with the world as he sat draped in a toweling robe, finishing his breakfast, sipping his second large cup of coffee, savoring the unique flavor of the freshly ground beans from De Bry. The sun glinted into the small dining room of his flat, and he could just hear May humming to herself in the kitchen.

He was on the late shift at Service Headquarters in that tall building overlooking Regent's Park, and therefore had the day to himself. Nevertheless, his first duty of the morning was almost complete, as the multitude of discarded newspapers proved—for, when he was on an office assignment, it was necessary for Bond to go through all the national daily papers, plus one or two of the provincial ones.

He had marked up three small stories that appeared in *The Mail, The Express,* and *The Times* that morning: one concerning the arrest of a British businessman in Madrid; a second consisting of three lines in *The Times* about an incident in the Med; and the third being a whole article in *The Express* by their constant, though often inconsistent, spywatcher, claiming the Secret Intelligence Service was in the midst of a huge row with its sister organization, MI5, over disputed territory.

"Have you no finished yet then, Mr. James?" May, her old and stubborn self, bustled into the room.

Bond smiled. It was as though she took pleasure in harassing him, chivying him from room to room when he had a free morning.

"You can clear, May. I've got half a cup of coffee to finish, the rest can go."

"Ooh, you and your newspapers." She swept a hand over the papers spread across the table. "There's ne'er a happy bit of news in them these days."

"Oh, I don't know . . ." Bond began.

"It's terrible, though, isn't it?" May pounced on one of the tabloids.

"What in particular?"

"Why, this other poor girl. It's spread all over the front pages, and they had yon head policeman on the breakfast television. Another Jack the Ripper, it sounds like."

"Oh, that! Yes." He had barely read the front pages. They were full of a particularly nasty murder that the police—so the newspapers said—linked to a killing earlier in the week. He glanced down to the headlines—TONGUELESS BODY IN WOODSHED. SECOND MUTILATED GIRL DISCOVERED. CATCH THIS MANIAC BEFORE HE STRIKES AGAIN.

He picked up *The Telegraph,* which had the story as a second lead.

The body of Miss Bridget Hammond (27) was discovered late yesterday afternoon by a gardener in a disused woodshed near her home in Norwich. Miss Hammond had been missing for twenty-four hours. A colleague from Rightline Computers, where she worked as a programmer, had called at her flat in Thorpe Road on Wednesday night, after she had failed to turn up for work that morning.

The police stated that the case was clearly one of murder. Her throat had been cut and there were "certain similarities" with the murder of 25-year-old Millicent Zampek in Cambridge last week. Miss Zampek's body was discovered mutilated on the Backs, behind King's College. It was revealed at the inquest that her tongue had been cut out. A police spokesman declared, "This is almost certainly the work of one person. It is possible we have a maniac on the loose."

An understatement, Bond thought, tossing the paper to one side. These days, perverted murder was a fact of life. Instant information, through the wonders of modern communications, simply appeared to bring it closer. Then, as the telephone began to ring, he felt a strange sensation—a prickling at the nape of his neck, and an extraordinary sinking in the pit of his stomach, as though he knew something very unpleasant was about to be—as they said in the Service—laid on him.

It was the ever-faithful Miss Moneypenny, using

her official voice and speaking in that jargon they had both mastered so well over the years.

"Can you lunch?" was all she asked after he recited his number.

"Business?"

"Very much so. At his club. Twelve-forty-five. Important."

"I'll be there." Bond cradled the receiver. Lunch with M at his club, Blades, was a rare invitation that did not bode well.

At precisely 12:40, knowing his Chief's obsession for punctuality, Bond paid off his taxi, taking the usual precaution of walking to Park Street, where that most coveted of gentleman's clubs can be found in almost mysterious splendor behind its recessed, elegant Adam façade.

Blades—as any book on London's clubland will point out—is unique; it was an offshoot of The Savoir Vivre, which was too exclusive to last after its opening in 1774. Its successor, Blades, came into being on the old premises in 1776, and, while noted for its exclusiveness and considerable expense, it has remained one of the few gentleman's clubs to flourish and maintain its standards right up to the present day.

Blades is still an all-male preserve. Its revenue comes almost entirely from the high stakes at its gaming tables, the food is still exceptional, and its half a dozen waitresses have continued to be the most beautiful in the city. They also keep the reputation of being, in the main, not averse to male blandishments, and it is not unknown for one or the other of them to linger on the premises in order to console a lonely soul in one of the twelve bedrooms available to members staying overnight.

Blades' membership includes some of the most powerful and wealthy men in the land, who have been shrewd enough to persuade visiting business associates—Croesus-rich Arabs, well-heeled Japanese, and billionaire Americans—to use the facilities as guests. Literally thousands of pounds still changed hands each evening—on the turn of a card or the roll of backgammon dice.

He pushed through the swing doors and walked up to the porter's lodge. Brevett—the porter—knew Bond as a very occasional guest at the club, and greeted him accordingly. Bond could not help thinking of the man's father, who had been the porter at the time of the great card game in which 007 had, at M's instigation, revealed the evil Sir Hugo Drax as a cheat. The Brevett family had been custodians and porters to Blades for well over a hundred years.

"The Admiral's already waiting in the dining room, sir." Brevett gave a scarcely noticeable hand motion to a young page boy who led Bond up the wide staircase, and across the stairwell into the magnificent white and gold Regency dining room, which has not altered over the years.

M was seated alone in the far left corner, away from windows and doors and with his back to the wall, so that he had a view of anyone entering or leaving the room.

He gave a curt nod as Bond reached the table, glancing at his wristwatch as he did so. "Bang on time, James. Good man. You know the rules, what d'ye fancy?—bearing in mind we haven't got all day."

Bond ordered grilled sole with a large salad, asking for the makings of a dressing, so that he could prepare it himself. M nodded his approval.

The food arrived, and M waited in silence as James Bond carefully ground half a teaspoonful of pepper into the small bowl on the tray of accoutrements. This was followed by a similar amount of salt and sugar, to which Bond added two and a half teaspoonsful of powdered mustard, crushing the mixture well with a fork before stirring in three full tablespoons of oil, followed by one of white wine vinegar, which he dribbled in carefully, adding a few drops of water before the final stir and pouring the mixture over his salad.

"Make someone a damned good husband, Bond." The clear gray eyes showed no apology for mentioning marriage—a topic people who knew Bond steered well clear of, and had done since the untimely death of 007's bride at the hands of SPECTRE.

Bond ignored his Chief's lack of taste, and began to attack his fish with the skill of a surgeon. "Well, sir?" He kept his voice down.

"Time enough, yet not enough time," M said coolly. "Words of our late Poet Laureate, not that you'd recognize Betjeman from Larkin, eh?"

Bond decided to rise to the irascible old spymaster's bait. "I know a few good ribald rhymes though, sir—The Jolly Tinker; The Old Monk of Great Renown? I can even recite you the odd limerick."

M chewed on his fish—he had ordered the sole also, but with new potatoes—swallowed, and looked at Bond, his eyes cold as a Siberian labor camp.

"Then recite me one about Seahawk, Bond. You remember Seahawk?"

Bond nodded. Five years had now passed since that operation. But Dave Andrews had been killed on Seahawk, and Bond would never forget the days and nights spent in the cramped quarters at the fore-ends of the Trafalgar Class nuke, trying to calm and comfort the two girls.

"There once was an Op we called Seahawk . . ." he began, but M held up a hand to stop any further impropriety.

"What if I tell you the truth about Seahawk?"

"If there's need-to-know, sir." All Bond knew in fact about Seahawk was what he had been ordered to do, and what had happened. Take off two agents, he had been told. He remembered Bill Tanner, M's Chief of Staff, saying the two Bond had to rescue were getting out in their socks—which in another language meant leaving in a hurry to save their very lives. Almost to himself, Bond said, "They were so damned young."

"Eh?" snorted M.

"I said, they were very young. The girls we got out."

"They weren't the only ones." M looked away. "We pulled the whole shooting match out over a matter of seven days. Four girls, a young man, and their parents. We did it. *You* brought a couple of the girls home. Now, Bond, two of the girls are dead. You probably read about it this morning. They had new names, new backgrounds, the whole works. Untraceable, the children—you're right, they *were* very young—and their families. But now someone's got to at least two of them. Brutally killed, with the added horror of having their tongues removed. You read about the maniac on the loose?"

Bond nodded. "You mean—?" he began.

"I mean that both the recently murdered young women were rehabilitated after doing sterling service for us, and there are still three out there waiting for the executioner who cuts out their tongues."

"A KGB hit squad, leaving us a message?"

"With each death, yes. They're slicing up *Cream Cake,* James, and I want it stopped—fast."

"Cream Cake?"

"Finish your lunch, then we'll take a stroll in the park. What I've to tell you is too sensitive even for the walls of this exclusive establishment. *Cream Cake* was one of the most audacious things we've done in years. I suppose that's why there's a penalty. Revenge, they say, is a dish best eaten cold. Five years is cold enough, I reckon."

"*Cream Cake* was a ploy to get our own back." M did not look at Bond as the two of them strolled—two businessmen reluctantly returning to their offices—through Regent's Park. "You know what an 'Emily' is?"

"Of course. The argot's a shade outdated, but I know what it means."

Bond had not in fact heard the word "Emily" for years. It was the name their American sister Service had used to denote special KGB-recruited operatives, mainly in West Germany. Emilies were usually single girls who had thought themselves into a situation common in certain kinds of young women, who imagine they will remain spinsters for the rest of their days. Indeed, some were held back because of an elderly parent, and the lack of romance in their lives was accounted for by the fact that they had little time to spare—work by day, coping with an ailing mother or father by night and early in the morning. But Emilies had something else in common: they usually worked for a government department, mainly in Bonn, and often as secretaries close to the BfV (Bundesamt für Verfassungschutz), the West German equivalent of MI5, but attached as a department of the Ministry of the Interior; or the BND (Bundesnachrichtendienst), which is the intelligence-gathering organization, working very much in harmony with the British SIS, the American CIA, and the Israeli Mossad.

The KGB had exploited numerous women in the Emily category over the years.

A man would suddenly come into an Emily's life, and quite quickly the drabness of that life would alter dramatically. She would feel wanted; she would find herself receiving gifts, being taken to expensive restaurants, theaters, cinemas, the opera. Then she would be so swept off her feet that the unbelievable would happen—she would sleep with the new friend. She was in love and nothing else mattered—not even when the beloved asked her to do little favors, like smuggling trifling documents out of the office, or copying some trivia from a dossier.

Click, she was trapped, and, before she knew it, an Emily was in so deep that, if things went wrong, she had to flee Eastward with her lover—who, as likely as not, disappeared when she was set up in a new life within the Communist DDR, or even in Russia itself.

"We decided to use the Emily ploy in reverse,"

M said, cutting through Bond's thoughts. "But our targets were very big guns indeed—senior officers of the HVA, who began the Emily business, after all, and even trained the seducer agents."

Bond nodded. M spoke of the Hauptverwaltung Aufklärung, or Chief Administration, Intelligence—the most efficient organization, next to the KGB, in the Eastern Bloc.

"Senior HVA officers; also, attached KGB officers—including one woman. We had several sleepers who'd been left unused—left so long that they were really past it. Husband-and-wife teams we thought would be of great use. In the end, we found their children would be the best bet. Five families were chosen because of their kids—all attractive, late teens to early twenties, over the age of consent, if you follow me?" M sounded embarrassed, as he always did when discussing sexual traps, or honeypot ops, as the trade knew them. "Sounded 'em out. Satisfied ourselves. Slipped in a bit of on-the-ground training—even brought two of 'em into the West for a while." He paused as they passed a gaggle of nannies wheeling perambulators.

"Took a year to set up *Cream Cake,* and we had great success. Very great success, with a little help from others. Put the bite on the woman, who was pure old-school KGB—or GRU; snaffled a couple of high-grade HVA men. Eating out of the palm of our hands; and there was one very big fish who could still be dangerous. Then it was blown. With little warning. You know the rest. Brought them home. Reconditioned all of them—gave them new lives, golden pat on the back, homes, training, careers. Got a lot out of it, 007. Until last week, when one of the girls was murdered."

"Not one that I—"

"No. But it alerted us. Couldn't be sure, of course. Couldn't tip off the police. Still can't. Now they've got a second one, the Hammond girl in Norwich." He took a deep breath. "They've signaled loud and clear by this bizarre removal of tongues. Could be KGB, might be HVA—even GRU. But there are still two young girls out there, and one personable young man. They've got to be pulled in, 007. Brought to a safe place, and put under protection until we've rolled up the hit team."

"And I'm the one who's going to pull them?"

"In a manner of speaking, yes."

Bond knew that gruff tone of voice only too well, and M pointedly looked away as he continued, "You see, it's not going to be an easy operation."

"There's no such thing." Bond realized he was trying to raise his own sinking spirits.

"In this case it's worse, 007. We know where two of them are—the girls you brought out, as it happens. But the young man's a different kettle of fish entirely. He was last known to be in the Canary Islands." M gave a frustrated sigh. "One of the girls is in Dublin, by the way."

"I can get the girls quickly, then?"

"It's up to you, James." Again, the use of his Christian name alerted Bond. "I cannot sanctify any saving operation. I cannot give you orders."

"Ah!"

"In the event of anything going wrong we will deny you—even to our own police forces. After the

Cream Cake debacle, the Foreign Office watchdogs gave strict instructions. The participants were to be Hoovered clean, given a face-lift, and then left alone. We were to make no further contact or aid. If I went to the Powers That Be asking for sanction to protect these people, and possibly use one of them as a tethered goat to deal with the hit team, the answer would come back as callous as the Black Death . . ."

"Let them eat cream cake." Bond spoke somberly.

"Precisely. Let them die one by one, and have done with it. No compromises. No connections."

"So what do you want, sir?"

"What I've told you. You can have names and addresses, I can point you in the right direction, let you delve into the files—even the murder reports, which, naturally, we have, er, acquired. After that, which should take you the rest of the afternoon, I can give you leave of absence for a couple of weeks. Or you merely carry on with your normal duties. Understand?"

"Point me." Bond's voice was gritty. "Point me and give me some leave. I'll pull them in . . ."

"Nothing official. I can't even let you use a safe house . . ."

"I'll see to that, sir. Point me and I'll get them, and the hit team into the bargain. With luck *nobody* will know what's gone on—except the hit team's masters."

The following silence seemed to go on forever. Then M took a deep breath. "I'll give you names, and the file numbers for Registry, as we walk back to the shop. After that, you're relieved of duty for two weeks. Good luck, 007."

3

Dare to Be Chic

The Headquarters Registry was on the second floor, guarded by girls as statuesque as models, and usually dressed in casual jeans and shirts. Until a few years ago the uniform was twin sets, pearls, and well-cut skirts purchased with Daddy's hard-earned cash at Harrods or Harvey Nichols. M rarely went near the Registry since the rules had been relaxed, but he had been as good as his word regarding the information Bond was to see.

In the park, M had rattled off names and file prefixes, made Bond repeat them, and then told him to take one more turn around the Inner Circle, in which Queen Mary's Gardens are enclosed, before returning to the high, anonymous building where the Service kept its darkest secrets.

Now a tall, unimpressible goddess jotted down the file numbers as Bond gave them to her, taking the slip of paper to the Watch Officer—a striking brunette who sat at a high desk overlooking the other girls, ranged in rows before their work stations. There were no questions, not even a raised eyebrow from the Watch Officer, whose name was Rowena MacShine-Jones—known to all as Registry Shiner. Ms. MacShine-Jones gave the nod, and the computers and digitizers went through their paces. Within five minutes, the goddess returned with a thick plastic file that was flagged in red, meaning CLASSIFIED A+, followed by the date and the magic words, *These documents must not be taken from the building. Return by 16:30 hrs.* Bond knew that, if he did not obey this command, one of the Registry guardians would seek him out and bring them back for shredding and burning, just as he knew the file's spine contained a "smart card" that would trigger a holocaust of alarms if he even tried to get them out of the file, let alone the building. High tech was the byword these days.

On his office desk he found a similar file, flagged with the same classification, except this one had to be returned to the eighth floor—which meant to M personally.

Within an hour, Bond had been through both sets, making mental notes that were now neatly pigeonholed in his well-ordered mind. He spent another hour rechecking his memory against the documents. After that, it was simply a case of returning the Registry file and taking the second one up to M's office.

"I think he'll see me." Bond smiled at Miss Moneypenny on entering the annex to M's private eyrie.

"More leave, James? He mentioned you might want to take some."

"Only for unexpected family business." Bond

looked her straight in the eyes, like any trained dissembler.

Moneypenny sighed. "Oh, that I could be part of that family. I know what sort of business it is when you fabricate this kind of leave." She shaped her lips into a mock pout.

"Penny, if that were true there's nothing *I'd* like better."

The intercom buzzed, and M's voice crackled through the speaker: "If that's 007, Moneypenny, send him in here."

Moneypenny gave Bond a rather soulful look, raising her eyes heavenward. Bond merely smiled at his Chief's crustiness and—seeing the small green light come on over M's door to signify that anyone waiting should enter—gave a small, courteous bow to Moneypenny, and went into the inner sanctum.

"Come to return the grisly papers, sir." He placed M's file on the desk. It contained the police reports on the two murders—complete with photographs. The two girls—Millicent Zampek and Bridget Hammond—had traveled the road to their respective ends via blunt instruments crushing their skulls from behind. The tongues, of which the press had made so much, had been removed with almost surgical precision after death—the police officer in charge of both cases had queried the *medical knowledge* of the murderer(s). There was little doubt, the reports said, that the same person, or persons, had carried out the executions.

M drew the file toward him with no comment. "Moneypenny said you'd put in an application for two weeks' compassionate leave, 007. True or false?"

"True, sir."

"Good. Then you can leave right away. I trust things'll work out for you."

"Thank you, sir. I think I'll visit Q Branch before I go, but I really do have to get into Mayfair before six."

M nodded, satisfaction flickering for a second in those iceberg-gray eyes. A look of tacit understanding passed between the two men, for they knew that, of the three remaining prospective victims, the nearest—Ms. Heather Dare—owned and managed a beauty salon just around the corner from The Mayfair Hotel. This was a pleasant coincidence, for Bond occasionally dined in that hotel's particularly good Le Château Restaurant, not merely for the excellent food, but for the security offered by its half a dozen special alcoved and very private tables that are well away from the eyes and ears of other clients.

M dismissed Bond with an almost cursory flick of his right hand, and 007 made his way into the bowels of the building where Major Boothroyd—the Armorer, as he was known—kept his iron hand on Q Branch. As it turned out, the Major was away ("In Dorset, looking at some nasty electronic hardware"), and Bond found the Branch operating under the expertise of the Major's assistant, the leggy, bespectacled, but unashamedly delicious Ann Reilly—known to everyone in the Service, somewhat obviously, as Q'ute.

In her early days with Q Branch, Bond and Q'ute had quite a thing going, but with the passage of years and Bond's unreliable timetable they had become mere kissing cousins.

"James, how nice," she greeted him. "To what do we owe the pleasure? Nothing new brewing, is there?"

"On a spot of leave. Couple of weeks. Thought I'd collect bits and pieces." He deliberately played it down. If he had been on normal leave he would have had to sign out with her for a CC500 scrambler telephone anyway. That justified his presence. In reality, he was there to pick her brains and maybe filch some small piece of technology.

"We've got one or two things on test. Maybe you'd like to take away a sample or three." She grinned, looking her most stunning, and Bond wondered if M, in his craftiest mood, had given her guarded instructions.

"Come into my parlor." She made it sound like an open invitation, and they walked briskly down the long room where shirtsleeved young men worked in front of VDUs or peered through huge lighted magnifiers at electronic boards. "Nowadays," said Q'ute, "everyone wants it smaller, with a longer range, and more memory."

"Speak for yourself." It was Bond's turn to smile, though the gesture did not even light up his eyes. His mind was full of the gruesome photographs of two young girls battered to death, even though he knew Q'ute talked of sound stealing, movement theft, concealment, and deadly devices—her stock-in-trade.

He left half an hour later with some small items, plus the obligatory CC500—which, under his current instructions, he would not be allowed to use, for both M and the Foreign Office would deny him entirely until he had everything neatly tucked away and the hit team—KGB, GRU, or HVA—disposed of or sent scuttling back to their homeland.

At the door of her office, Q'ute put a hand gently on Bond's arm. "If you want anything from here—if you *need* anything—just call and I'll bring it to you myself."

He looked into her face and saw that he had been right—instructions of one kind or another had been given to Q'ute by M.

The participants were to be Hoovered clean, given a face-lift, and then left alone, M had said—by which he meant that everybody who had been operationally active during *Cream Cake* was to be debriefed, provided with a foolproof new identity, and then disowned. Bond knew what *that* meant. It was like being cut out of some rich relation's will, and, if he fouled up, the same fate would fall on his head like a load of manure.

In the Bentley Mulsanne Turbo, tucked away in the underground car park, he readied himself for what the instructors called street work—checking the ASP 9mm automatic, its spare clips, and the hard steel telescopic operations baton. His getaway case—containing spare clothes for at least a week—was in the boot. So prepared, James Bond started the engine, and the car glided smoothly out of its parking slot and up the ramp into the spring sunshine of London's streets.

Some twenty minutes later, having handed the car over to one of The Mayfair Hotel's blue-liveried doormen—the one with a discreet Parachute Regiment badge in his lapel—Bond walked by Langan's Brasserie in Stratton Street, its garish red neon blazing even in the afternoon. From there, Dare to Be Chic, which lay on the Piccadilly end of Stratton Street, was but a few steps away.

"Dare" he could understand, for the girl's German family name—true or false—had been Wagen, so this was a literal translation. Where the Heather had come from, heaven and the Service resettlement officers alone knew.

The windows of the beauty salon, which had become popular and successful in the last couple of years, were black, the lettering gold with a logo—art nouveau: a bobbed-haired woman sporting a cigarette holder positioned below and to the right of the bold script that dared you to be chic.

Inside the neat single door was a minute foyer, deeply carpeted and with one picture—a Kurosaki woodblock print that, to Bond, resembled a magician's box opened in front of highly regular pyramids. The Kurosaki hung to the right of a gold elevator door, the button of which was neatly labeled with the Dare logo.

He pressed, stepped into the mirrored cage, and was whisked silently upward. Like the foyer, the elevator sported a deep crimson pile carpet. For a finger-snap of time Bond thought it would be a wonderful place to make love to a beautiful woman. Then the cage came to a gentle halt and he was in another foyer. Double doors led to the rooms where women subjected themselves to heat, facials, the expert fingers of hairdressers, and the professional hands of masseurs. The carpet remained red, another Kurosaki hung on the wall to his left, there was a door marked PRIVATE to the right, while in front of him a golden blonde dressed in a severe black suit and blazing white silk shirt sat at a kidney-shaped desk.

The blonde looked as though every pore on her

face had been cleaned out by Dyno-rod, and each strand of hair accurately grown and set for all time by a sculptor. Her lips parted in an encouraging smile while her eyes asked what the hell a man was doing in this woman's preserve. To Bond it was rather like the greeting one had when visiting his sister Service, MI5.

"Can I be of help, sir?" The words came out in that terribly painful, overemphasized drawl that Knightsbridge shop assistants confuse with upper-crust speech, turning "can" to "Ken," and "sir" to "sah."

"Quite possibly." Bond gave her his second most radiant smile—his first was reserved only for the genuine article—"I wish to see Ms. Dare."

The encouraging look became fixed as she said she was most terribly sorry, but Ms. Dare was not in this afternoon. Bond watched her eyes as she said it, noting the tone of voice collapsed slightly, as though she had learned the words by heart. The reply lacked conviction and the eyes flicked a fraction toward the door marked PRIVATE.

He sighed, took out a blank card, leaned over, wrote one sentence on it, and pushed it toward the girl. "Be a darling and take this to her. I'll mind the store. It *is* very important, and I'm sure you wouldn't want me to walk in on her without being invited."

When the girl hesitated, he added that Ms. Dare could look at him on the monitor—inclining his head toward the security camera high up in the corner by the door—and if she did not like what she saw he would move on. The blonde still could not make up her mind, so he added that it was official and flashed his ID—the impressive, fully laminated one with colored lettering, not the real thing, which was plain plastic in a little leather folder.

"If you'll wait one moment I'll see if she's come back. Ms. Dare was *certainly* out earlier this afternoon." She disappeared through the private door and Bond turned to face the camera. On the card he had written, *I come in peace with gifts. Remember the gallant submariners.*

It took five minutes but it worked like a charm. The golden girl showed him through the door marked PRIVATE, along a narrow corridor, up some steps to another very solid-looking door. "She says to go straight in."

Bond went straight in to find himself staring down the wrong end of a piece of gunmetal blue that, by its size and shape, Bond recognized as a Colt Woodsman—the Match Target model: a plinking pistol, as they would say in the US, but a plinking pistol can still kill, and Bond was always respectful in the presence of any such weapon, particularly when it was held as steadily as this, and pointed directly at his most trusted and best friend.

"Irma," he said in a slightly admonishing tone. "Irma, please put away the gun. I'm here to help." As he spoke, Bond assured himself that there was no other exit and that Heather Dare, née Irma Wagen of Operation *Cream Cake,* had placed herself in the correct position—legs slightly apart, back against the left-hand side of the rear wall, eyes open and uncompromisingly steady.

"It *is* you," she said, but did not lower the pistol.

"In the flesh," he obliged with his genuine number-one smile, "though to be honest I wouldn't have recognized you. The last occasion we spent time together you were a bundle of sweaters, jeans, anoraks, and fear."

"And now it's only the fear." She looked very solemn, and, for the first time, Bond realized all manner of things about her.

Heather Dare's accent held no trace of her first language—German—which meant she was the complete professional as far as the secret world was concerned; she was also a very poised, attractive lady—dark of hair and eyes, with a tall, slim frame, most of which, he considered, was taken up by her legs. Her elegance went with the business she had managed to build up over the past five years. All in all, a lady who would turn heads even on the most exclusive beach. Bond also caught an inkling of something else—a grittiness, maybe even a deeply ingrained stubbornness.

"Yes, I understand about the fear," he said. "That's why I'm here."

"I didn't think they'd send anybody."

"They didn't. I was simply tipped off. I'm on my own, but I do have the training and skills. Now, put the gun down, so that I can get you away to somewhere that's safe and under wraps. I'm going to haul in all three of you—the three that are still alive."

Slowly she shook her head. "Oh, no, Mr. . . ."

"Bond. James Bond."

"Oh, no, Mr. Bond. The bastards have got Franzi and Elli, I'm going to be certain they don't get my other friends." The Hammond girl's true Christian name was Franziska—hence Franzi, Franzi Trauben; while Millicent Zampek had been known, in her life within *Cream Cake,* as Eleonore Zuckermann.

"That's what I said." Bond took a pace forward. "A place of safety, where nobody's going to find you. Then I'll take care of the bastards myself."

"If that's the case, where you go, I go. Until it's over, one way or another."

So, it was a combination of toughness and rock-like stubbornness that motivated Heather Dare. He had experienced enough about women to realize that this mixture could be neither fought nor reasoned with.

He looked at her for a moment, pleased with her slender build and the femininity that lay under the veneer of clothing—the well-cut gray suit, set off at the throat by a pink blouse and thin gold chain with pendant. The suit looked very French: Paris, he thought, probably Givenchy. It would be true to form for Heather to be dressed by the same designer as Frau von Karajan. "You have any ideas how we should handle it then, Heather? I *do* call you Heather, don't I—not Irma?"

"Heather," she breathed very low. A two-beat pause—"I'm sorry, I gave you the other names in their original form. Yes, I've thought of myself as Heather ever since your people sent me out into the real world with a new name. I have difficulties in thinking of the old gang in new guises."

"On *Cream Cake* you were interconscious? I mean, you knew one another? Knew what each target was?"

She gave a brief nod. "By real names, and by street names. Yes, we were interconscious, as you put it—of one another, of the targets, of our control. No cutouts, that's why and how Emilie and I were together when you picked us off that little beach." She hesitated, then frowned, shaking her head. "Sorry, I mean Ebbie—Emilie Nikolas is Ebbie now."

"Yes, Ebbie Heritage, right?"

"Correct. It happens that we're old friends. I spoke with her this morning."

"In Dublin?"

Heather smiled. "You *are* well informed. Yes, in Dublin."

"On an open line? You spoke on an open line?"

"Don't worry, Mr. Bond."

"James."

"Yes. Don't worry, James, I said three words only. You see, I spent some time with Ebbie before this place got going. We made a pact, complete with all the old secret trappings. I told her, 'Elizabeth is sick.' She replied, 'I'll be with you this afternoon.' "

"Meaning?"

"The same as 'How's your mother,' which was the *Cream Cake* warning, slipped into a conversation—'mother' was the trigger: *You're blown. Take the necessary action.*"

"The same as it was five years ago."

"Yes, and we're about to take that necessary action again now. You see, James, I've been in Paris. I flew back this morning. On the plane I saw the paper—the murder, *murders.* It was the first I knew of it. Once would have put us on guard, but twice—and with the . . . the tongue . . ." For the first time she sounded unsure, even shaken. She swallowed, visibly pulling herself together. "The tongues made it certain. It's a charming warning, yes?"

"Not subtle."

"Warnings, and orchestrated revenge killings, are seldom subtle, James. You know what the Mafia does to adulterers within a family?"

He gave a sharp nod. "It's not pretty, but it makes its point." For the blink of an eye his mind recalled the last time he had heard of such a murder, with the man's genitalia hacked off.

"The tongue makes a point also."

"Right. Then what does 'Elizabeth is sick' mean?"

"That we've been blown; it is dangerous; meet me where we arranged."

"Which is?"

"Which is where I'm going—on the Aer Lingus flight from Heathrow at eight-thirty tonight."

"Dublin."

Again she nodded. "Dublin. Hire a car and head for where Ebbie will have been waiting since this afternoon."

"And you did the same for Frank—Frank Baisley—or Franz Belzinger? The one now known as Jungle?"

She was still tense, but she gave a little smile. "He was always a joker. A bit of a risk-taker. His street name was Wald, German for Forest. Now his nickname is 'Jungle.' He finds it amusing, and no—no, I could not get a message to him because I don't know where he is."

"I do."

"Where?"

"Quite a long way off. Now *you* tell me—where are you meeting Ebbie?"

She hesitated for a second, probably weighing up the safety of such a breach of their private security.

"Come on," Bond rapped out, "I am here to help.

I'm coming with you to Dublin anyway. I have to. Where do you plan to meet?"

"Oh, we decided a long time ago that it would be best to hide in the open—Ashford Castle, County Mayo. A grand hotel—the place where President Reagan stayed."

Bond smiled. It was sound professional thinking—The Ashford Castle Hotel *is* grand, and expensive, and the last place on God's earth a hit team from either Russia or one of the satellites would think of looking, unless they were on your heels and following. "Can we look as though we're having a business meeting?" he said casually. "And can I use your telephone?"

She took a seat behind her long desk, the Woodsman disappearing into some safe place. Then she spread papers around and pushed the telephone toward him. Bond dialed Heathrow and asked for the Aer Lingus reservations desk, was given another number to call—which shows how wonderfully organized they are at Heathrow—dialed the second number, and booked himself onto EI 177, Club Class, in the name of Boldman.

"My car's just around the corner," he said as he put down the receiver. "We'll leave here at about seven. It'll be dusk and, I presume, all your people will have gone."

She glanced at her watch—a neat Cartier—and her eyebrows rose. "They'll be finished very soon now—" and, as though on cue, her telephone rang.

It was the blonde, Bond presumed, because Heather said yes, they should all leave, lock the doors, usual things—she was working late with the gentleman who had called. Yes, she would see them all in the morning.

So they sat, as the glowing spring day took on a chill of evening, and the grumble of traffic from Piccadilly dwindled slightly. And as they sat, they talked, Bond gently probing her about *Cream Cake* and learning nothing he did not know from the files of that afternoon, except that Heather Dare held herself responsible for the panic call to all five participants: "I'm sorry, Gustav has canceled dinner." She herself had been working their prime target, Colonel Maxim Smolin, who during that period was the second man in the East German madhouse of secrets, the HVA.

She told him, unwittingly, a great deal about herself, and a lot more concerning the inner workings of *Cream Cake,* alerting him to a few deceits left out, or degutted, in the files.

At five minutes to seven he asked if she had a coat, and she nodded, going to the small, built-in wardrobe and slipping into a white trenchcoat that was far too easily identifiable, and very definitely French, for only the French can make raincoats that have flair. He ordered her to lock up the Woodsman. Then, together, they left her office, switching out the lights as they went.

Into the elevator cage, hissing down to street level.

The lights went out of their own accord just as they reached the small ground-floor foyer, and, as the doors opened onto gloom, Heather screamed and the attacker came at her like a human typhoon.

4

Ducking & Diving

The man who hurled himself into the elevator cage must have been absolutely certain that Heather was alone. Later Bond thought that all the attacker could have seen from his lurking point in the foyer was the white trenchcoat—for Heather had taken a step forward toward the doors as they opened.

Bond was thrown against the glass side of the cage, off balance. He felt his back crack into the glass, saw that the assailant had one hand firmly on the shoulder of Heather's trenchcoat, spinning her around, with his other arm raised high. Dimly Bond could just make out an object that looked like a large hammer held aloft. The whole business had taken a split second—all fury and violence.

Desperately fighting the natural forces of gravity, Bond struck out with his right leg—a hard, straight blow with his heel forced forward and in the direction of the intruder's lower legs. He felt his shoe hit and heard a muffled grunt as the man was deflected from making an accurate downward stroke, missing Heather by inches.

The rear mirror glass of the cage shattered as the wielded hammer struck. It was the attacker's turn to recover his balance. By this time, Bond had made his move, tugging the collapsible baton from its holster on his right hip, flicking down so that the telescoped steel clicked into place—forming a formidable weapon with which he struck out toward the target's neck.

The killer went down without even a cry—just a dull thud as the steel of the baton connected, followed by a scraping noise as the man's head went straight into the already splintered glass, as though following the exact trajectory of the mallet blow.

Suddenly the fury was gone, leaving only the sound of Heather breathing heavy little choking sobs. Bond reached out to see if there was an emergency light switch inside the elevator cage. His hand touched the control panel and, at first, the doors tried to close and then open as the safety buffer came into play, for the sprawled assailant's legs stretched out into the foyer.

The same thing happened three times before Bond's fingers hit some override button and the cage flooded with light.

Heather was shaking, hunched in the far corner away from the inert body, which was clad, from head to foot, in black—jeans, a turtleneck, and gloves. Even the man's hair was dark, but it looked as though some hairdresser had tried to give it a punk style by putting in crimson streaks. The sharded rear mirror reflected the gory patches—the great star-like cracks giving an odd, kaleidoscopic picture of black and red.

With his right foot, Bond heaved the body over,

turning it faceup. The man was not dead. His mouth had fallen open and there was a sharp pattern of slashed cuts, from hairline to mouth, where his face had hit the glass. You could hear the quick breathing, and the blood seemed to be flowing normally. Enough, but nothing to worry about. When consciousness returned, he would probably feel more pain from Bond's blow than from the slashes.

"Couple of aspirins and he'll be right as rain," Bond muttered.

"Mischa," Heather said, aloud and with some violence.

"You know him?"

"One of the heavies they kept in Berlin. Moscow-trained. Jack-of-all-trades, as long as the trades have something to do with causing pain, maiming, or killing." As she spoke, Heather seemed to be trying to press her back through the side of the elevator cage, as though attempting to put as much space as possible between her and the man she recognized as Mischa. All the time, the doors kept closing, hitting Mischa's legs, rebounding open again, quiescent for a few seconds, then having another go.

"Persistent things, elevator doors." Bond bent over the unhappy Mischa, probed around, and finally pulled—from under the thug's body—the weapon meant for the back of Heather's skull. "A nice carpenter's mallet." He hefted it in his hand, a large, heavy wooden hammer with a king-size head. "Brand new. Unused," he said after examining it, before wiping the handle off with his handkerchief and putting it back on the floor. Bending again, he began to go over the body, searching and feeling wherever another weapon might be concealed.

"Not even loose change, or a pack of cigarettes," he announced, straightening up. "Do we, by any chance, have another way out, Heather? A fire escape or something?"

"Yes. A metal zigzag thing at the back of the salon. It's to do with fire regulations. I had it put in when we refurbished the place." She paused, looked around her, scowled at the thumping elevator doors, and asked, "Why?"

"Because, sweet, lucky Heather—and you've been damned lucky—friend Mischa did not come alone. Not if comrade Colonel Maxim Smolin orchestrated everything for the other two girls and intended you to go by the same unpleasant route."

"But Maxim wouldn't . . ." she began, then changed it to another questioning "Why?"

"Mischa carries nothing else on him. Just the instrument to bludgeon you to death. There's no knife; no little medical gizmo for the swift removal of tongues—and that's the trademark, isn't it?"

She gave a small frightened nod; Bond, kicking the mallet to the back of the cage, grabbed the unconscious Mischa by the scruff of his turtleneck and lifted him without effort, dumping him into the foyer.

Heather had the wit to hold the elevator button, and once the unconscious killer was free of the doors, Bond slammed the heel of his hand onto the UP button.

They made the silent ascent to the beauty salon's entrance, where Heather did things with security alarm switches in a neat metal cupboard set into the wall. Then, with a quick "Through here!" she pushed open the double doors.

"No lights," Bond ordered. "Lead me there," and he felt her hand, remarkably cool for one who had just escaped death, clasp his own palm, as she negotiated her way past the handbasins and dryers of the hairdressing salon, then into a corridor punctuated with doors that stood out clearly in their clinical white.

A final door—EMERGENCY EXIT visible in red overhead—opened with a push-bar safety lock, and the cool of the evening hit them as they emerged onto a metal platform—a black square studded with holes—from which you could almost reach out and touch the other buildings. To the right, narrow and swaying steps zigzagged down.

"How do we get out? At the bottom, I mean." Bond looked down, seeing nothing but a tiny courtyard—square, surrounded by the backs of buildings.

"Only key holders can use the exit," she panted. "We have four sets, one for each of my head people: hairdressing, beauty consultant, massage—and one for me. There's a door to a passageway that runs alongside the car showroom, and a door at the other end. Same key for both doors."

"Locks?"

"Yales. The far door takes you into Berkeley Street."

"Go, then! Go!"

She turned toward the fire escape, one hand on the guardrail, and at that moment Bond heard heavy running feet thudding toward them from the other side of the door. "Get on with it." He did not raise his voice. "Just get down and leave the doors open for me. There's a British Racing Green Bentley

Turbo parked opposite The Mayfair. Go into the foyer and watch for me. If I arrive in a hurry, with both hands in view, run straight to the car. If my right hand's in my pocket, and I'm taking my time, lose yourself for half an hour, then come back and wait. Same signals at half-hour intervals. Now, move!"

She seemed to hesitate for a second, then went down the metal stairs, which seemed to shake precariously as her speed increased, while Bond swiveled toward the exit, drawing his 9mm ASP, holding it low against the hip. Friend Mischa, the mallet man, had not come alone.

The thudding of feet grew louder, and, when he thought the distance right, Bond pulled back sharply, opening the door.

He did it the textbook way, leaving just enough time to be certain his targets were not friendly policemen—who were liable to be unfriendly if they thought he was some criminal intruder.

By no stretch of the imagination were these men police: unless London's finest had taken to using Colt .45 automatics without warning.

The men who had been pounding down the passage slithered to a halt as soon as he showed himself. Oddly, they had put lights on in the corridor, so they could be seen quite clearly—though Bond was aware that he was an equally good target, even turned sideways as they taught on the yearly field small-arms course.

There were two of them—well-muscled trained hoods, one moving fast behind the other, each hogging a different side of the narrow corridor.

It was the one ahead, to Bond's right, who fired, the big .45 sounding like a bomb in the confines of the corridor. A huge piece of the doorjamb woodwork, to his left, disintegrated, leaving, a large hole and sending splinters flying. The second shot passed between Bond and the jamb. He felt the crack of the bullet as it cut the air near his head, but by this time he had also fired—low, to miss or do damage to feet and legs with the horrific little Glaser slugs with which he always loaded the ASP.

The hoods would have been easy meat for that kind of ammunition—hundreds of No. 12 shot in liquid Teflon within the soft bullet—but Bond had no desire to kill anybody: M had been clear enough—*In the event of anything going wrong we will deny you—even to our own police forces.* He had no intention of being denied by his Service if up for murder at the Old Bailey, so he squeezed the trigger twice, one shot to each wall, heard a yelp of pain and a shout, then turned about and hurtled down the fire escape, glancing below to see there was no sign of Heather.

He thought there was another shout from above him as he reached the first door, which Heather—he thanked heaven—had left open. Bond went through it as though trying to beat all existing records, slammed it after him, and put up the Yale catch before barreling down the passage to the street door. Seconds later he was in the street itself, turning left and left again, both hands in sight.

Within seconds the hotel doorman had come over with the car keys and unlocked the Bentley. Bond tipped him a shade lavishly and smiled casually at Heather as she came across the road from the hotel entrance.

The car was parked facing Berkeley Street, and they slid away, first left, then around Berkeley Square, bearing left again, then right, past that doyen of hotels, The Connaught, and left into Grosvenor Square, Upper Grosvenor Street, and the heavy traffic of Park Lane.

"Keep an eye open," he told Heather, who sat—silent—at his side. "You're trade, like me, so presumably you can spot a tail. I'm going through the park, down Exhibition Road, and then right, toward the M4. I presume you've been trained, so I really don't have to tell you the rules, but in case you've forgotten—"

"I don't forget," she cracked back, like a whip. "We are ducking and diving, yes?"

"That's what the rule book says. Never fly straight and level for more than half a minute; so never walk around without watching your back; always make it difficult for them to follow; always mislead."

"Even when they know you're there," she added tartly.

"Right." Bond smiled, though the streak of cruelty still played around his mouth. "What, incidentally, were you going to do about luggage, Heather?"

"I had a case packed at home. No way, now."

"Have to buy a toothbrush at the airport. Anything else'll have to wait until Ireland. You booked under your own name?"

"Yes."

"Well, you're going to unbook it. Then hope like hell the wait list isn't too long. We'll stop at the service station. We can only presume the other two were also Smolin's men—expecting to find your battered corpse, and do the tongue removal. I got a glimpse of them, and they seemed to be the kind of people who'd enjoy that sort of thing."

"Did you . . . ?"

"Kill them? No, but at least one of them's hurt. Maybe both. Didn't stop to find out. Now, think of a good alias."

"Smith?"

"No. House rules—not Smith, Jones, Green, or Brown. Something with polish."

"Arlington," she said. "Like Arlington Street. Very smart and West End."

"Like the American cemetery," Bond snapped. "Probably a bad omen, but it'll do. We still free of company?"

"There was a Jag XL back there that I didn't like the look of, but it turned off into Marlowes Road. I think we're clear."

"Good. Now listen, Heather. You cancel your Dublin booking, and try to get on in the name of Arlington as soon as we arrive. I'll take care of anything else. Right?"

"Whatever you say." She was reasonably calm, only a razor-thin edge under the cool, collected voice. It was impossible for Bond to deduce how good she really was.

They stopped at the first service station on the M4 Motorway, three miles or so from the Heathrow Exit. Bond shooed her into the one telephone booth that was free while he loitered by the next one, in which a woman was dialing a series of numbers from a little black book. In the end, Bond was able to take Heather's place. She nodded to him, confirming that she had canceled her Aer Lingus flight, and Bond, with a handful of change, delved into his telephone number memory and dialed the British Airways desk, inquiring if there were seats available on the 20:15 shuttle to Newcastle. Assured that there were, he asked them to hold two in the names of Miss Dare and Mr. Bond.

Back in the parking area, using the car for cover, Bond opened the boot and slid the baton and his ASP pistol into the special, lined compartment of his getaway case, where they were 100 percent safe from airport scanners, and 99.5 percent secure from search. If worse came to worst, he would have to use his Service permit, but then every Special Branch officer of the Irish Garda would know he was in the Republic.

Fifteen minutes later he had the Bentley stashed away in the secure long-term park, his getaway case out of the boot, and stood—two paces behind Heather—in the queue for the Terminal Connection Bus. He reflected, not for the first time, on the inappropriateness of the use of the word "terminal" for airports.

During the short drive from the service station to Heathrow, he had explained the diversionary tactics to Heather. "They're remarkably inaccurate about passenger listings on the internal shuttles." He smiled, having pulled the trick before. "You also have to go through the same airside main gate to get to shuttles or the Irish flight." He went on to tell her exactly what to do, including emergency procedures in the event of her not being able to get a seat on Aer Lingus 177.

In the first stages they were to go their separate ways, meeting up only when, as Mr. Boldman, he checked in at the Dublin desk. He also suggested that she try to buy a small carry-on flight bag and the bare essentials. "Not that you'll ever be able to buy anything *really* essential at Heathrow," he added, his mind darting back to those halcyon days when airports and railway stations could provide practically everything around the clock.

They got off the bus at Terminal One. It was just twenty minutes to eight, and both of them moved with some speed—Heather to the Aer Lingus Dublin desk, Bond to the shuttle area, where he picked up the tickets booked in their real names and paid for with his own credit card. Clutching his small bag, he walked briskly back to the Aer Lingus check-in, collected his ticket in the name of Boldman, and loitered until Heather reappeared, carrying a small, very new-looking bag. "Toothpaste, brush, spare undies, and some scent." She grimaced.

"Good." Bond nodded. "Now for the Newcastle shuttle."

As they passed down the ramp and through the gates to the walkway, brandishing tickets at the security guards, Bond checked the departures monitor to satisfy himself that already EI 177 was loading at Gate 14.

There was the usual crush around the shuttle check-in, and he took the boarding cards for both of them. They did not even have to put on an act in order to slip quietly to the back of the queue, and then away through the door and out into the walkway again, this time switching tickets for the Aer Lingus flight, and parting from one another—Bond allowing Heather to go well ahead of him toward Gate 14. If anyone came looking, they would at least show as having bought tickets for the shuttle, and even checked in.

If M had broken the rules further, and had someone watching at a discreet distance, they would not discover the Dublin booking until too late. But he was thinking more of Smolin's people, who could well be searching the airport, and making inquiries already.

That sixth sense, acquired over long years of playing Hare and Hounds with SMERSH, SPECTRE, and a dozen other organizations, was well tuned, and Bond's mental antennae picked up nothing of note. If anyone was on the watch—particularly lurking on behalf of Comrade Smolin—Bond neither felt, nor saw them.

They boarded EI 177 separately, and sat three rows apart, not joining up again until they had gone through the green customs channel at Dublin Airport an hour later.

Outside it was raining and dark, but Bond, undeterred, felt quite ready for the lengthy drive to County Mayo and the famous Ashford Castle.

There were no signs of a reception committee at Dublin, so while Heather went off to see if the main airport shop—which they both knew sold clothes—was open, Bond sauntered over to the car rental desk and organized a car. They had a Saab available—his preference, a Bentley Turbo, was way out of the question—and he filled in the necessary forms, using his Boldman license and credit card. A red-uniformed girl smiled a Colleen-type smile, and had just told him she would take him down to the car, when he turned to see Heather, seven or eight yards away, leaning against a pillar. She looked stunned:

her face was chalk-white. As Bond closed in on her, he saw a copy of the Dublin *Evening Press* dangling from her hand. "What is it, Heather old love?" he spoke gently.

"Ebbie," she whispered. "Look," raising the newspaper for him to see the headlines, "it must be Ebbie, the bastards."

Among the chatter and throng of the airport main concourse, Bond felt the hairs on the back of his neck rise. In bold print, four inches high, the headlines shouted their warning—MYSTERY GIRL BATTERED TO DEATH AND MUTILATED IN HOTEL GROUNDS.

He scanned the small print. Yes, it was County Mayo. Yes, it was The Ashford Castle Hotel. Yes, the girl—unidentified—had been battered to death. Yes, one report—unconfirmed—said a part of her body had been mutilated. Yes, Bond thought, it had to be number three—Ebbie Heritage, also known, in another world and time, as Emilie Nikolas, if he remembered the file correctly. Smolin—if, indeed, it *was* the famous Colonel Maxim Smolin behind the murders—must have two teams operating. This, Bond knew as he glanced at the trembling Heather, meant they were not safe anywhere. "Move," he told her, softly. "Move fast. Now! Follow the nice lady in the red uniform."

5

Jacko B

It was not what in Ireland is called "soft weather." This was the hard variety, lashing against the windscreen so that you could barely see the taillights of other vehicles. Bond drove with excessive care while Heather sat, hunched, next to him sobbing, her words blurred by grief—"My fault . . . it's my fault. Three of them now. Ebbie now. Oh, Christ, James . . ."

"It's *not* your fault. Get that out of your head." But he knew how she felt, for Heather had told him the whole sorry tale as they waited in the little office high above the intersection of Stratton Street and Piccadilly a few hours, and yet a lifetime, ago. With the news of another violent death spread over the front page of the *Evening Press,* Bond knew it would be folly to head straight for Ashford Castle now. He turned onto the airport exit road, was narrowly missed by a battered yellow Cortina with a wire coathanger for an aerial, and then turned off before reaching the main road that runs into Dublin from the North. The sign said INTER-

NATIONAL AIRPORT HOTEL, and he knew that place of old.

Tucking the car away in one of the vacant slots near the entrance, he turned off the engine and looked at Heather. "Stop crying." It was a quiet command. Not ruthless, or uncaring, but a command nevertheless. "Stop crying, and I'll tell you what we're going to do." At that moment, if pressed, he wouldn't have been able to tell anyone what he expected to do, but he needed the girl's confidence and cooperation.

She sniffed, turning her red eyes toward him, the scarlet accentuated by the hotel park lighting. "What *can* we do, James?"

"Book into this hotel. Now, here, just for the night. I'm not taking advantage of the situation, Heather, but we book *one* room, okay? One room and I lie across the door to guard you—or on a sofa pulled across the door. I also make a couple of telephone calls. We are Mr. and Mrs. Boldman, got it? They'll need only my signature, but you have to know what this is about. I'm taking a double room for your protection and your protection only. Right?"

"Whatever you say."

"Then do something with your face. Tidy up, and we'll go in looking like an ordinary English couple—or maybe an Irish couple, depending on what sort of voice I'm in."

Inside, Bond managed the soft brogue of Southern Ireland and a Dublin accent, booking the room, commenting on the weather, and backchatting the somewhat straitlaced girl at RECEPTION.

The room was functional. A one-night resting

place between planes or onward travel: comfortable, but without any frills.

Heather flopped onto the bed. She had ceased crying, but looked weary, tired, and frightened. Meanwhile, Bond had made some quick decisions. M had given him the push toward this job, and underlined that he had no official status; but Bond had his own contacts, even here in the Republic of Ireland, and as long as he did not cross lines with the Embassy, he saw no reason for not taking advantage of them.

"We'll get food shortly." He grinned at Heather, probably a shade too conspiratorially. "In the meantime, why don't you freshen up in the bathroom while I make a couple of calls." Even if it was Smolin, with the entire HVA, GRU, and KGB backing him up, it was unlikely the telephones of the International Airport Hotel had an intercept on them.

Dredging his memory, Bond dialed a local number and was answered, after three rings, by a woman.

"Inspector Murray in?" Bond asked, mentally crossing his fingers.

"Who wants him?"

"One of his lads, tell him. He'll be knowing when he speaks." Bond still used the Dublin accent.

She made no comment, and a few seconds later the deep chuckling voice of Inspector Norman Murray, of the Garda's Special Branch, came on.

"Norman"—Bond smiled to himself as he spoke—"Jacko B here."

"Oh? Jacko, is it? And where are *you,* Jacko?"

"Not over the water, Norman."

"Lord love you, what the hell're you doing here,

then? Not mischief, I hope—and why didn't I know you were in the country?"

"Because I didn't advertise. No, not mischief, Norman. How's the charming Mrs. Murray?"

"Bonny. Rushing around all day and playing squash half the night. She'd be sending her love to you if she knew we'd talked."

"Don't think she should know."

"Then you *are* on mischief. Official mischief?"

"Not so you'd notice, if you follow me."

"I follow you."

"You owe me, Norman."

"That I know, Jacko. Only too well. What can I do for you?" A slight pause, then, "Unofficially, of course."

"For starters, the Ashford Castle business."

"Oh, Jesus, that's not in our court, is it?"

"Depends, and even then, it could be unofficial. Have they identified the girl yet?"

"I can find out. Ring you back, shall I?"

"I'll call *you,* Norman. You're there for the next hour or so?"

"You'll get me here. Home after midnight. I drew the late shift this week, but the wife's out with her squash pals."

"You hope."

"Away with you, Jacko. Call me back. Ten, fifteen minutes, okay?"

"Thanks." He quickly closed the line, praying that Murray would not run a check with the Embassy. You could never really tell with Branch people on either side of the water. He dialed another number.

This time a jaunty voice answered—chirpy, but oddly guarded.

"Mick?" Bond asked.

"Which Mick would you be wanting?"

"Big Mick. Tell him it's Jacko B."

"Jacko, you rogue," the voice roared at the other end of the line. "Where are you then? I'll bet you'll be after sitting in some smart hotel with the prettiest girl any red-blooded man would fancy right there on your knee."

"Not on my knee, Mick. No. But there is a pretty girl." He glanced up as Heather came out of the bathroom, face scrubbed. "A very pretty girl," he added, for Heather's benefit. She did not smile, but grabbed her handbag and retreated into the bathroom again.

"There, what'd I tell you?" Big Mick's voice gave a great guffaw. "And if there's a woman in the picture, Jacko B, then there's trouble, or I don't know you at all."

"Could be, Mick. Just could be."

"What can I do for you, Jacko?"

"Are you in work, Mick?"

Another guffaw. "Sorta in and out. This and that, if you know what I mean."

Bond knew what he meant. He had known Big Mick Shean for the best part of fifteen years, and while the Irishman walked a very slender tightrope as far as the law was concerned, Bond had a dozen reasons to trust him—or any one of his companions—with his life. In some ways, Bond had trained him in certain nefarious dealings, like back-watching; on-the-ground surveillance; and how to get rid of dubious people who showed more than a passing interest.

"Would you have any wheels, Mick?" he asked, knowing that if Big Mick did not have a car he could soon get one—or three—and have them clean and respectable within twelve hours.

"I might have."

"You'll need, maybe three. With a couple of fellas to each."

There was only a slight pause—half a beat too long. "Six fellas and three sets of wheels. What's in it?"

"Couple of days' work or so. Usual rates."

"Cash?"

"Cash."

"And danger money?"

"If there's danger."

"With fellas like you there's always danger, Jacko. What's the deal?"

"Straight and true as a dog's hind leg. I might be needing you to look after me and the girl—at a distance."

"When?"

"Probably in the morning. As I say, two days, maybe three."

"Give us a ring about midnight, Jacko. If it's you, the cars have to be respectable . . ."

"And reliable."

"I was just going to say that, so."

"A nice little country drive, that's all."

Big Mick appeared to hesitate again; his voice had dropped and become very serious when he next spoke. "It's not to go into the North at all, Jacko, is it?"

"The opposite direction entirely, Mick. No worries on that score."

"Lord love you, Jacko. We don't do politicals, if you follow me."

"I'll call back around midnight."

"You do that."

Bond cradled the telephone just as Heather came out of the bathroom again. She had repaired her face, and the hair now looked fabulous.

He smiled at her, the kind of smile guaranteed to get cooperation. "Pity, you look so good, Heather."

"Why a pity?"

"Because I'd like to take you out to dinner, Dublin boasts some excellent restaurants. Unhappily—"

"We daren't show our faces."

"No. I fear it'll have to be sandwiches and coffee up here. In the room. What's your fancy?"

"Could we make it a bottle of wine instead of coffee?"

"Whatever you say."

In the end he called room service and discovered they made smoked salmon sandwiches, with which he ordered the best bottle of Chablis they seemed to have. He also retrieved the baton and his gun from the getaway case—it was the thought of someone coming to the room with the sandwiches, for the oldest trick in the book was to substitute a man for the waiter. One of the few things they got right in bad movies. But, before the waiter arrived, Bond picked up the telephone and called Inspector Murray as he had promised. Their conversation was short and fairly sharp. In the field never trust anybody, they taught, and he knew exactly how long it would take Murray to get a trace on his number, and therefore pinpoint him at the International Airport Hotel.

"Norman? Jacko. You have anything?"

"It'll be in the morning papers, Jacko. But there's something else I want to talk to you about."

"Just give me what's going in the papers."

"Local girl, Jacko. No form. Part-time chambermaid, name of Betty-Anne Mulligan."

"Ah. They got any ideas down there?"

"None at all. Good girl. Twenty-two years. No current boyfriends. Family's cut up no end."

"And the mutilation?"

"I think you know, Jacko. You've had a couple on your side of the water. Betty-Anne Mulligan was sans tongue. Head bashed in and not a tongue in her mouth. Removed after death. Very surgical—professional—they tell me."

"So. Nothing else?"

"Only the clothes she was wearing. The raincoat and headscarf."

"Well?"

"Not hers, Jacko me boy, not hers. Belonged to a guest at the hotel. Lovely bright day when Betty-Anne went in to work. The rains came midafternoon, and she had a long walk. Two miles and no coat or covering for her head. Guest took pity on her . . ."

"Name?"

"Miss Elizabeth Larke—with an 'e,' Jacko. Would you be knowing anything about that?"

"No," Bond answered honestly, "but I might by tomorrow. If I do I'll give you a call."

"Good man, now—"

"No, Norman. No time. Will the guest's name be in the papers?"

"It will not. Neither will the tongue."

Bond had been looking hard at his watch. He had about thirty seconds to get him clear of a trace. "Good," he snapped. "Your questions'll have to wait. Oh, and Norman, this *is* completely unofficial. I'll be in touch."

He heard Murray cry out, "Jacko—" as he closed the line. For a full minute he sat looking at the telephone, then the room service waiter knocked on the door, breaking the mood.

"Heather, did you often have meetings with Ebbie? I think I asked you before, but I need more details."

They munched at the pile of sandwiches, washing them down with a '78 Chablis that cost a fortune. Certainly it was a good year, but not at that kind of price.

"We met two or three times a year." Heather held out her glass for more.

"And observed precautions? Field rules?"

"Yes. Very careful. Booked hotels under names we concocted . . ."

"Such as?"

"She was always Elizabeth. I was Hetty. Surnames were birds and fish—she was a bird, I a fish."

"Ah. You kept a list?"

"No. Each time we met we arranged the name for the next meeting." She laughed, a jolly laugh, the kind you got from girls who hung around horses, rode, and talked of sales, and roans, and chestnuts. "Ebbie and I were very close. Best friend I ever had. In my time I've been Miss Sole, Miss Salmon,

Miss Crabbe—with an extra 'b'-'e'—we always added, if possible, like Miss Pyke spelled with a 'y.' "

"And what are you this time?"

"You've made me Miss Arlington, but I would have gone as Hetty Sharke—with an 'e.' "

"What about the bird?"

Her eyes brimmed and he thought she was about to break down again; he told her to take her time, sounding supportive. She nodded, gulped in air, and tried to speak, then had another go and it worked, but with only a little voice. "Oh, we laughed a lot, she's been Elizabeth Sparrow, Wren, Jay, Hawke—with an 'e.' "

"And this time?"

"Larke."

"With an 'e,' naturally."

She gave a little nod, then giggled as though the wine was getting to her. "We steered clear of Tits, James."

"Yes." The wine was definitely getting to her: a strange mixture of a girl for a former field agent, part completely naïve amateur, and part sharply professional. So, Miss Larke, safely staying at The Ashford Castle Hotel, was Ebbie Heritage. There were other questions, though. Had she just been kind, lending the poor little chambermaid her raincoat and scarf? Had she spotted someone, and if so, would she now get out fast?

"You have a fallback if anything went wrong?"

Heather nodded. "Every time." The professional status was rising again.

"Yes?" He was asking the pertinent question.

"This was an emergency. We made plans for something like this the first time we met after our rehabilitation. If something went wrong, or I didn't show, she was to have gone to Rosslare—the big hotel that looks over the harbor, The Great Southern. In case we had to make a dash for it on the ferry. But, now . . ." she trailed off, the tears close again.

Bond looked at his watch. It was gone eleven. For a second he wanted to put Heather out of her misery—tell her that Ebbie was alive and well and living in—where? But no. Experience told him to play Ebbie's situation very close to his chest.

"Look, Heather, tomorrow's going to be a tough day. I'm going downstairs for a few minutes. You are not to open the door to anyone except me, and I'll give you a Morse V knock—tap-tap-tap-bang, twice. Anyone else, just stay silent. And don't answer the telephone if it rings. Get yourself ready for bed. I'll avert my eyes when you open up—"

"Oh, Lord, James, I'm a big girl. I've been in the field, remember. I'm not shy about you seeing me in my scanties, as they so coyly say." She giggled again, and Bond felt a small signal of worry. This was a trained field agent, who had been entrusted with, possibly, the most important target of *Cream Cake,* yet she appeared to be slightly drunk on less than half a bottle of Chablis. *That* just didn't ring true, like many other things. Very enthusiastic amateur trying hard for professional recognition.

He slipped into his jacket. "Right, Miss Heather Dare. No door, except for my knock. No telephone. I won't be long."

Downstairs, Bond went into the bar and bought a vodka and tonic, offering an English ten-pound note. The change came strictly in Irish money, as though there was no difference in the rate of exchange, so he leaned lightly on the barman for three pounds' worth of ten-pence pieces to feed one of the telephone boxes in the foyer.

There was nobody suspicious either in bar, coffee shop, or foyer—he took his time checking, walking even into that odd well, spaced out with black imitation leather seats, set back in booths, that occupied most of the foyer like some kind of bunker.

Not a smell. Nothing untoward, as his old friend Inspector Murray would have said. When he was absolutely certain, he went over to the telephone near the door, looked up The Ashford Castle Hotel, County Mayo in the directory, and dialed the number standing with the handful of coins in his other hand.

"I'd like to speak to one of your guests—Miss Larke," he told the distant switchboard operator. "Miss Elizabeth Larke."

"Just one moment." A click on the line, then, "I'm sorry, sir, Miss Larke checked out."

"When? I'm really calling for a friend who was to meet her at your hotel, a Miss Sharke, S-h-a-r-k-e. There wouldn't be a message left for her?"

"I'll have to put you through to Reception." There was a click, and another voice announced that she was "Reception."

Bond repeated his query. Yes, Miss Larke *had* left a message to say she had gone on ahead.

"You don't know where?" Bond queried.

"It's a Dublin address." Reception paused, as though uncertain if she should give it, then relented and rattled off Ebbie's normal Dublin address, near Fitzwilliam Square.

Bond thanked her—wondering what Ebbie had really been up to with an address as good as that—then closed the line and dialed the Garda Special Branch number, right up there in Dublin Castle where all the action was.

"Jacko again, Norman," he said when Murray came on the line.

"You just caught me, I was getting out early. Hang on a minute." The minute stretched a little. Murray was putting a trace on the call.

"Right, man, I wanted a word with you anyway."

"That you'll get, probably tomorrow, Norman. One question: do you think the boys in Mayo will have finished with Miss Larke—the guest who was so kind with her raincoat?"

Pause. One, two, three. He was holding on to give the engineers time. "Well?" Bond chivied.

"I suppose so. If they had her forwarding address. I spoke to the Super in charge of the case. She was no suspect. Gentle as a lamb, he said. Lamb and Larke, eh?" An explosion of laughter.

"Thanks, Norman." Bond quickly put down the phone. Murray knew him as Jacko B on a very official basis. They had worked together a couple of times, and the Special Branch man had no illusions concerning the Service he was dealing with when Jacko B contacted him. They had an edgy, suspicious, though firmly defined relationship. In all probability, Murray would now—after three conversations, and no idea of his whereabouts—be on to the Resident at the Embassy in Merrion Road. Jacko B had been Bond's contact telephone crypto for the Republic of Ireland—his "blower name," as old hands called it—for a long time. In fact, he considered, it must be wearing a shade thin now, but nobody had thought of changing it.

Not yet midnight, Bond thought, but Big Mick was never very far away from a telephone. Piling the loose change on top of the public telephone, he dialed the number. Mick came on straightaway.

"I have the cars and the men," he said, once the bona fide codes were established. "Just give me the details, Jacko."

Bond gave him the number of the self-drive hire car, then, "I should say around ten, maybe ten-thirty, tomorrow. You'll pick us up somewhere around the Green. We'll be parked, and walking up from Grafton Street. What've you got, Mick?"

"A Volvo, maroon; a dark blue Audi; and an old Cortina, dun-colored, with plenty of go under the hood. Where're we going, and how d'you want us?"

"We'll be going to Rosslare—the direct route. I want someone well ahead, let's say the Cortina; with the Volvo and Audi close up to me. Box me in if you can, Mick. Not too tight, nothing out of the ordinary. Flash me if we've got any persistent company. Flash twice if you mark a dark-complexioned man with close-cropped hair, square face, struts rather than walks—"

"He won't be doin' much strutting in a motor," Big Mick sounded caustic.

"Military. German. That's the only description I can give you," Bond said wearily, realizing that a verbal picture of Maxim Smolin was not the easiest thing to paint over the telephone. He had seen the man only once, in Paris about three years ago. Seen him once, and been through his file a dozen times. There were seven covert photographs in the file and even they did not help. "Anyone who looks out of place is a danger," Bond said. "See you tomorrow, and thanks, Mick. Money from the usual place, okay?"

"You're a gentleman, Jacko. Tomorrow, then."

He cradled the telephone, and was about to go up to the room again, when he thought of one more chore—suspicious, perhaps, but necessary, for he felt most uneasy. On the way to the elevator he paused by the internal guest telephone and dialed their room number, scowling as it gave the engaged sound. Heather had disobeyed him, and the thought added more worry to his already overloaded anxiety.

Back at the bedroom, Bond gave the Morse code V knock twice, quickly. The door opened, and a vision of pink and white scampered away, back into the bed. He closed the door, put on the chain, and turned to look at her, lying, with a half smile on her face. The telephone on the bedside table was off the hook. He nodded toward it.

"Oh." She smiled again, moving from under the bedclothes so that they dropped back revealing a bare arm, shoulder, and part of one breast. "I'm terrible with phones, James. Can't stand not answering them, so I took it off the hook." She replaced the instrument and looked at him from the bed, the sheet and blankets falling to reveal both breasts. "If you want to sleep here, James, I wouldn't complain."

She looked so vulnerable that it took a great deal of willpower for Bond to refuse the offer. Heather merely shrugged—a gesture that allowed the covers to fall even lower. Bond recalled some song he had heard, which described breasts, "like virgin moons."

"You're a sweet girl, Heather, and I'm flattered. Bushed, but flattered, and tomorrow's another day. A tough old day as well."

"I just feel so . . . so—alone, and bloody miserable. Oh, you probably think I'm just a tart. What the hell." And, with that, Heather Dare, née Irma Wagen, turned over, pushed her head into the pillow, and pulled the sheets up.

Bond quietly removed one of the spare pillows from the bed, took off jacket and trousers, wrapped himself, first in the short silk robe from his getaway case, then in a blanket he found in the wardrobe. James Bond then literally stretched himself across the doorway, one hand resting lightly on the butt of his automatic pistol.

Sleep eluded him. Heather gave little snorts, as though having a bad dream, but Bond's dreams were reality, there in the darkness, as he thought about the operation that had been called *Cream Cake,* the incongruities of the situation, and the ruthlessness of the man called Maxim Smolin.

He drifted into sleep, waking with a start. It was five o'clock, and someone was gently trying the handle of the door.

6

Basilisk

Silently, James Bond rolled out of his blanket, drawing the pistol as he did so. The door handle continued to turn, then stopped, but by the time it had done so Bond was at Heather's side of the bed, his gun hand shaking her naked shoulder, while the other pressed gently over her mouth.

She made small grunting noises as he bent low and whispered that they had company—she should keep silent, get onto the floor, and lie out of sight. She nodded and he took his hand away, returning to the door, keeping to one side, because more than once he had seen what bullets did to people through doors.

He slipped the chain gingerly and then, standing well back, sharply pulled the door open.

"Jacko? Hello there." Even in the light from the corridor, Bond recognized Inspector Murray's tall frame and the smiling, shrewd face peering into the room.

"What the hell!" Bond moved behind him, shutting the door, snapping the lights on, and pushing the Garda Special Branch man just hard enough to put him off balance, all in one fast movement.

Murray stumbled forward, grabbing for the bed, but Bond had him in a neck choke, the ASP's muzzle just behind the policeman's right ear. "What the blazes are you playing at, Norman? You'll get yourself killed creeping about like that. Or have you got an armed posse surrounding the hotel?"

"Hold it, Jacko! Hold it! I come in peace. Alone, and unofficially."

Heather's frightened face slowly appeared from the other side of the bed, her eyes looking straight into the Inspector's merry face.

"Ah," he said, the mouth splitting into a friendly smile, as Bond slightly relaxed his grip. "Ah, and this would be Miss Arlington, would it, Mr. Boldman?—or may I call you Jacko B?"

Keeping the pistol close to Murray's head, Bond released him from the choke, moving his free hand and finding the Garda-issue Walther PPK in a hip holster. He removed the gun, sliding it across the floor, well out of reach. "For a man of peace, you come well prepared, Norman."

"Oh, come on, Jacko, I *have* to carry the cannon, you know that as well as I—and what's a wee gun, between friends?"

"Death." Bond sounded cynical. "You knew I was here all the time, then?—and Miss Arlington?"

"Ach, man, of course. But I kept it to myself. We just happen to have a red alert on at the moment and your face came up at the airport. Lucky I was on duty at the Castle when it came in on the Fax. I telephoned old Grimshawe—who we all know is the Brits' head spook in Merrion Road—and asked if he had any extra bodies over here, or expected any. Grimshawe tells me the truth. We work better that way. It saves a lot of time. He said no—no spooks, and no extracurricular activities, so I believed him. Then you rang me, and I got interested." His eyes twinkled as he turned back toward Heather. "You wouldn't be Miss Larke's friend, Miss Sharke, would you, dear?"

"What?" Heather's mouth hung open.

"Because, if you are, then it's bloody bad security, and not up to the high standards we've come to know and love. Names like Larke and Sharke attract attention. Stupid—which *we* are not."

Bond stepped back. "Mark him well, dear, stupid he is not," he said, mimicking Murray's accent, which was more lowland Scots than Dublin—as Murray always said, "I was born in the North, educated in the South, holiday in Scotland or Spain, work in the Republic, and don't feel at home anywhere."

"It was a shade idiotic, Norman, to come trying my door handle at this time of night."

"And when else should I try it? Not in broad daylight, when I have to account for every movement I make."

"You could have knocked."

"I was going to knock, Jacko. Another thirty seconds and I'd have knocked. Tap, tap, bloody tap."

The men looked at each other, neither believing the other. "I'm not here for the fun of it." Inspector Murray produced his cheerful smile. "I'm here because I owe you."

"Not because you're as nosy as any other copper?"

"I think your London policemen are wonderful, too. I owe you in a big way, Jacko, and I always repay."

That was true enough. Four years ago, Bond had saved the Garda SB man's life—up on the border, just on the Republic's side, not far from Crossmaglen, but the facts of that would remain buried in secret archives.

Heather still crouched on the floor. Now she pulled the clothes off the bed, wrapping them around her, and trying at the same time to pat her ruffled hair into some reasonable shape. Both men gazed at her in silence.

When she was decent, Murray sat himself on the bed, swiveling his body in a vain attempt to watch both Bond and Heather at the same time. "Look, girl," he addressed Heather, "Jacko'll tell you that you can be trusting me."

"Don't even think about trust, Miss Arlington." Bond's face remained impassive.

Murray sighed. "Right. I'll just be giving you the facts, then I can get home to a cup of cocoa and sleep."

They sat as though staring each other out. Finally Murray spoke again. "Your Miss Larke, now—the one that lent the poor young girl her coat and scarf—"

"What . . . ?" Heather began, but Bond shook his head almost viciously, telling her to say nothing.

"Well, your Miss Larke now appears to have, as they say of foxes, gone to earth."

"You mean she's not—?" Heather began again.

"Shut up!" Bond clipped out with some venom.

"My God, Jacko, can't you be the masterful one

when you've a mind?" Murray grinned, took a breath, then started to speak again. "There was a Dublin address." He looked around, first at the girl and then at Bond, his face a picture of innocence. "A nice little address near Fitzwilliam Square."

Silence, as though he was still waiting. No replies, so, with a shrug, he continued, "Well, as they would say in London, somebody's gone and turned over that particular drum."

"You mean this Dublin address given by someone called Larke?" Bond asked.

"Whose name is not Larke, but, I suspect, Heritage. Ebbie Heritage, and what sort of a name is that, I ask you? Sounds like one of these romantic novelists. *Her Heart Lies Bleeding* by Ebbie Heritage."

Heather could not stop herself from letting out a stifled gasp.

"Enough of bleeding hearts." Bond sounded decidedly crusty. "This woman—Larke, or Heritage . . . ?"

"Ach, come on, Jacko, don't play the goat with me. You know bloody well, if you'll pardon me, Miss . . . er—Sharke?"

"Arlington," Heather provided, appearing to have herself under control.

"Yes." He did not believe a syllable of the name. "I've told you, the address provided by Miss Larke really belongs to a Miss Heritage. Both are missing. The apartment—the flat—near Fitzwilliam Square's been done over."

"Burglary? Vandalism?" Bond was exceptionally curt.

"Oh, a bit of both. It's one hell of a mess. Professional, but dressed up to look like enthusiastic amateurs. Interesting thing is that either the owner never had a piece of correspondence, or never kept any—or it was purloined by whoever took the place apart. They even ripped up loose floorboards. Now what d'you think of that?"

"You've come out here, at dawn, just to tell me this?" Bond asked.

"Well, you showed interest in the Ashford Castle business. Thought you should know. Besides, me knowing what kind of work you're engaged in, I thought there was something else I should put your way."

Bond nodded, as if to say, "Go on, then."

"Did you ever hear of a fella called Smolin?" Murray asked, all honey and disinterest. "Maxim Smolin. The Branch in London, ourselves, so I presume the people you work for as well, have him under a stupid code name—*Basilisk.*"

"Mmm," Bond grunted.

"You want this joker's life history, or do you know it already, Jack?"

Bond smiled. "Okay, Norm—"

"And don't you be after calling me Norm, either, or I'll have you in the Bridewell on some trumped-up charge that'll ban you from the Republic for life plus ninety-nine years."

"Okay, *Norman.* Maxim Anton Smolin. Born 1946 in Berlin of a German lady called Christina von Geshmann, by a Soviet General—whose mistress she was at the time—name of Smolin. Alexei Alexeiovich Smolin. Young Smolin took his father's name and, oddly, his mother's nationality. There is some corner of a Russian field that is forever German, if you follow me."

"I'm ahead of you, lad."

"Educated in Berlin, Moscow, and then Berlin again. Mother died when he was only a couple of years old. That your man, Norman?"

"Go on."

"Entered the military via one of those nice Russian schools, I forget which one. Could have been the Thirteenth Army. Anyway, he was commissioned young, then into the Spetsnaz Training Center—the élite, if you like that kind of élite killer. One thing's for sure, young Maxim found his way, by invitation, into the GRU, because that's the only way you get into the GRU—unlike the KGB, who'll take you off the streets if you make them an offer. From thence, by a series of postings, Smolin came back to Berlin—East Berlin. And he returned as a high-ranking field officer of the HVA—the East German Intelligence Service."

"Our Jacko's got one of those photogenic memories, as my old mother would say," Murray muttered.

Bond took no notice, hardly pausing for breath. "He's everything, our Maxim. A mole within a warren of moles: working with the HVA, which has to work with the KGB, yet all the time he's doing little jobs on the side because he's really a member of the GRU—that most secret arm of Military Intelligence."

"You have the man to a T." Murray beamed at them. "You know what they say about the GRU, which in many ways is to be feared more than the jolly KGB? They say it costs a ruble to join, and two rubles to get out of. Almost an Irish saying, that. Very difficult to become a GRU officer. Bloody difficult to jump over the wall once you're in, because there really is only one way out—in a long box. They're also very fond of training foreigners, and Smolin is only half Russian. They tell me he holds great power in East Germany. That even the KGB men there are in awe of him."

Bond half nodded. "That's really a matter for speculation, but who better to be well placed in the East German Secret Service? Him being a member of the Russian Military Intelligence with a lot of experience?" He stopped for four beats. "But what of this little man, Norman? Have you something to tell us about him?"

"You know, Jacko, the whole world imagines that we have but one problem on this divided island—the North and the South; the lads and the forces of law and order. They're wrong, and I'm sure you're aware of it, so. Your man—Basilisk—arrived in the Republic two days ago. Now, Jacko, when I heard of that terrible thing at Ashford Castle, I recalled there'd already been two just like it over the water, and a little quotation came to mind."

"Yes?"

"There's something most pertinent been said, and written, about your Soviet General Staff Chief Intelligence Directorate—your GRU. The fella was writing about people who can't keep quiet; who leak secrets. He wrote, *The GRU knows how to rip such tongues out!* Name of Suverov, that fella. GRU defector. Interesting, Jacko?"

Bond nodded, looking solemn. The amateur and professional historians of the secret world always tended to dismiss the GRU as having been swallowed by the KGB. *The GRU (Soviet Military Intel-*

ligence) is completely dominated by the KGB, one such writer had maintained. *It is an academic exercise to consider the GRU as a separate entity,* another had written. Wrong, on all counts. The GRU fought hard, and constantly, to keep a separate identity.

"Penny for them, Jacko?" Murray was making himself comfortable on the bed.

"I was merely thinking that the cream of the GRU are richer—and more deadly—than their KGB counterparts. Men like Smolin are better trained, and have no scruples at all."

"And Smolin's here, Jacko, and"—he paused, the smile wiped from his face to be replaced by the look of a hard man—"and we've lost the bugger, if you'll pardon the language again, Miss Dare."

"Arlington," Heather mumbled without conviction. Bond saw that she looked both nervous and a little sad.

Norman Murray lifted his hand and tilted it. "Dare, Wagen, Sharke, so who's counting?" He yawned and stretched. "It's been a long night. I must away to my bed."

"Lost him?" Bond asked.

"He did the vanishing trick, Jacko. But Smolin's always been good at vanishing—he's a proper little Houdini; and talking of Houdini, Smolin's probably not the only one of his breed that' s on the loose in the Republic."

"Don't tell me you've lost the Chairman of the Central Committee as well?"

"It's no time to be caustic with me, Jacko. But we've had a small tip-off. Nothing elaborate, mind you, but a strong straw in the wind."

"A straw to clutch at?"

"If it's the truth, you wouldn't be after clutching at this one, Jacko B. This one's a walking mortal sin that doesn't go by any fancy cryptonym. Just a word, that's all."

"Well?" Bond waited.

"The word is that someone much higher up the ladder than Smolin is, at present, in the Republic. I've no collateral; nothing firm. But the word's strong enough. Someone from the top; now, that's all I can give you." He rose, walked to the corner, and retrieved his Walther. "I'll be saying goodnight to you both, then. And sweet dreams."

"Thanks, Norman. Thanks a whole bunch." Bond walked him to the door. "May I ask you something?"

"Ask away. There's no charge."

"You've lost sight of Comrade Colonel Smolin . . ."

"This is true. And we haven't even had a sniff at the other one—if he's here at all."

"Are you still looking for him—them?"

"We are that—in a desultory way, of course. Manpower, Jacko B, manpower's your problem."

"What would you do with them if you cornered either one?"

"Put them on an airplane to Berlin. But those fellas'd complain and dodge into that den of iniquity in Orwell Road—you know, the one that's got about six hundred bits of aerial and electronic dishes on the roof. Bit of irony, isn't it? The Soviets having their embassy in Orwell Road, and building a forest of communications hardware on top of it. That's where your man'd hide."

"And he's not there at the moment?"

"How would I know, so? I am not my brother's keeper."

"But you *are,* Norman. That's exactly what you are."

They came into St. Stephen's Green from Grafton Street, with Heather clutching shopping, the carriers announcing to the world that she had bought all a girl needs at Switzers and Brown, Thomas & Co.

Bond walked two paces behind her and a shade to the left. He carried one small parcel and his gun hand hovered across the front of his unbuttoned jacket. Ever since Norman Murray had left the hotel Bond had worried—anxious about a dozen matters that just did not add up.

At first, Heather had nagged him, furious that he had not told her Ebbie was alive and not victim of the mallet and scalpel—maybe some special curved surgical instrument, he thought.

"But you didn't tell me, you bastard. You knew how I felt. You knew she was alive—"

"I knew she was *probably* alive."

"But why couldn't you have the decency to tell me?"

"Because I wasn't one hundred percent certain; and because your precious operation *Cream Cake* strikes me as having been a lash-up from start to finish—and it's still a lash-up!" He stopped himself from saying more, for his temper was rapidly fraying at the edges.

After a few more exchanges, Bond finally told

her to shut up and get at least an hour's more sleep. "You're going to need it."

She dozed off, but Bond remained awake, turning the problems over and over in his mind.

In theory, *Cream Cake* was a good operation, but if Heather was typical of the five young people chosen to carry out the seductions, the Operations Planners were criminally at fault.

The germ of the idea had been fair enough: after all, the HVA and KGB had been seducing little Emilies working for West German Government agencies for years—had not they even seduced old Willy Brandt's confidential aide? Though you could hardly call him an Emily.

The trouble with *Cream Cake* lay in its team—four young girls and a youth: there would never have been time to train them properly. Their parents were in place, as the Planners liked to say, so that was considered to be enough.

Their names spun in Bond's head like a gramophone record revolving with the needle stuck in a groove—Franzi Trauben and Elli Zuckermann, both dead, skulls crushed and tongues neatly removed; Franz Belzinger—who liked to be called Wald—and, of course, Irma Wagen herself, and Emilie Nikolas, a real Emily who should be in Rosslare.

He told himself that he must start thinking of them all by their refurbished English names—much good those had done them. Then he asked himself why Franz—Frank, he corrected himself—liked being nicknamed Wald? No, he had to think in English—the dead Bridget and Millicent. The living Heather and Ebbie. The presumably living Jungle Baisley.

Four young girls and a youth—tethered honeypots—plunged headlong into an Emily ploy that came unstuck. He would go over it again with Heather. He must go over it again.

And, in those early hours of sleeplessness, while the five characters in this drama called *Cream Cake* came and went in his head, Bond was conscious of the other dark figures, appearing out of all proportion, as is often the case within an active mind half awake just before dawn. The sixth actor—Maxim Smolin, whom he had seen so many times in grainy surveillance photographs, or jumpy films, distorted through fiber-optic lenses, and once—once only—in the flesh as he came out of Fouquets on the Champs-Elysées.

Bond had been sitting almost opposite—at a pavement café with another officer—and, even at the distance provided by that wide street with the distractions of its traffic, the short, tough, military figure of Smolin had a profound effect on him. It was possibly the way he carried himself—like a professional soldier, but more so; or, maybe it was his look, the eyes never still, the hands held just so, one fist clenched, the other flat as though making a tough cutting edge. In those few brief moments when Bond saw him, Smolin appeared to radiate energy and a malevolent power.

Then there was the seventh protagonist, the someone higher up the ladder than Smolin, unnamed by Norman Murray. The possibility that an even more senior officer—GRU or KGB—was here threw a considerably darker shadow over the entire business.

But those were predawn thoughts, when the enemy

assumed near-nightmare proportions. Now it was day, and their car was parked on the far side of St. Stephen's Green; Heather had bought everything, from the flesh out and then some, and, before that, Bond—to Heather's amazement—had gone through his ritual exercises and eaten his predictable breakfast, commanded, rather than ordered, from room service, and sent back twice until they got it right.

The rain had gone, yet there was a chill in the air and drifting gunfire-smoke clouds raced each other over the rooftops.

En route to the parked car, they paused for the traffic lights, and Bond caught a glimpse of the piratelike, black-bearded, tousled-haired Big Mick Shean at the wheel of a maroon Volvo. The Irishman showed no sign of recognition, but he was sure to have already identified the parked car, and Bond with the girl as they waited for the lights to change.

They crossed the road on the green light and began to walk slowly—"Don't rush it," he had told Heather. "It should be the same routine you use when lighting a fuse on an explosive charge: walk away, never run, lest you trip." She nodded, and obviously knew something about explosives, so there had been *some* training out of the field, Bond judged. During the ride to Rosslare he would go through it piece by piece.

They did not cut across the Green, but sauntered along the North side, heading East—for the car was parked on the Eastern side of the square that forms that Dublin landmark.

As they drew level with The Shelbourne Hotel, Bond almost froze. He glanced across at the renowned hostel—once Noël Coward's favorite, and often likened to New York's Algonquin because of its attraction for the arty and international set—and saw, for only the second time in the flesh, the precise, compact figure of Colonel Maxim Smolin, accompanied by two men who could only be described as thickset, and even that was an underestimation. "Don't look toward the hotel," he muttered under his breath. The three men were now descending the steps, looking left and right as though for expected transport. "No, Heather, don't look," as she reacted by starting to disobey his order. "Just keep walking," quickening his pace, "your ex-lover just came out of his cave."

To himself, he thought, Basilisk is here, now, and deadly.

7

Accident

There was no point in trying to hide or run. Smolin knew Heather by sight. He could have recognized her, clothed or unclothed, at half a mile in a Scottish mist; and Bond reckoned that the HVA man would know *him* on sight as well. After all, his photograph was in the files of practically every intelligence agency in the world. All he could pray for was that, in the traffic, and with Smolin's obvious concern over his own transport, he would not have spotted them. But with a man like Smolin he knew the chances were slim. Smolin was not just a professional, but a hyperprofessional, trained to single out the most unlikely faces among a crowd of thousands.

Gently taking Heather's arm, Bond guided her around the corner, turning right—their backs to The Shelbourne now—not hurrying her unduly, but almost imperceptibly increasing their walking pace toward the car, which was parked, nose inward to the pavement, on one of the many meters that stood like detection devices along the East side of the Green.

He felt the familiar, unpleasant tingling around the back of his neck—like a dozen small, deadly spiders unleashed in the nape hair. It was not 100 percent accurate, but Bond was realistic enough to know the odds were very high on Colonel Maxim Smolin's eyes watching their retreating backs. He was also probably smiling at the coincidence of catching sight of his former lover in the middle of Dublin. Or, Bond wondered, was it simple coincidence? In this business coincidence was usually a dirty word. M always maintained there was no such thing, just as Freud had once said that, in conditions of stress and confusion, there was no such thing as an accident.

They reached the car and, once in, Bond scanned the mirror while twisting the key in the ignition and clipping his seat belt on. The traffic was heavy, but he just caught the flash of a dun-colored Cortina passing behind them, with a dark blue Audi close on its bumper. Already he had seen Big Mick at the wheel of the maroon Volvo, so all the cars were circling the Green. The trick would be to get out and onto the road to the outskirts of Dun Laoghaire, then on along the coast. The route would take them through Bray and Arklow, Gorey and Wexford, then down to Rosslare—that untidy crop of buildings that stood above the harbor. A trick it certainly would be, for they might well have to circle the Green more than once to get into position: and that meant passing The Shelbourne again.

Gently, Bond started to back out into the traffic, waiting with not a little impatience for a gap to appear. When one finally did he reversed the car unforgivably fast, slamming the gears into first again and taking off at some speed. Seconds later he was tucked neatly in behind the Audi.

They circled the Green once and there was no sign of Smolin and his two large associates outside The Shelbourne. The Cortina left at that junction, going straight on, heading for Merrion Row and Baggot Street.

By the time they reached the same point a second time, Big Mick was behind them, so that they were tightly boxed in—with the Cortina well ahead and out of sight as the forward scout. Bond, glancing in the mirror, saw Big Mick's craggy face split into a grin at the successful fast linkup of the team. Behind them, in the back seat, Heather's purchases rolled around, slipping and sliding as Bond threw the car from one lane to another. He wanted to get out of Dublin's main environs as soon as possible.

"Why did he like to be called Wald?" Bond asked suddenly. They were now well away, mixed up in a steady stream of traffic, but approaching Bray with its great, ugly church dominating the small town, looking almost French and certainly too large for the community.

Heather started in her seat. She had been silent, allowing Bond to concentrate.

"Wald? You mean Franz? Jungle?"

"I'm not talking about the Black Forest, old love." Bond drove like a fighter pilot, eyes scanning the road ahead, the mirrors and instruments, making regular checks at least every thirty seconds. Yet his mind was balanced between driving, watching, and the short interrogation he wanted to conduct.

She paused, as though she needed to think of the answer. "It was odd. You've seen his photograph?

Yes, well, he was so good-looking—blond hair, clear skin, fit, tall and slim, strong, and with a fine face. He looked like those old photographs you see of Hitler's ideal Germans—a true Aryan."

"So why did he like to be called Wald?" There was impatience in Bond's voice, and it showed. Her description was colored by her new business interest—the beauty salon—not her old profession as tethered honeypot. "Why Wald?" he repeated.

"He was vain." She made it sound that simple.

"And what's that got to do with it?" They had stopped for some traffic lights, Bond's car close on the Audi's rear, with Big Mick's Volvo separated from them by two trucks.

"About the work, he was vain. He said he could always hide from anybody. He had this idea that no one could ever find him if he didn't want to be found—like searching a dense forest. I think it was Elli who said we should call him Wald, and that pleased him. He is a little full of himself—is that the right phrase?"

Bond nodded. "Hence Jungle Baisley now. Looking for him would be like looking for a particular tree?"

"That's about it. Or like a needle in a haystack."

Now Bond was even more concerned. "You say Elli gave him the nickname. The five of you met together regularly?" That would have been almost suicidally bad security, he thought. But there were many things about *Cream Cake* that pointed toward bad security.

"Not a lot of times, no. But there were meetings."

"Called by your case officer—your controller?"

"No. Swift saw us one at a time. We had regular

meetings. Safe houses. Rendezvous in shops or parks. But you must understand that we all knew each other—since children."

Bond thought they were almost children when this monstrous plan was conceived. Two were dead for sure, the others had prices on their heads and their tongues. Smolin would not rest until they were all safely in their coffins. And what of Swift, their case officer, their control? There had been a great deal about Swift in the files M had put his way. Swift was a street name, and the real identity was carefully hidden, even in the official documents. But Bond knew the man behind the masked name—a legend among case officers; one of the most experienced and careful people in the business. So much so that he was cryptoed Swift because of the speed at which he worked on his clients: swift and surefooted. Not the kind of man to make errors. Yet, if Heather had told him the truth about how *Cream Cake* had come to its chaotic end, Swift's judgment had let him down at last.

They passed through lush green countryside, littered with trees and the occasional cottage sending up calm and drifting smoke signals from its turf-burning fire. It was a land that appeared tranquil, if untidy—just as untidy as *Cream Cake.* Quickly, Bond went through it again in his mind, thinking of the network by their English names.

All five had parents who had been, if not sleepers, then dozing agents—men and women who handed over the odd piece of useful intelligence; yet all of them very well placed. Bridget's father was a lawyer, with some bigwig officials among his clientele; Millicent's parents were both doctors, with a number of intelligence community people on *their* books; the other three came from military or paramilitary families—Ebbie's father was an officer with the Vopos; Jungle's and Heather's were in the thicket of secrets—German officers working out of Karlshorst, that area of East Berlin that housed both military barracks and intelligence buildings as well as the Soviet HQ in Eastern Germany.

It was easy to see how—a few years ago—those five young people had glistened like gold when the Planners thought up the idea of compromising people in East Germany: just as the Soviet and East German agencies had done to intelligence departments in the West.

Bridget was to set her cap at a member of the East German Politburo; Millicent was to "make herself available" to one of the seven KGB officers serving under a paper-thin "advisory" cover at Karlshorst; Ebbie had a Major of the East German Army in *her* sights; while Jungle and Heather were in charge of the greatest prizes—Fräulein Captain Dietrich, the woman officer in charge of the civilian executive staff of the HVA, well known for her taste in younger men; and Colonel Maxim Smolin, to whom some referred, with a dark gallows humor, as The Plague Master of the HVA—for Smolin was responsible for rooting out and destroying clandestine agents of the Western organizations. Next to the Director of the HVA—and the leading politicians—he was probably one of the most powerful men in East Germany, with a hire-and-fire brief that made his law absolute in the seamier, and more deadly, side of the secret labyrinth—except, perhaps, for this more senior officer hinted at by Murray.

But back to Maxim Smolin, who had fallen for Heather—hook, line, and proverbial sinker. Or so the record said. Bond recalled every detail of *that* file—*Basilisk set the girl up in a small apartment, five minutes' drive from the Karlshorst Headquarters, where he spent most of his off-duty hours with her. After any "business" trip abroad he brought back luxuries*—there had followed a list that ranged from expensive hi-fi equipment to what the French term "fantasy" gifts from Paris. The list, attributed to Swift, was amazing in its detail: dates and items given in one column, time that Basilisk spent away in another, with a full list of his movements. It was the only one so itemized.

Fräulein Captain Dietrich also gave presents to Jungle, but Swift did not appear to have such good and knowledgeable intelligence about those. There was, also, far less information concerning the relationships between the other three *Cream Cake* operatives and their targets. From the beginning, Bond had wondered if this was really a team business, or were they only after two people—Dietrich and Smolin—with the rest merely makeweights, or even distractions?

Bearing in mind the way Swift had misjudged the operation, Bond had to go over the whole thing, again and again.

"Tell me about it one more time, Heather." They were passing through a village that looked as though it had a cathedral, twelve garages, twenty bars, and around five hundred inhabitants.

"I've told you. All of it." She spoke in a small voice, weary, as though she did not want to speak of *Cream Cake* ever again.

"Just once more. How did you feel when they told you?"

"I was only just nineteen. Precocious, I suppose. I saw it all as a joke. It wasn't until later that I realized how deadly the whole business really was."

"You were a virgin?"

She gave a little snort. "Of course not."

Bond did not pursue that line. "But you felt excited?"

"It was an adventure, for God's sake. If you were just nineteen and they told you to seduce a not unattractive woman older than yourself, wouldn't you have been excited?"

"Depends which way my political feelings ran—uphill or down."

"What's that supposed to mean?" She was showing shredded nerves now.

"Were you a politically aware young woman when they approached you for this exciting adventure?"

She gave a long sigh. "If you really want to know, I was disenchanted with the whole political scene. To me, everyone talked pigswill—East, West, North, South, whatever—the Communist Party, the Americans, the British. Maxim used to say, 'When it comes to politics and religion, it's a fairground.' "

"Really?" He was surprised at this sudden revelation about Smolin's views. "And what did he mean by that, I wonder?"

"He meant you paid your money and took your choice. But he used to say that once you'd taken that choice it bound you hand and foot. He said that Communism was the nearest thing in politics to the Roman Catholic Church. Both of them had rules from which you could not deviate."

"But you were trying to deviate him. You were doing your best to make him a convert."

Another sigh. "In a way, yes."

Bond grunted. "You had met him before—Smolin?"

She sighed. "I've told you. He was a regular visitor—social functions at the house, of course."

"And he'd shown an interest?"

"Not particularly." She stopped, then launched into a long speech—yes, Colonel Smolin may not have been the greatest-looking man around, but he *was* attractive. Not really a physical thing at first sight, but he had *something*. She used the word "indefinable." Then Smolin had appeared even more attractive when the matter was fully explained to her, first by her father, who had said he was fighting against the powers that had split her rightful country in two; then by the man she had come to know as Swift, her controller. He had been more blunt with her.

"He's a bastard," Swift had said at her first briefing. "A grade A, platinum bastard who wouldn't think twice about hanging his own mother with piano wire. He's a professional spycatcher, spyhunter, and spykiller who doesn't mind if he's wrong from time to time. We're asking you to get yourself into his bed, make him rely on you, share his thoughts with you, share his fears, and, at the last, his secrets."

"Maxim wasn't really as bad as Swift painted him." She still clung to some hidden, probably sentimental, sadness about the affair with Smolin. Bond had sensed it before.

"I expect the executioners' mistresses at Auschwitz and Belsen said similar things while they ate their *Kirschtorte* as their loved ones were operating the gas chambers," Bond said brusquely. He had no time for sentiment as far as men like Smolin were concerned.

"No!" Heather almost shouted. "Read my report. It's all there. Maxim was an odd mixture of a man, but a lot of the stories about him are just not true."

"So that's why he's got a team out now—hunting down your friends, and yourself? That's why he's tearing tongues out?"

She remained silent, staring ahead. Bond gave her a quick glance. He could have sworn that there were tears glistening in her eyes.

"What were they really after?" Bond asked after a while, though the question was as much to himself as to Heather. Already he had a theory about *Cream Cake.* It was not just a series of dangling honeypots to turn a handful of East German bigwigs into doubles, or to compromise them in such a way as to make them run so hard that they would never be any trouble again. There was some more devious motive. Again, aloud—knowing that Heather had not the remotest idea about what they were after, for the whole thing had ended in chaos—"And you just went out and caught him, netted him, bedded him, and reported the pillow talk back to Swift?"

"I've told you!" she almost shouted at him. "How many more times, James? Yes, yes, yes. I hooked him. I even became fond of him. He was good to be with: kind, thoughtful, gentle, and very loving. Too loving."

"Because you misjudged the moment of truth?"

"Yes!" Angry now. "Yes, must I go through it again and again? I told Swift that I thought he was ready. God . . ." She *was* near to tears, and they were on the Arklow road now. "Swift told me to bring him home. Lay the news on him. His actual words were, 'Spear him and drag his soul to me.' "

Bond concentrated on the road. He had first read the bones of the story in the files, and heard the inside guts of the events from Heather in the offices of the beauty salon, Dare to Be Chic, high above Piccadilly, a lifetime ago—yesterday. Now he needed to hear it again. "Spear him and drag his soul to me." "And what happened when you laid the news on Maxim Smolin? When you tried to spear him and drag his soul to Swift?"

She took a deep breath, opened her mouth, and, as she did so, they started to go into a bend leading onto a long stretch of open road flanked by scrubby hedges. Big Mick, a couple of hundred yards behind, suddenly flashed his lights, and in the driving mirror Bond saw two cars at speed, squeezing in on the Volvo so that the whole road was filled with the three vehicles. Though he had not driven this route for years, Bond had an odd sense of déjà vu. In his mind there was a picture of an accident, flashing blue lights, police flagging them down. Before even seeing what lay ahead, he knew and felt the fear tighten in his stomach. Behind, the two flanking cars appeared bent on squashing the Volvo.

Then they were round the bend and onto the mile or so of straight road that was—just as he expected—not empty, but littered with debris, warning signs, and the flashing lights of catastrophe. He shouted to Heather, yelling at her to brace herself. Ahead, there was a Garda car, an ambulance, the remains of a dun-colored saloon that could have been a Cortina, and an Audi on its side crushing the hedge. There was also a heavy truck across the road. Bond was in no mood for trucks. He braked, left-footed, and tried to spin the car, even though he knew that by now the road behind him would be blocked by a crushed Volvo—unless Big Mick had supernatural powers.

Heather screamed, the car slewed sideways on, and then just kept going, gathering speed in spite of Bond's attempts to control it. Too late, he realized that the road surface had been neatly treated with a thick slick of oil.

The group of mangled vehicles—plus the ambulance and Garda patrol car—seemed to be coming up with amazing speed. Bond fought the wheel, feeling the rear coming round much too fast, and knowing there was no way to avoid collision. When it came, there was almost a sense of anticlimax—a grinding crunch and a sudden stop, taking them from around fifty mph to zero in a split second.

He automatically reached for his gun, but even that was too late, for the doors were wrenched open and, with professional ease, two men in Garda uniform had both Heather and Bond out of the car, each using a neat armlock that caused considerable pain. Dazed, Bond wondered where his gun had gone—disappeared like some magician's prop. He tried to shake off the pain and resist, but, almost unaware of the movement, he found he and Heather were both being hustled into the ambulance, where four other figures waited to take over.

For members of an ambulance team, they did not appear to be at all concerned about injuries. In fact, one of them seemed more intent upon causing pain than preventing it, for by this time Heather was screaming fit to wake the dead. Then she stopped, suddenly and completely as one man chopped her expertly on the side of the neck with the cutting edge of his extended hand.

She went down just as the doors closed and the ambulance began to move, but the man who had hit her also caught the falling body and hoisted it onto one of the two stretcher beds on either side of the interior.

From the gloom up front a fifth man appeared, yet they seemed in no way crowded. Later Bond realized that it was a very large ambulance—probably a resprayed, refurbished military vehicle.

The ambulance picked up speed, its siren hee-hawing. Above the wail, the fifth man spoke.

"Mr. Bond, I believe. I'm afraid there's been a small accident, and it's necessary to get you away from the site as fast as possible. I'm truly sorry to inconvenience you, but I fear this is essential to all of us. I'm sure you understand. So, if you would just sit down and remain quiet, we'll get along nicely, I'm certain."

There was no doubt about it—Colonel Maxim Smolin had a great deal of charm, even when it was laced with threats.

8

Cockerel or Weasel

The ambulance swayed and bounced, slowed, swayed again, then accelerated. Bond reckoned they had very quickly left the main road and were probably doubling back—possibly edging up into the hills, maybe even climbing through the wild and craggy Wicklow Gap.

Bond glanced at Heather, who lay unmoving on the stretcher bed, and hoped that the force of the blow had not done any serious damage.

"She'll be fine, Mr. Bond. My men had orders not to kill, merely to render unconscious." Close up, Smolin seemed an even more commanding figure, and his quick response to Bond's anxious look showed an intelligent and observant awareness.

"And your people're well trained in how to kill and not *quite* kill, I'm sure." He almost added Smolin's name, but held back.

"Trained to perfection, my dear fellow." For a man of his background, Smolin spoke near-faultless English, though the trained ear would undoubtedly pick up the fact that it was just a shade too perfect.

There was a charm in his manner that took Bond by surprise; yet, behind the charm, one sensed a diamond-hard interior: not so much a ruthlessness as a feeling of absolute power and confidence—a man who expected to be obeyed; one who knew, without second thoughts, that he could maintain his balance at the sharp end of life.

He was a shade taller than Bond had realized from his previous two sightings, and his body was strong, fit, and well-muscled under the casual—if expensive—anorak, cavalry twill trousers, and turtleneck.

Smolin now looked hard at Bond, and there was the trace of a bright twinkle in his dark, slightly oval eyes, while the smile around his mouth appeared not mocking but amused.

"Might I ask what all this is about?" Bond had to speak loudly above the engine noise and rattling as the ambulance continued to sway, accelerating, then slowing. The driver was either unused to handling such a vehicle, or they were, indeed, on a difficult mountain road.

The smile turned into a chuckle—short and almost pleasant. "Oh, come on now, James Bond, you know well enough what it's about."

"I know that I was giving a lift to a lady friend of mine, and suddenly I find we're kidnapped." He paused, then added with mock puzzlement, "And you know my name! How the hell do you know my name, anyway?"

This time there was a full-blooded belly laugh. "Bond, my dear good fellow, don't make me into a fool." He nodded his head toward the still-unconscious Heather. "You know who your lady friend is, and what she's done? I suspect you know *exactly* what she's done, and *exactly* who I am—after all, my file is with many foreign agencies. Surely the British Secret Intelligence Service has a dossier on me just as my own Service has one on you. Try telling your grandmother to suck eggs, James Bond. You know everything about the operation called *Cream Cake*, and I would be most surprised if you did not have all the details of the punishment at present being dealt out to its protagonists."

"*Cream Cake?*" Even Bond was pleased with the way the words came out in a cross between question, puzzlement, and surprise.

"Operation *Cream Cake*." Smolin paused for breath, then laughed again as though he found the whole thing as funny as a Marx Brothers' movie.

"I know nothing about cream cakes, or chocolate éclairs!" Bond was pacing himself now, allowing time to build up a good, healthy anger. "I do know that Heather here asked me to give her a lift—"

Smolin gave a rueful smile, his laughter diminishing. "Would this be after the little problem in her beauty salon last night?"

"What problem?"

"You're trying to tell me that you were not the man who was with her when some ill-advised idiots tried to kill her in London? That you're not the man who drove her to the airport . . . ?" The smile had faded into just a hint of uncertainty.

"Bumped into her in the departure lounge." Bond locked eyes with him. "I mean, I've only met her once before. Look, what's this really all about? And how did you set up that police roadblock? You a terrorist or something? To do with the North?" He was sizing up the opposition while playing a somewhat ridiculous game for time. Heather still lay unconscious, Smolin sat quite close to him, and the other four hoods were ranged around the ambulance—two up front, the other pair by the doors: all clinging on because the ride was more like being on a rollercoaster than in a large vehicle. They had disarmed him, and he could not drag the charade on for much longer, or even contemplate escape as yet.

"If I didn't *know* who you are, and had not watched you set up your own security precautions, I might just wonder if I'd got the wrong man." Smolin was smiling again. "But the setup, together with the weapons you were carrying. Well . . ." He allowed matters to hang in the air.

"And what of *your* setup?" Bond asked, seemingly without guile.

"I suspect they were exactly what you would have arranged in similar circumstances. We had a backup watching you, in radio contact while we went on ahead. Then we simply closed off the far end of the road, a mile or so on; and shut off the road behind you when you passed into our zone of operations—the old funnel principle, with plenty of debris, an oil slick, and some fancy-dress Garda uniforms."

Bond could dissemble no longer. "They teach you those kinds of skills in that center of yours on the old Khodinka airfield, do they, Colonel Smolin? The place where most of you end up, one way or another—in the crematorium, either neat in a box, or alive and screaming because you've betrayed your service—the organization you jokingly call The

Aquarium?" He said calmly, "Or do you learn them at your offices on Knamensky Street?"

"So, Bond, you *do* know about my service—you know about GRU. And you know about *me* also. I'm flattered—but happy that I was right about you."

"Of course I know, together with anyone who takes the trouble to read the right books. We have a saying in *my* Service, that the tricks of our trade are far from secret; you only have to find the right bookshops in Charing Cross Road, or Piccadilly, and you can learn it all—tradecraft, addresses, organization. It takes only a little reading."

"A little more than that, I suspect."

"Possibly. The GRU likes to let the KGB have the glory, pretending to be backseat boys who bow to the gray men of Dzerzhinsky Square. Yes, we do know you're more fanatical, more secretive, and therefore more dangerous."

Smolin's smile was overtly happy. "Much more dangerous. Good, I'm glad we know where we stand. It has been a long ambition of mine to meet you face-to-face, Mr. Bond. Was it you, perhaps, who concocted the idiotic *Cream Cake* business?"

"There you have me, Colonel Smolin. I know nothing of such an operation."

One of the hoods shouted something from the front of the ambulance, and Smolin said, almost apologetically, that they would soon have to take measures to ensure silence and blindness. "We're coming up to the point where we change cars." The smile seldom left his lips, as though it had been neatly cut to shape by a plastic surgeon.

The ambulance slowed down, lurched, leaned heavily to the left, so that everyone had to grab on to whatever was at hand in order to remain either upright or seated. Gradually they rumbled to a halt on what Bond presumed was rough ground.

From the front came the sound of the cab door being slammed shut. Then the rear doors opened and a short, red-faced man dressed in the dark uniform of an ambulance driver peered in.

"They are not here yet, Herr Colonel." He addressed Smolin in German.

The Colonel merely nodded in an offhand way, and told them to watch and wait. Bond craned his neck in an attempt to see out of the back, but only glimpsed trees, backed by rocky slopes that bore out his original feeling that they had taken a route into the bleak Wicklow hills.

"Get the girl ready." Smolin half-turned his head, giving the order to one of the men up front. The man fumbled with a briefcase, and Bond saw a hypodermic being made ready. He made a slight threatening move toward the syringe-bearer, whose partner immediately performed a small magic act with an automatic pistol. One moment his hand was empty, the next it was full of gun, the one-eyed muzzle of which pointed steadily at Bond.

Smolin raised an arm, as though both protecting and restraining Bond. "It's all right. The girl will not be harmed. I merely think she should be put under a mild sedation for a while. We have a long drive ahead, and I really don't want her to be conscious. You, friend Bond, will lie on the floor in the back of the car that will arrive at any minute. You will have your face covered, and as long as you behave no harm will come to you." He paused, smiled, then added, "Yet!"

There was a long silence, during which Heather moved slightly and groaned, as though regaining consciousness, and the hood with the syringe quietly prepared her for the injection, which he gave with some skill, the needle sliding through the skin of her bared forearm at a neatly calculated angle.

"So, James Bond, you say that you know nothing of any operation coded *Cream Cake?*"

Bond replied by shaking his head.

"And I suppose," Smolin continued, "you've never heard of Irma Wagen?"

"Not a name known to me."

"But you do know Heather Dare?"

"I met her once, before the airport departure lounge, yes."

"And where did you meet her, *once before the airport departure lounge?*"

"At a party. Through friends."

"Friends, as in professional friends?—I believe, in the jargon of your Service, friends are other members of that Service. Or, at least, your Foreign Office refers to them as The Friends."

"Ordinary friends. A couple called Hazlett—Tom and Maria Hazlett." He added an address in Hampstead, knowing it could be checked out with impunity, for both Tom and Maria were an active alibi couple. If asked—even in a roundabout way—whether they knew either Bond or Heather they would answer, "Yes, and isn't Heather wonderful?" or, "Of course, James is an old friend." They would also have a surveillance team on to the questioners in double-quick time, for both had that particular knack of second-guessing friend or foe, and covering for people in the correct manner. After all, that was what the Service had trained them to do.

"So, in that case you would claim you did not know Irma Wagen and Heather Dare—of the Dare to Be Chic beauty salon—are the same person?"

"I've never heard of any Irma Wagen."

"No. No, of course you haven't, James—you must call me Maxim, by the way. I do not respond to the diminutive, Max. No, you haven't heard of Irma, nor the doomed *Cream Cake* operation." His smile did not alter, but the disbelief shone through his words. Then he came out and said it aloud, "I just do not believe you, James Bond. I do not, cannot, believe you."

"Please yourself." Bond gave the impression of complete disinterest.

"Then where were you driving the fair Fräulein Wagen, whom you know as Heather Dare?"

"Enniscorthy."

"So, why should she want to go to Enniscorthy?" He shook his head, as though to underline his disbelief. "And where were you going that enabled you to give such a service to this—this damsel in distress?"

"She was in no distress," Bond said levelly. "We merely recognized each other at the airport, and sat next to one another on the plane. I told her I was going to Waterford and she asked if she could cadge a lift. What she actually said was, 'Can I bum a ride?' "

Smolin wrinkled his nose.

"Yes, I agree. Nasty phrase." Bond smiled back pleasantly.

"And what were you going to do in Waterford?"

Smolin remained comfortable on the other stretcher bed, beside Bond.

"Buy glass, what else? I'm very fond of Waterford crystal."

"Of course you are. And it's so difficult to buy in London, isn't it?" With heavy sarcasm like that, Smolin betrayed his Russian side.

"I am on leave, Herr Colonel Smolin. I repeat, I know of no Irma Wagen, and have never heard of an operation called *Cream Cake*."

"We shall see," Smolin replied smoothly. "But, just to clear the air, I will tell you what we know of this ludicrously named operation. It was what used to be called a honeytrap. Your people baited it with four very young and attractive girls." He held up four fingers, grasping one for each name, as though ticking them off. "There were Franzi Trauben, Elli Zuckermann, Irma Wagen, and Emilie Nikolas." He laughed his pleasant chuckle again. "Emilie—a good name, when you consider that we always spoke of *our* honeytrap *targets* as Emilies—but you know all that." He ran a hand through his dark hair. "Each of these girls had a well-placed target, and they might just have got away with it, but for the fact that I was included among the targets." Quite suddenly his whole demeanor altered. "They used *me* as a target for their games. *Me*, Maxim Smolin, as though I could be caught and netted by a slip of a girl with about as much idea of how to set up an entrapment as a raw recruit." His voice rose, "That's what I can never forgive your people for doing! Putting an amateur onto me! So amateur that she gave the game away within minutes of her first pass at me, and eventually brought down the whole nasty little network. *Your* Service, Bond, took me for some kind of a fool! A professional would have been different, but an amateur, like her"—his finger rose, pointing toward the prone body of Heather—"an amateur I can never forgive!"

So, Bond thought, this was the real Smolin—proud, arrogant, and unforgiving.

"Surely, the Glavnoye Razvedyvatelnoye Upravleniye also uses casual labor from time to time, Maxim?" He asked the question with the ghost of a smile.

"Casual labor?" A fine spray of spittle clouded the air in front of Smolin's lips as he spat the words out with utter contempt. "We would *train* casual labor. But *never* would we use casual labor against a target of my importance."

There he had it. *My importance*. Colonel Maxim Smolin regarded himself as inviolable; essential to the smooth running of the second most dangerous of the secret organizations within the structure of the Soviet Union—the first being Bond's older enemies, the one-time SMERSH, now totally reorganized as Department 8 of Directorate S following their total loss of credibility as Department V, as in Victor.

Smolin was breathing heavily, and Bond felt that old and ice-cold hand trace an invisible finger down his spine, an indication of fear. The chiseled stone face of a killer, the hard muscular body, that brightness in the dark eyes.

From far away came the sound of a car's horn. Three short blasts followed by a longer one.

"They're here." Smolin returned to his native German.

The ambulance doors opened, fully revealing the view of green slopes, strewn with the gray of rock outcrops, and the half circle of trees in which they were parked, well off the road down which two cars—a BMW and a Mercedes—were making slow progress toward them.

Bond looked at Smolin and cocked his head toward Heather. "I truly have no knowledge of this *Cream Cake* business." He spoke quietly, hoping that in his moment of rage Smolin might even believe him. "Sounds more like a BND job rather than our people . . ."

Smolin turned. "It *was* your Service, James Bond. I have proof. Believe me, just as you must believe we'll sweat you until your very bones turn to water. There are still a couple of mysteries that need solving, and I'm here to solve them."

"Mysteries?" The cars were near now, and two of the hoods had descended from the ambulance, readying themselves for the transfer of their prisoners.

"We have dealt with two of that nest of bottled spiders—the Trauben girl, and the Zuckermann bitch. You might recognize them better as Bridget Hammond and Millicent Zampek. Small fry, but squashed. This girl—*my* girl—might hold some of the answers in her pin brain; and there's another yet to come. The Nikolas cow—Ebbie Heritage. Those two, with yourself, should fill in the gaps, and put the final pieces into the jigsaw before the three of you go to hell and damnation." Smolin started to chuckle, and the chuckle turned into the old belly laugh.

If he wanted Heather and Ebbie alive, why the thug with the mallet, and the chase down the fire escape—the shooting and dicing with death in London? Smolin had spoken of the incident earlier as "some ill-advised idiots trying to kill her."

The most devious of ideas began to permeate Bond's brain as he watched while two of the hoods carried Heather to the Mercedes. He was also surprised to see the ambulance driver loading the pile of packages they had bought in Dublin into the boot. They had moved with great speed, Bond thought, to get everything out of his rented car in what seemed to be so short a time. But, then, the GRU were organized on military principles, and all true members were trained soldiers—but for recruited talent operating in foreign countries.

In Moscow, they worked out of that decorative mansion at 19 Knamensky Street—once the property of a Tsarist millionaire—and were at constant loggerheads with the KGB, who always claimed to have the upper hand, even though the GRU, by virtue of its military roots, was effectively set apart from the larger and better-known intelligence and security service.

He felt Smolin's arm on his shoulder, hearing him hiss, "Your turn, Mr. Bond."

They frog-marched him to the car, drew a thick sack over his head, handcuffed his wrists securely behind his back, and forced him onto the floor of the BMW. The sack smelled of grain, drying his throat in a matter of minutes.

He heard the sound of the ambulance starting

up, and then Smolin's feet pressing down on his back as the Colonel took his seat. A moment later, the car started, and they began to move away.

Why? Bond asked himself. Smolin had said that the "honeytrap" was "baited . . . with four very young and attractive girls." Only four had been mentioned. Only the four girls. He had not even bothered with Jungle Baisley, né Franz Wald Belzinger, and his target—Fräulein Captain Dietrich—whom Heather had described as one of the two prime targets. Why? The germ of a terrifying and sinister scenario became more clear in Bond's mind as he concentrated on trying to deduce their speed, mileage, and direction. Was Jungle an undiscovered and successful member of the network? Had M performed a neat piece of misdirection when briefing him, or was something more dangerous at work here in the peaceful lush greenery of the Republic of Ireland? Did it all have something to do with Norman Murray's rumor that an officer, more senior to Smolin, was in the field? Was Smolin under pressure?

He also remembered Murray's smiling face—"Maxim Smolin . . . a stupid code name—*Basilisk*." Now, Bond delved into what little he knew of mythology. The Basilisk, he remembered, was a particularly revolting monster—hatched from a cockerel's egg by a serpent. Even the purest human perished at a glimpse from the Basilisk's eyes. The creature would lay the whole world to waste but for its two enemies, the cockerel and the weasel. The weasel was immune, and the Basilisk died at the sound of the cock's crow.

Bond wondered what he was—a cock, a weasel, or neither.

9

Schloss Gruesome

By Bond's reckoning, they drove for roughly three hours. After eighty minutes or so he lost all sense of direction, except that his instincts told him they were crossing their own path time and again. In the dark choking stuffiness of the sack, with his body unnaturally curled, cramped, and uncomfortable on the floor of the car, he tried to clear his mind, concentrate, and work out exactly what headings they were on. When he was forced to abandon this, he began to examine the various theories that had first come to mind back in the ambulance.

He did not doubt that Smolin's threat, to get a full rundown on *Cream Cake* from Bond and Heather, was in any way idle. The man's reputation was enough.

It was quite possible—if Norman Murray's vague and obscure information was accurate—that Smolin was not entirely his own man. If the huge arrogance he had shown in the ambulance had been dented, it could be that the GRU officer might well act irrationally, and that could be Bond's lever.

Somehow, he knew that it was now up to him to make things happen.

Bond could not know that, the longer they were on the road, the more difficult and complex the situation was to become.

They stopped once, and Smolin—who did not leave the car—spoke calmly to Bond. "Your lady friend appears to have woken up, so they're taking her for a short walk. She is quite safe." He gave an amused snort. "She should remain docile for a while yet."

Bond moved, trying to shift his position, but Smolin's heel came down hard on one shoulder, almost causing him to yelp with pain.

When it came, the interrogation would probably not rely on the more sophisticated methods of that dark art. Rather, it would be conducted in the atmosphere of brutality.

Eventually, they seemed to leave the smoothness of a well-made road—Bond had sensed they had been climbing for some eight or ten minutes—and moved onto a rougher track, going at around thirty miles an hour and bouncing a good deal.

Then they were back on a good surface, turning slightly and coming to a halt. There were the sounds of engines dying and doors opening. He felt fresh air on his body, Smolin moving, and hands pulling away the sack and unlocking his handcuffed wrists.

"You can get out of the car now, Mr. Bond." Smolin was obviously already out, and Bond blinked, adjusting to the bright lights as he tried to massage life back into his arms.

Stiffly, he pulled himself onto the seat and then

through the door. His legs felt as though they did not belong to him, while his back and arms ached so that he could hardly move, and had to clutch at the car to steady himself.

It took several minutes for him to even stand properly, and he used the time—making more of it than necessary—to examine the surroundings. They appeared to be on a large turning circle in front of a great gray solid building, oblong but decorated with a square tower at either end. Above the roofline the top of the walls—like those of the towers—were castellated: great rows of thick toothlike battlements.

The main front door was of heavy oak, set in a Norman arch, while what windows could be seen were also built within ornate arches. The whole, Bond thought, added up to one of those strange buildings erected in Ireland during the late Georgian or early Victorian period by landed gentry who felt it necessary to refer to their homes as castles.

This one, he noted quickly, had a number of twentieth-century refinements, like a large number of antennae sprouting from one tower, and a big satellite dish aerial on the other.

The whole pile was set in a green bowl at least three miles wide, with the ground curving upward in sloping hillocks on all sides. All traces of trees, or other cover, had been neatly removed.

"Welcome." Smolin was in peaceful mood now, seemingly at his most charming.

As he spoke, Bond saw Heather being helped from the Mercedes parked in front of them. He was also aware of the undisciplined barking of dogs coming from behind the front door, together with the sound of bolts being drawn back.

Seconds later the doors swung open, and three dogs crashed onto the graveled turning circle—German shepherds to whom Smolin called, "Hey, Wotan, Siegi, Fafie. Hey-hey!"

The dogs—big, sleek-coated creatures—bounded toward Smolin with obvious pleasure. Then, as they sensed Bond, one of them turned and bared its fangs, growling with some menace.

"Good, Fafie, good! Stay! Watch!" All this in German, then to Bond, "I should not make any sudden moves, if I were you. Fafie can be particularly vicious once I've told him to watch someone. They're well trained, these animals—all with good killer instinct—so take care." He stopped petting the other two shepherds, quietly motioning toward Bond. "Siegi, Wotan. Watch! Yes, *him*. Watch!"

Two men had come through the door, then there was a female voice and a young girl, pert with fluffy blond hair, appeared. She was dressed in a claret-colored tight silk shirt, and a pleated skirt that lifted and flared around her legs as she started to run toward Heather, calling out in German, with eyes twinkling and her face a picture of happiness. She looked a wholly delightful child of nature, Bond thought as he watched her: the breeze blowing at her skirt, showing the tantalizing molding of her thighs. She turned, moved, and stood with an almost innocent sexuality, as though unaware of her body and its beautiful proportions.

Then Bond's heart sank as he heard her words—"Heather—Irma—they have you safe as well. I thought we were going to be left out in the cold.

But they haven't let us down. I always said the British wouldn't let us down." She was close to Heather now, embracing her.

"A small deception, I'm afraid." Smolin looked at Bond, as Heather gasped, "Ebbie? What—?"

"Inside!" Smolin's voice cut loudly across the mix of conversations that had started up between his men, and also the bewildered girls. "Everybody inside! Now!"

The hoods closed in, the dogs circling as though on guard. They seemed to be particularly concerned with Bond and the two girls, moving them like sheep through the door, into a vast, high hallway, flagstoned and surrounded on three sides by a gallery fashioned in stripped pine, as was the wide staircase that reached up to it, curving down to the far right of the hall.

Heather appeared to be quite calm—the effect of the drugs, Bond supposed—but Ebbie trembled visibly, horror in her wide blue eyes as she looked toward Bond. Recognition slowly dawned as she recalled that night, five years before, when Bond and the Special Boat Squadron men had plucked Heather and herself from the German coast.

"Is he—?" Ebbie spoke loudly, turning toward Heather, half raising a hand to point accusingly at Bond. Heather shook her head and said something quietly, glancing quickly, first at Smolin and then at Bond, whose eyes flicked around the hallway, taking in everything: the dark blue velvet of the drapes, the three doors and one passage that led off to other parts of the castle; the large paintings—eighteenth-century men and women staring sightless from their oil-created eyes, trapped on canvas and set within ornate gilt frames.

Smolin snapped orders at the two men who had come out with Ebbie, while the other group—the four men from the ambulance, plus the pair of thugs who had driven the Mercedes and BMW—stood near the door.

All were armed, you could see it in their manner and in the clothes they wore—the distinct bulges beneath either uniforms or jeans and short denim jackets.

Armed to the teeth, Bond thought, and, as though the very idea produced proof, he saw a folded machine pistol appear from behind one of their former drivers' backs. There would be more of those, and probably other men as well—watchers on the rim of the grassy bowl in which the castle stood. Men, guns, and dogs; locks, bars, and bolts; plus a long haul across open ground even if they were to get past this lot. All his senses were directed toward the possibility of escape, while at the back of his mind, buried in that constantly working computer of the brain, he still examined the various theories that had first come to him in the ambulance.

"Irma, my dear, bring Emilie over here, though I think she knows Mr. Bond." Smolin called across to the girls, and Bond was pleased to note that Ebbie had regained wit enough to cloud her face with a puzzled expression—"I don't think . . . ?" she began.

Smolin spoke coldly, "Remiss of me. Mr. Bond, you do not know Fräulein Nikolas—or Miss Ebbie Heritage, as she now prefers to be called?"

"Haven't had the pleasure." Bond walked over

with his right hand outstretched to give Ebbie a comforting, reassuring squeeze. "And it *really* is a pleasure." He meant this last remark, for, now that he was close to Ebbie Heritage, Bond sensed a desire he rarely felt at first meeting a girl. Through his eyes he tried to convey that all would be well, a difficult task as the three German shepherds moved with him, not growling or showing signs of attack, but letting him know they were there and ready.

"Strange," Smolin rasped, "I could have sworn that she recognized you out there, Bond."

"He . . ." Ebbie began. Then, as a tincture of confidence returned, "He reminded me of someone I used to know. Just for a second. Now I see he's English, and I've not met him before. But, yes, for me also it is a pleasure." A flash of static seemed to pass between them.

Good girl, Bond thought to himself, glancing toward Heather and trying to pass on a reassuring look to her. Heather's eyes did not appear to be properly focused, but she managed a firm and very confident smile. For a moment, Bond could have sworn that *she* was trying to give *him* a message not merely of hope, but also something deeper. It was as if they had already reached a mutual understanding.

"So." Smolin was standing beside them. "I suggest we all eat a hearty meal. A full stomach before work, eh?"

"What work, Colonel Smolin?" Bond saw the glint of evil deep in the man's eyes.

"Oh, Maxim. Please call me Maxim."

"What kind of work?" he repeated firmly.

"There is much talking to be done. But first you

must see your quarters. The guest accommodation is good here in . . ." He paused, as though stopping himself from giving away their actual location. Then, "Here, in Schloss Varvick," a contented smile. "You recall Schloss Varvick, James?"

"Familiar." He nodded.

"As a boy you probably read of it—Dornford Yates, I forget the book, but one of his many improbable tales of derring-do included such a castle."

"So, for the want of a better name, Maxim?"

Smolin nodded. "For want of a better name."

"Your base in the Republic of Ireland? Schloss GRU?" Bond did not smile. "Or, perhaps, Schloss Gruesome."

Smolin exploded in a burst of laughter at Bond's rather heavy-handed humor. "Good. Very good. Now, where is our housekeeper? Ingrid!" He shouted, and again, "Ingrid—where is the girl? Somebody get Ingrid."

One of the retainers disappeared through a door that obviously led into the bowels of the castle, if you could dignify the bizarre place with such a name. In a few seconds, he returned with a tall, angular woman, dark-complexioned, jet-black hair worn long and tidy; but with a face so sharp that there could be no other description for it but hatchet.

Smolin ordered her to show his guests to their quarters, adding that Miss Heritage was already nicely settled in. "You'll not be cramped." He stood, hands on hips and head thrown back. "There is a communal sitting room, but you each have a separate bedroom, so all will be kept decent."

Two of the hoods closed in on them as Smolin ordered Fafie to follow, and the thin figure of Ingrid moved up the stairs silently, as though she was on a cushion of air. Yet there was no grace about her, rather something sinister, all sharp angles under her long black dress, a veritable Mrs. Danvers from Daphne Du Maurier's *Rebecca*.

"It *is* very comfortable." Ebbie's voice was strong and pleasant, with no hardness in her accent. "I quite enjoyed it last night—but, then, I thought it to be sanctuary." Her English was not quite as flawless as Heather's, but she did seem, on the face of it, to have a more outgoing personality. For all her svelte, dark, model-girl appearance, Heather—he felt—had disappeared into the shell of her long legs, slim body, and attractive mask of a face. Ebbie, on the other hand, was full of fun, laughter, and with a sense of her own sexuality. She held her shoulders well back, as though to show off her fine, obviously unrestrained breasts, which pushed out hard against the silk of her shirt.

The little group, followed by Fafie, climbed to the gallery and turned right, treading on polished pine boards until they came to an open corridor that ended, some ten paces from its entrance, at a heavy door, also in pine.

This, in turn, led into a large sitting room, heavily decorated—flock wallpaper, a large, buttoned settee with matching chairs, and solid-looking side tables. What space remained against the walls was taken up by other pieces of furniture—a card table with ball-and-claw feet; a Gothic breakfront bookcase reaching almost to the ceiling, containing nothing but magazines crushed and piled into the shelves; and a very big, equally Gothic bureau, the top of which came to just under Bond's chin.

It was all very Germanic, as were the three pictures that hung lowering on the walls—dark prints of mountain scenes, clouds gathering between valleys—Victorian German in great, ugly wooden frames. The floor was of the same polished pine, but sported a number of thick rugs, placed haphazardly around a larger center oblong rug. Bond was always deeply suspicious of rugs. It also concerned him that the room had no windows.

Not counting the entrance, there were three doors—one to each of the walls—which Bond took to be the bedrooms.

"I have the one over here." Ebbie went to the door set almost opposite the entrance. "I hope nobody minds this?" She looked straight at Bond, hard in the eyes, then through slightly lowered lashes, as though inviting him to use the room with her. She stood with one leg forward, bent at the knee, once more showing the curve of thigh under the thin material of her skirt.

"First come, first served, as my old Nanny used to say." He nodded at her and then, turning to Heather, he told her to take her pick. She shrugged and went to the door on the left. Sinister, Bond thought, recalling the old theatrical tradition of the pantomime devil making his entrance stage left—*a sinister*, the side of the evil omen.

The whole caldron of theories, left bubbling on the back burner of his mind, came into the open again together with the possible answers to many questions—where did Jungle Baisley fit in? Had M misled him? Had *Cream Cake*'s former controller—Swift—really made a terrible error of judgment in telling Heather to activate Smolin? How was the said

Smolin so well briefed concerning his movements? and why had he felt it necessary to distance himself from the so-called London incident, when Heather had almost died like the two other girls from the network? Had the fluffy and edible Ebbie lent her raincoat and scarf to one of The Ashford Castle Hotel chambermaids on purpose?

He entered the bedroom, which had a bathroom *en suite*—as they said in the best middle-class estate agents' advertisements—and found the furniture as oppressive as anything in the castle. A huge bed, the head in solid oak, carved with intricate whirls and circles; a freestanding wardrobe, solid and ornate; and an old-fashioned washstand, complete with a solid marble top that had once carried a bowl and jug, doubling as a dressing table.

The bathroom was modern—two-star hotel, in unlikely avocado green, with pine laminates around the tiny cupboard, a tub built for a midget, and even a bidet squeezed between bathside and sink.

Bond went back into the bedroom to find one of the hoods standing in the doorway, holding his get-away case.

"The lock is, I fear, broken." The man's English was far from good. "The Herr Colonel ordered the contents inspected."

The Herr Colonel can stick it, thought Bond. Aloud, he thanked the man. It was highly unlikely that they had found anything to interest them. After all, his two overt weapons—the ASP and the baton—had been removed, but they had left him cigarette lighter, wallet, and pen, all three of which he had from Q Branch with Q'ute's blessing.

Another thought struck him. It was odd that, so

far, Smolin had not subjected him to a body search, which could easily have revealed items secreted in his clothing. Smolin was a dedicated and careful operative, and this oversight was well out of tune with his reputation.

They had wrecked the locks on his case, and he was about to open it when he heard the two girls talking loudly in the sitting room.

Quickly he went out, motioning them to stop, pointing at the telephone, two standard lamps, and the overhead lighting in order to remind them that the suite of rooms was almost certainly bugged—though not, he felt, in those obvious and traditional places.

There had to be some way of talking unheard with the girls, for he needed a lot of information—the three key questions Heather had been instructed to ask Smolin, as well as some pertinent details concerning their case officer, Swift.

Traditionally, they should have crowded into one of the bathrooms, turned on all the taps, and talked—but that old dodge had long gone out of the window with modern filtering systems that cut out extraneous sound. Even talking in whispers with a radio on at full volume was no longer safe.

Quickly he strode to the bureau and tried the flap. It was not locked, and sure enough writing paper and envelopes had been left in the pigeonholes. Taking some of the paper, he gestured at the girls to sit down near one of the heavy side tables and carry on talking while he went to the door and peered out. They must have been very sure of themselves, he thought, for the door was unlocked and there appeared to be no guards in the corridor.

Back at the table—seated between the girls—he bent over the paper, taking out his pen and writing quickly, trying to make some logic of his own confused suspicions, and set questions in a definite order of importance.

The girls were flagging, their conversation becoming stilted, so he asked Ebbie how she had been picked up.

"The telephone. After the terrible thing that happened. Heather says you know about it, the girl's murder." Ebbie moved a fraction closer to him, a hand brushing his arm.

Bond started to write his questions, two to each sheet of paper, and double sets—one for Ebbie, another for Heather.

"They telephoned you?"

"*Ja*—yes. They said I was to leave as soon as the police had no use for me. I was to drive to Galway—to The Corrib Great Southern Hotel—they would contact me there." She allowed her shoulder to press hard against his arm, leaving in its wake a tingling sensation that he found decidedly pleasant.

Bond passed two sheets of questions to Heather, and a couple more to Ebbie, miming for them to write replies. Heather had a pen, but Ebbie looked lost, so Bond gave her his, carrying on the conversation, as though desperate to know the answers. "And they said they were from Britain?"

Hesitation, for Ebbie was trying to write. Then, "Yes, they said from the people we used to work for." She smiled at him, revealing small, perfect teeth and the pink tip of her tongue.

"You had no doubts?"

"None. They seemed *very* English gentlemen. They

promised one night at a safe place, then an airplane would come. I would go to some other place." She frowned and continued to write, still allowing her arm to press against Bond's shoulder.

"They say anything about your friend here—Heather?"

An agonizing silence while she wrote some more. "Safe. They say she is safe and will be coming soon. I never . . ."

He turned to Heather, who had been writing quietly, and seemingly efficiently. "You were unconscious in the ambulance." He gave her a broad wink, so she would not be disturbed by what he was going to say. "Smolin talked to me about something called *Cream Cake*, you know about that?"

Her jaw dropped, the mouth starting to form the word "but"—as in, "but you know all about *Cream Cake*, James," then she realized it was for the listeners, and said she was not to speak of it. The whole business had been a despicable trick; that neither she nor Ebbie was responsible for this thing. "A mistake," she repeated, "a most horrible mistake."

Bond leaned over and began to read what they had already written, his eyes moving quickly, first down one page, and then the other.

As he read, so the worm of suspicion and deception, which had sprung to life earlier, started to move in his brain, and at that moment the door burst open to reveal Smolin, flanked by two of his men. There was no point in trying to hide the papers, but Bond drew them off the table, trying to misdirect Smolin's gaze by rising to his feet.

"James, I'm surprised at you." Smolin's voice was

soft, almost soothing, and therefore more threatening. "You think we only steal sound from what we call our guest suite? *Son et lumière*, my friend. Sound and pictures." He gave one of his regular laughs. "You will never guess the times we've compromised important people in one or another of these rooms. Now, be a good fellow and hand over the papers." One of the men stepped toward them, but Heather snatched the sheets from Bond and headed for her bedroom door, light and very fast on her feet.

The hood sprang at her in a rugger tackle, missed, and ended against the wall as her door slammed, followed by the noise of the key turning in the lock.

Both Smolin and the still-upright hood had automatics in their hands, and the man who had fallen was back on his feet, pounding on the door, shouting in German for her to come out. But there was no sound until, eventually, the lock clicked and Heather—haughty as ever—stalked into the room. From behind her door, smoke curled out of a metal waste bin. "They're gone," she said in a matter-of-fact tone. "Burned. Not that they could have meant much to you, Maxim."

Smolin took one pace forward and lifted his arm, hitting her hard in the face, first with the back of his hand, then the palm, smashing into her cheeks. She rolled with the blows, staggered, and then straightened up, her face scarlet.

"That's it. Enough!" Smolin drew in a breath through his clenched teeth. "We won't wait for food. I think the time has come to talk—and talk you will. *All* of you." He turned back to the door, shouting for more of his men, who came noisily up the stairs, weapons drawn.

"You first, I think, James." Smolin's finger was aimed like a dagger.

There was little point in struggling as two of the men locked Bond's arms and hustled him out along the corridor and down the main staircase.

The angular Ingrid stood near the front door, as though overseeing the whole thing, like a thin black insect, while the dogs growled, ranged around her. Then they pushed Bond through one of the other doors and down another pine staircase. Along a passage and into a small room, bare but for a chair bolted to the floor.

They sat him down, snapping cuffs on wrists and ankles, shackling him to the arms and legs of the chair, which, he quickly discovered, was made of metal.

He was conscious of the two men standing behind him, preparing Lord knew what, and of Smolin, face set in a burning cold anger, directly in front of him.

Bond braced himself for physical pain, or even that worse possibility—the thing the Soviets always spoke of as a chemical interrogation. He emptied his mind, did all the things they had taught him, putting in layers of rubbish, forcing truth deep into his subconscious.

Then, when it came, Bond was shocked into mind-bending fear, for Colonel Maxim Smolin of the GRU, the main target of *Cream Cake*, spoke very quietly. "James," he began. "When M took you to lunch, and then for that walk in the park, explained *Cream*

Cake to you, and bluntly said they would deny you if anything went wrong—now, James, what was your first thought?"

Smolin had begun at the point that Bond had neatly hidden away, and would have given to his interrogator only under the heaviest of pressures—physical or drug-induced.

10

Interrogation

For what seemed an eternity, Bond felt as though his mind had been struck by a whirlwind—the enormity of the situation exploded in his brain as he tried to put some logic into Smolin's question. Listening devices planted in M's club, Blades? directional microphones? sound stealing in the park? a penetration of M's office? Impossible. M himself? Equally impossible.

Yet Smolin *knew*. There was no getting away from that central point. In the beginning was M's private briefing in the park. The beginning was the last thing Bond would have revealed. But Smolin had it, and if he was party to that knowledge, what else did he know, and how?

Bluff would not last long—"What briefing? What park?" Spin it out, he thought. All ideas of taking any initiative dissolved rapidly.

"Come, James, we both know better than that. I'm a GRU officer with considerable experience. Case-hardened, you might say. We're both aware of the way our organizations can be—have been—

penetrated. Let us just say that *Cream Cake* was detected long before we allowed the four girls to discover they were blown."

"As I know nothing of this *Cream Cake*, I can't be any help to you." *Four girls*, he thought—still only four, and no mention of the one man.

Smolin shrugged. "Do you want me to do it the hard way, James? We all make mistakes from time to time. Your people made a mistake with *Cream Cake*. We made a blunder in letting the network get away in their socks, as your people say." He gave his most unpleasant laugh. "In the case of *Cream Cake*, I suppose we should say they got away in their stockings, eh?" His eyes locked with Bond's, and it was as though *he* was now trying to pass some secret message. "*All* of them being young women, eh?"

What about Jungle? Bond's mind still spun in disbelief. "I don't know what you're talking about," he said quietly. "I haven't the faintest idea what this *Cream Cake* business is, or was. I gave a lift to a girl I met at a party, and ended up with the GRU around my neck. I haven't denied what you obviously *do* know—that I'm a member of one of Britain's supposedly secret departments. But we're not all privy to every harebrained scheme that goes on. We work on a need-to-know basis . . ."

"And your most secret Head of Service—M—decided that you had need-to-know, James. Yesterday, in Regent's Park after lunching at his club, he told you the whole story, with many of its twists and turns—not quite all of them, though. Then he said he'd be obliged if you'd tidy things up—bring in the members of the *Cream Cake* team, and make them safe. Defuse the time bomb. He offered you the information, but said he could give you no sanctification. If you got into a mess neither he, nor the Foreign Office, could bail you out. On the contrary, they would deny you and, unlike Saint Peter with Christ, not just thrice, but for all time." He twisted the left side of his mouth in a smirk. "It was up to you, and like the headstrong field man that you are, you took him up on it. Now, my question was, what did you feel when he laid that little lot on you?"

"I felt nothing, because it didn't happen." This was surely a nightmare. Any minute he would wake in his comfortable flat, with May preparing breakfast.

There was a long pause as Smolin sucked in air through his teeth. "Have it your own way. I'm not going to play any games. No strong-arm stuff. We'll do it with a small injection. I haven't got time to waste. My report has to be ready by later tonight when a *really* important visitor is expected." He turned, speaking to the pair of guards in a mixture of German and Russian. From what Bond could understand he was telling them to bring in the medical tray, then leave him alone to do the work.

The taller of the two men asked if he did not need assistance. "I shall do my own recording. The prisoner is secure. Now get on with it." Smolin's commanding manner made them jump to obey, and one was back in a few seconds wheeling a small medical trolley, like a butler serving tea.

Smolin dismissed the man, and once the guard had left, the GRU officer moved into Bond's line of sight, toward one of the walls. For the first time, Bond saw a row of small switches, which Smolin carefully threw down, turning back to the medical trolley and starting to do things with a hypo. As he worked, so he spoke, very softly, not even looking in Bond's direction.

"I've turned the sound off, so that we cannot be overheard. One of those guys is KGB—very bad news; and there are others planted in the team I've been given—only two of them can be trusted as GRU men, and even they might find themselves in a situation where they cannot obey my orders. While I'm getting things ready, you should know that the injection is to be nothing more worrying than distilled water. It was the only way I could engineer matters so that we could be alone." The eyes lifted slightly in a conspiratorial glance.

"What the hell're you talking about?" Bond found his own voice dropping to a whisper, realizing that in the one short sentence, Smolin had revealed yet another persona.

Careful, he cautioned himself. When you sup with the devil use a long spoon.

"I'm speaking to you about truth, James Bond." He lifted the hypo and a small vial, slid the needle through the skin of the vial, filled it, and squirted a small spray from the hypo to clear any air. "I'm talking about how I escape—with Irma. I'm sorry, I mean Heather. I've been able to hide the fact that Wald Belzinger—your Jungle Baisley—was ever part of the *Cream Cake* network. I did that to shield both myself and Susanne."

"Susanne?" Bond queried as Smolin readied his arm to take the injection.

"My colleague, Susanne Dietrich. I hid her little affair, and the conspiracy. I also warned the four girls, so they could get out before KGB caught up with them. That was none of Heather's doing—though, of course, she imagines it was her fault: that she made the final play for me too soon." He slid the needle home and Bond did not even feel it go in. "If anyone else should arrive in this room, act as though you're doped to the eyeballs. In fact, it would be a good idea if you just let your head go back and closed your eyes, anyway."

"As I understand it," Bond still talked in almost a whisper, "it was you, the so-called Plague Master of the HVA, and resident GRU mole within that organization, who blew the whistle on the girls." Christ, into the trap, he thought. I've admitted it.

Smolin bent low, near his ear, pretending to make the supposedly drugged Bond comfortable. "Yes, I *had* to blow the whistle, as you put it. Believe me, James, I only blew it a matter of seconds before KGB sounded their own alarm. And now? Well, I can't keep the heat off much longer. First, it *is* a KGB team—two teams, to be exact—who are quietly killing off the former members of *Cream Cake*. Also, I should imagine that, when our honored guest arrives tonight, he will bring with him tidings that the fifth, hidden and male, member of the network has—as I understand the London criminal fraternity would say—had it away on his toes with my good colleague and close friend Fräulein Captain Susanne Dietrich."

"Really?" Bond wanted to listen, not comment. Already he had gone too far.

"She went on leave two weeks ago, and has not returned. The KGB officer in charge of sweeping up the case will have put two and two together by now, and there will be, like in American gangster movies, an APB out on friend Belzinger, or Baisley, or Wald, or Jungle. It also puts me right in focus, which means I too must jump, as I have promised, if the going gets rough."

"Promised whom?"

"My dearest Heather, for one. Her case officer—Swift—for another. And your own beloved Chief, M, for good measure."

"You're trying to tell me, Maxim, that you have been a defector in place for the last five years?"

"Quite."

"And you expect me to believe you? *You*, the half-Russian, half-German scourge of the DDR's intelligence service? *You*, hated by more people than either of us would care to count? The dedicated officer with allegiance only to Moscow? I can't buy that, Maxim. There is no way I can buy it. Just doesn't add up."

"That is exactly *why* you should buy it, James. It is the only thing you can buy, because if you don't you're dead—so am I, come to that. You, Heather, Ebbie, myself, and, eventually, Susanne Dietrich and her lover Jungle Baisley. We're all booked for oblivion if you don't buy it and act on it."

"Prove it to me, then, Maxim. Give me proof."

"Haven't I done that, James? Haven't I done it by asking you the question about your reaction to M's very private briefing? There was no way for me to get that except from the horse's mouth. I can give you chapter and verse if you want."

Bond waited, the voice within still telling him to take care. He felt no ill effects from the injection, but that didn't mean a thing. Now he dug deep into his mind, focusing attention on Smolin at the same time as he examined his own mental and emotional state. No, he was not drugged. This was all very real, and the likelihood of Smolin's story became more probable as each second passed.

"James, the job we're in—it's like living within a set of Chinese boxes and never knowing exactly who or what is in which box. I know about the telephone call you received yesterday morning; your lunch at Blades; your walk in the park; your afternoon spent going through the files; and the incident at Heather's beauty salon." He paused, looking very serious now. "I tried very hard to head off that bloody KGB team of assassins, but it was too late. I know about the escape; your double switch at Heathrow; your telephone conversations with friends here—including Inspector Murray of the Garda Special Branch." He leaned both his hands on the chair arms, putting his face close to Bond. "You see, I have committed the cardinal sin within any intelligence organization. I *knew* what Heather was when she made her first pass at me; I checked out the others. At any moment I could have hauled them all in, but I did not."

"Why?"

"Because, when I was approached I *wanted* to be approached. I wanted to get out; knew it; had to live with it. Heather offered me a way of escape and, like a fool, I took it. And what happened? They asked me to stay in place; to become even more of a monster than ever before. What better cover, James?"

"Who asked you?"

"Heather, whom I love dearly. Then Swift, and, last of all, your own boss—M."

"Where?"

"In a safe place on the West side of the Wall. A day trip. He agreed to keep Heather under wraps. I agreed to work for him. In Berlin we set up codes, contacts, cutouts, and so it was, until the KGB began to sniff around what had really been going on five years ago within their sister service in the DDR. It is only a matter of time before they find my name computes with *Cream Cake*. After that, unless I can jump, it's Moscow, a quick bullet if I'm lucky; one of the cancer wards or the Gulag if I'm not." He wagged a finger in front of Bond's nose. "The same goes for you, James. For all of us."

In spite of his feelings, Bond had yet to be convinced that this was the whole and complete story. "If this is true, why wasn't I told?" For a stomach-churning second, he again realized that even in discussing events with Smolin he was answering questions, providing a skilled interrogator with all he required.

"Need-to-know. Your cunning old M is too wily a bird. You were the man for the job, but you did not *have* to know about me. It was a chance in a million that we would meet. M's instructions to me were to watch from afar and let you get the girls out—then pick up Jungle." His eyes narrowed below a wrinkled forehead, replete with anxiety. "I don't think he realized that I was so surrounded by KGB; and I couldn't call off their hit team. Also, up to late yesterday, he had no idea of the latest developments. We spoke during the early hours this morning—first through Murray, who had contacted him, and later on a secure line. M thought I might still have a chance of staying in place. That is what *he* reasoned. But he is wrong; I've been blown, James—or, at best, almost blown—and I must get out, and to get out I need your help, because we have not just been penetrated by KGB, but impregnated by them. I've told you—at least one is in my team: most probably more than one. The real threat, here in the castle, is that bitch of a housekeeper, Ingrid. She's very definitely KGB. Black Ingrid, as they call her in certain circles, is deputy, and, I suspect, mistress of the man who is running the rout of your *Cream Cake* team. Beware of her, my friend. It might look as though those damned dogs regard me as their master, but I assure you the dogs are also doubles, and Ingrid's their real case officer. She can countermand my orders to them in a second, and they will obey." He gave a humorless smile. "And before you ask it, yes, the dogs *were* trained in that almost windowless complex you have described—the one outside Moscow, behind the walls and wire on the old Khodinka airfield."

What had he to lose—Bond thought—or for that matter, what to gain? "If I believe you, Maxim, what do you need from me? You have a plan, have you? Like getting me to take you, and the girls, to Jungle Baisley's hideout so you can put the lot of us in the bag?"

"Don't be stupid, James. You think KGB won't know where he's hiding out by now? You think they won't have double-checked Susanne's movements?

I should imagine that, by this time, those two're probably as near to being in the bag as we are."

"And who's this honored guest you've been talking about? The one due in tonight?"

"I thought you'd never ask, James." He stopped, his eyes clear and calm, but Bond had the impression that this was the kind of terrible calm you get before a hurricane strikes.

"Well?"

"You know *me* as Basilisk, yes? Cryptonym, Basilisk, yes?"

"Yes."

"Do you, then, James, happen to know the cryptonym Blackfriar?"

Bond felt his heart thump and stomach turn over wildly. "Christ!"

"Quite. Our guest is Blackfriar."

It took a few seconds for Bond to assimilate the information.

"Konstantin Nikolaevich Chernov. *General* Chernov." Smolin supplied the real name.

"Christ," Bond repeated. "Kolya Chernov?"

"As you say, James, Kolya Chernov—to his few friends. The Chief Investigating Officer of Department Eight, Directorate S, which was once Department V, and before that—"

"SMERSH!"

"With whom you have had dealings on several occasions." Smolin spoke slowly, as though each word had a hidden meaning. "And Konstantin Nikolaevich has a reputation that makes my own appear as blameless as Little Red Hooding Ride."

"Riding Hood," Bond corrected. He had noticed

that Maxim Smolin's faultless English had developed flaws under the stress of their conversation. Bond's brow crinkled, for he was not only aware of General Chernov's reputation, but knew his file intimately. Kolya Chernov was responsible for dozens of black operations, causing death and mayhem within both the British and American intelligence communities. He was also a man of crude and cruel cunning—hated, Bond guessed, by many within the Russian services as well as abroad. Blackfriar was a living nightmare to Bond's Service.

In his mind he saw the set of photographs that took up several pages of the file they held at the Regent's Park Headquarters. A slim man, tall, with his body well-honed by much exercise, Blackfriar was a known health fanatic who neither smoked nor drank alcohol. His IQ went off the scale, and he was well established as a dirty-trick planner of immense ingenuity. He was also a tenaciously shrewd investigator, and his file showed that he had sent at least thirty members of both the KGB and GRU to either their deaths or the Gulag for both major and minor infringements of discipline. "Being what he is, Blackfriar has the knack of scenting even the most tiny deviation at ten paces, and he follows it up like a hellhound," one defector was on record as saying.

Bond closed his eyes and let his head droop. Suddenly he felt both exhausted and fearful: not for himself, but for the two girls. "It *must* be important if he's actually coming into the field," he murmured.

"It is the first time in my own memory." Either Smolin was a very good actor, or he was filled with dread by even discussing the General. "Let me tell you, James, when I first blew *Cream Cake*—admittedly not for simply altruistic reasons—it was a matter for the Germans, for HVA and, naturally, GRU, me being who and what I am." Another humorless smile. "Or what I was. It has taken time for KGB to sniff out the more devious moves, the hidden secrets of *Cream Cake*—the existence of Jungle; the turning of Susanne Dietrich; and, of course, the turning of Maxim Smolin." He banged his own chest with a balled fist.

"It's taken them five years." Bond's voice was flat, as though his mind worked elsewhere.

"Four, to be exact. It was last year that KGB reopened the files and decided to investigate the case, going over our heads. They do not like GRU to feel they are an élite body; they dislike our methods, our secrecy, our way of recruitment from within the Army. I have heard Chernov himself say that we smack of the hated SS from the Great Patriotic War."

At first, Smolin said, the reinvestigation had been fairly low-grade—"A few simple dates, some cross-checking here and there." Then, out of the blue, General Chernov—Blackfriar himself—arrived in Berlin, "like an insidious disease. I flashed warnings to your people, but I dared not make a move. After only a week there were a number of field changes, and it didn't take great intellect to deduce that KGB were boxing me in. James, I have been watched and monitored for the past six months. It is Chernov's own revenge team who are on the loose, and Chernov's orders are that the girls are to be rooted out, killed in a particular way, and left with their tongues cut from their mouths—as the French say, *pour encourager les autres.*"

"So you do all in your power to assist Blackfriar, eh, Basilisk? You pick up Ebbie, and go to great lengths to trap Heather and myself on the road."

"On Chernov's orders, and only on *his* orders. I've told you, they're all around us, KGB. I thought of botching the job, but how could that help? James, I want your help. I need to get out *now.* Take you and the girls with me. Naturally, in front of the others I have to keep up a pretense—I must be seen to obey Chernov's orders. But not for long now."

"So, if you're giving me proof of your intentions, Maxim, tell me where we are. The location of this castle?"

"Not all that far from where we picked you up. The track to the road is about two miles. At the entrance we turn left, and it's straight downhill until we reach the Dublin–Wicklow road. An hour, two hours at the most, we can be at the airport and away."

"If I accept your version"—Bond still lay back, with his eyes closed—"I also need help."

"You have it. Don't move suddenly, but I'm unlocking the cuffs now. I have your gun with me—a nice piece of work the ASP 9mm. There . . ." Bond felt the heavy metal drop into his lap.

"So we just shoot our way out?"

"I fear we would be a little outnumbered. It is possible we could bluff most of my own men, but certainly not Black Ingrid, and those whom Chernov has infiltrated."

"Again, assuming I accept your word, how long

have we got?" Bond's hands were free now. He could feel the cuffs drop away.

"An hour. Hour and a half with luck. He has to land here while there is still light."

"And the girls, where are they being housed?"

"They've been locked in the guest suite, I should imagine. Those were my orders. The problem is getting to them. After such an interrogation as I am supposed to be making, you would be semi-conscious. They'll be waiting with a gurney trolley to take you along the passage. Then they'll carry you up the stairs. There." Bond felt the shackles on his legs being freed.

"Any suggestions?" Bond slid his hand onto the ASP, weighing it carefully to be certain there was a real magazine in place. It was something he had practiced many times—even in the dark—with empty magazines, or ones loaded with blanks, and the real thing. It *was* fully loaded.

"There is one way . . ." Smolin began, then stopped, his head and body turning as the door smashed open to reveal Ingrid, still in her Mrs. Danvers drab garb, but with the three dogs straining at their leashes.

"Ingrid!" Smolin used his most commanding tone.

"It's all been very interesting." Ingrid's voice was distinctly unfeminine—like her face, it was thin and sharp. "I have made certain changes to the interrogation room since you were last here, Colonel—on General Chernov's orders, naturally. For one thing, the switches, in here for the recording facility, have been reversed. He's going to be fascinated by the tapes. But we have listened long enough. The General will be here soon, and I want you *all* tightly locked away before he arrives."

As though reading each other's thoughts, Smolin leaped to the left, while Bond rolled out of the chair, moving right, as Ingrid shrieked, in German, at the dogs—*"Wotan, Rechts! Anfassen! Fafie, Links! Anfassen!"* The dogs sprang, snarling and, as Fafie's teeth fastened on his gun arm, Bond had a fleeting view of men standing behind Ingrid, and the third dog—Siegi—straining at the leash to go in for the kill.

11

Dog Eat Dog

He felt a tearing rip of pain as Fafie's jaws fastened on the lower part of his arm, making the fingers of his right hand open involuntarily, so that the gun dropped heavily onto the floor.

Beyond the pain, Bond was aware of several things—Ingrid's raw voice shouting above the snarling of the dogs; Smolin cursing in both Russian and German; the stale, stinking smell of Fafie's breath on his face, and the dog's weight as he held on—still growling—head moving from side to side as though trying to wrench Bond's arm from its socket.

He reflexed, like any trained man, smashing his free hand with full force into the dog's genitals. That's what you were taught, but training was different—for one thing, your arms were well protected, and you did not follow through on the blows. The trainer was always around and, once you had gone through the moves, he called the animal off. But this was for real, and he felt Fafie react to what must have been an exquisitely painful contact. The growl changed into a yelp of unexpected pain, and for a second the jaws relaxed.

Bond used that brief moment to roll and bring his right hand up to the animal's throat—thumb and fingers finding the windpipe and pressing as though he wished to tear out the dog's larynx. His left arm whipped around, catching the beast by the scruff of the neck but, by this time, the shock of pain and the full instinct of real danger had given Fafie renewed strength.

The yelp changed back into a series of chilling snarls and it took all of Bond's depleted reserves just to hang on. He could feel the deepening pain where Fafie had lacerated his arm, and the weakness that came from it. But, like the dog, he knew he was fighting for his life, and he increased the pressure with thumb and fingers—"You never throttle anyone, or anything, like they do in the movies, with both hands. Always use the one-handed choke for good results." He could hear the little leathery instructor from the training school as clearly as he had heard him long ago, during the first of many kill-or-be-killed courses.

Screw in with the hand on the windpipe and use all your strength at the back of the neck with the other hand—he put action to the thought, as Fafie was thrashing around in an attempt to pull clear. It was like wrestling with a tiger, and for one brief, darkened moment, Bond allowed his natural love for animals to creep into his consciousness, but for no more than a second. This *was* life and death.

As he wrestled, aware of the pain, noise, and confusion around him, Bond's mind clung to the one thing that would keep him going—Fafie wanted blood. His blood and his death.

"*Fafie! Anfassen! Anfassen!*" Ingrid shrieked over everything—"Fafie! Hold him! Hold him!"

But Bond had summoned a last great surge of strength, his fingers cutting in through the thick fur of Fafie's coat, the left arm pressing with increased power.

He could feel the animal begin to lose consciousness. Then, almost with lightning suddenness, Fafie's jaws relaxed, and the body became a dead weight.

Though he knew he had won this round, Bond continued to act as though he was wrestling with the dog, glancing sideways to lock on to where the ASP had fallen.

He rolled, grunted, and moved, trying to give the impression that Fafie was still fighting him. He felt strangely cool and calculating now, conscious of pain, but determined to get his hands on the automatic that lay to his right, just within his grasp.

He relaxed, looking toward Smolin to see, with some horror, that the GRU man was lying back, with Wotan covering him, fangs bared ready to be buried into his victim's throat if Smolin showed further resistance. That one look told Bond that the Colonel was not going to risk even the twitch of an eyebrow, for there was also Siegi being held on a choke chain, in reserve. After Siegi, there would be the men he had seen crowding in behind Ingrid. The moves would have to be carefully calculated and coordinated—all this was seen, digested, and comprehended in the wink of an eye.

There was no question of choosing the right moment, for the right moment was any moment.

Using the now dead Fafie as his only available shield, Bond broke through the barrier of pain that leaped from his damaged arm. He rolled to the right, reached for the weapon, rolled again, and fired—two shots for the straining Siegi; another single round as Wotan turned from his captive, catching the full force of a Glazer slug—knocking the vicious, trained killer animal back against the wall—then a fourth shot, low and toward the door, where it struck the jamb, carving a great hole through wood and plaster.

The sudden, unexpected deaths of all three animals had frozen Ingrid in the doorway, shock rooting her to the floor; but the men behind her had scattered.

"No more!" Smolin shrieked, on his feet now, lunging toward Ingrid, catching one wrist and jerking her arm down hard, then toward him and away, so the luckless housekeeper hurtled across the room, thudding into the far wall with a bone-cracking sound.

As she hit, Ingrid made an odd noise, part scream, a commixture of rage, frustration, and agony. Then she silently slid down the wall to sprawl, a black heap, on the floor.

Smolin had an automatic in his hand and was shouting toward the shattered doorway: "Alex! Yuri! I know you're good and sworn GRU men. I am your senior officer. KGB have mounted a despicable plot against us. You are with KGB men now. Turn. Turn on them. They are traitors and can only bring discredit, and death, upon your heads. Turn now!"

For a couple of seconds, silence hung in the passageway, like some deadly gas, then there was a cry, followed by a shot and the sound of blows.

Smolin nodded at Bond, signaling for him to take up a position on the right of the door, while the GRU man pressed himself against the wall on the opposite side.

Another shot. A shout, and the noise of a struggle, the unmistakable sound of a fist pounding against flesh and bone, and a voice calling in Russian, "Comrade Colonel, we have them. Quickly, we have them!"

Smolin nodded toward Bond, and together they threw themselves into the passage. As they jumped, so Smolin yelled in English, "Get them *all*, James! All!"

He needed no second bidding. On his side, to the right of the passage, one man lay unconscious while two struggled with a fourth, attempting to overpower him.

It required three quick shots from the ASP to dispatch the group. The terrible, efficient Glazer slugs did their work—the first exploded in the right side of one of the struggling men, spreading half its load into the stomach of the one grappling with him; the second took out the man on the floor; while the third dispatched the fourth man, who did not even have time to know what hit him.

The noise of the shots was deafening within the narrow passage walls. Doubly so, as Smolin loosed off two rounds from his automatic. Bond turned, to see he had also scored, the couple of fresh corpses—one spread-eagled, the other an untidy pile of remains—bore witness to the GRU officer's accuracy.

"Pity," Smolin muttered. "They were good men, Alex and Yuri."

"There are times when you have no option." Bond looked grimly at the carnage, realizing that he felt more for the dogs he had been forced to kill than for the thugs. "How many upstairs, Maxim?—You've proved yourself now."

"Two; I should think they're with the girls."

"They'll be down any minute, then."

"I doubt it. Up there, you don't hear much that goes on down in this basement." He was breathing hard. "We've used it many times, James. Strong men have screamed down here while people in the rooms above have made love and heard nothing."

Bond could hear Smolin, but the world around him began to swim and go out of focus. He was aware of the hot stickiness of his arm and a blinding pain that started at the source of the heat and spread throughout his body. He retched twice, heard Smolin calling his name from a long way off. Then the darkness covered him.

He dreamed of snakes and spiders. They slithered and crawled around him as he tried to get out of a dark and twisting maze, ankle-deep in the revolting creatures. He had to make it, and there was light, dim at the end of the tunnel. Then the end would disappear, and he was back where he had started, far below the earth, surrounded by a red glow. There. There it was again, the light at the end, but a large snake was dragging at his legs. He had no sense of fear, just the knowledge that it was essential for him to get out. But another snake had joined the first, while smaller reptiles wrapped themselves around his legs, pulling him down, hissing as he lost his balance.

Now, one of the reptiles had him by the arm, squeezing, sinking fangs into it, causing a pain that broke through the blackness. He looked, and a nest of spiders crawled into the wound made by the snake. Other spiders—large, fat, and furry—were on his face, stuffing themselves into his nostrils and prizing their way into his mouth so that he had to cough, splutter, and spit them out.

He was gagging on the spiders, but somehow he must have managed to get nearer to the tunnel's end, for light was hurting his eyes and a voice called his name—"James! James Bond! James!"

The snakes and spiders were gone, leaving only a wrenching pain where they had ravaged his arm, and something else was swimming into his vision—a face. The face of a girl. An angel? Was he dead? The lips moved. "James? Come on. It's okay." The face went out of focus and said, "Heather, he's coming round."

"Thank heaven for that."

Bond's eyes fluttered, opened and closed, then opened fully to see the pert pretty face of Ebbie Heritage filling the entire screen of his vision.

"What?" he said.

"You're okay, James. It's okay now."

He moved and was aware of the throbbing in his right arm and a feeling that something was constricting it.

"There's not much time." It was Maxim Smolin, easing Ebbie to one side. "You'll be fine, James, but . . ." He looked at his wristwatch.

Everything came flooding back in sharp detail, as

though someone had opened a set of gates in his memory.

Smolin straightened up. He stood looking down at Bond, one arm around Heather Dare's shoulders.

Bond took a deep breath. "Sorry, did I pass out on you?"

"Not surprisingly." Smolin smiled. "That damned dog's teeth went deep. How does it feel?"

He moved his arm. "Numb. Uncomfortable, but I can use it."

"Ebbie played Florence Nightingale." It was Heather speaking now. "We all have a lot to thank you for, James. Maxim's told us what happened down there."

"I only cleaned the wound." The Sirens, with their sweet, alluring, and seductive voices, must have sounded like Ebbie, Bond thought, stupidly dazed, as she continued, "The dogs were in good condition. I don't think there's any danger of poison. We used the strongest antiseptic known to man."

"And the most expensive." Smolin gave a wry smile. "The last of the Hine 1914 vintage. Smooth. Very smooth."

Bond groaned, "Smooth, magnificent, and far from intoxicating. I'm sorry."

"It went for a good cause," Smolin said with a nod. "Can you sit up? Stand?"

Unsteadily, Bond eased himself up. They had laid him on the settee in the guest suite. He tried to stand, but his legs felt as though they had been filleted. At first he had to cling to one of the settee arms to steady himself. Ebbie rushed to his side, her hands strong and experienced.

"Thank you, Ebbie. Thank you for everything." He moved with care, trying the muscles and thinking he must look like a small child learning to walk. Slowly the power returned. "Thank you, Ebbie," he repeated.

"We're in *your* debt. This was nothing."

"The others?" Bond turned to Smolin again. "Your men up here?"

"Taken care of." The GRU man's face went blank, reminding Bond of his own mind and emotions when a nasty piece of work had been done. It was always best to erase that kind of thing from memory. People who recalled too much either started to enjoy it and were engulfed by madness, or cracked under the guilt.

"Ingrid?" he asked, just for the record.

"Alive. Resting. Conscious, but she won't be going far. Several bones're broken." He became urgent. "James, we have to get out. You remember? Blackfriar? He could arrive anytime. We really should try to be away before he lands."

"Who's Blackfriar?" From a startled Ebbie.

"Satan himself." Smolin's mouth was set grimly. "General Chernov. From KGB's darkest side of the moon."

Bond nodded. "I'll be okay. Blackfriar is as Maxim says. Evil, clever, and very good at his work—which he appears to enjoy." He took several deep breaths and glanced, smiling, at Ebbie. She looked less sophisticated than Heather, but Heather appeared to have abandoned her haughty side as she now gazed at Smolin with wide, dark, and adoring eyes.

"Yes, I'm sure you'll be okay, James." Smolin had developed some acid in his manner. "You're the one who's had an injury, but you'll survive. I'm thinking of the rest of us."

"The cars are . . . ?"

"Here, yes." The Colonel gave a petulant shake of his head. "We have cars, James. What you don't seem to realize is that we're sitting in a natural bowl of earth. It's overlooked on all sides and there are, to my knowledge, at least ten men out there with sniperscopes, automatic weapons, the full works. They're also KGB, not GRU. Four of them at the main entrance alone. We start to drive away, they'll want to know why, and I really don't think they'll stop to question us. KGB have special men for that. The guys up on the rim of those hills—and at the entrance—are not questioners, either; they're shooters, killers."

"Dog eat dog, eh?"

"Shoot first. Worry about the questions later."

"Would they shoot at a really prime target?"

"Yes. You, me, or the girls. No doubts at all. Blackfriar has been in constant touch with this place—its real name is Three Sisters Castle, incidentally, and it's been used by KGB and GRU for the past ten years. But he's been on the radio link. I've had a look at the scratch pads in the Communications Room. Your name's been passed along the line. So has mine, and his last order was that nobody leave until he gets in. Anyone who tries *must* be stopped."

"I said *prime* target," Bond repeated. He was gradually starting to feel better, his mental processes becoming sharper. "Really prime—like General Konstantin Nikolaevich Chernov. Would they endanger his life? Put him in the line of fire?"

"You mean take him with us? Wait, and grab him?"

"Why not?"

"Because he will not be alone."

"Well, why not simply use him as cover? How's he coming in?"

"Helicopter. He's got plenty of unofficial transport over here—all *very* legal of course; the Republic's not the kind of place to play games using illegal transport. But he won't risk coming in when it gets dark—there are no facilities here for light aircraft or choppers once the sun's gone."

"He'll land near the castle?"

"We usually come in directly in line with the main entrance and fly up it. Then land out in front—close to where the cars are now."

"Who'll be with him?"

"At least two bodyguards—possibly more—his adjutant, and a skilled interrogator. They'll be armed. And they're all highly efficient."

Bond thought for a moment, and his arm gave a sudden stab of pain, making him wince.

"James, you all right?" Ebbie was at his side, one hand resting on the injured arm, her face troubled.

She had the kind of deep blue eyes in which a man would not reject the chance of drowning, and lips that cried out to kiss and be kissed. Bond nodded, saying it was just a twinge, nothing serious.

"We've *got* to get out." He reluctantly dragged his eyes from Ebbie, back to Smolin. "So we have to run the gauntlet, whatever the risks. Strikes me that the risk is lessened if we go just as the General arrives. Which of the cars, Maxim?"

"The BMW. It's good to start with, but this one's been souped up a little, as I believe they say."

Bond began to pat his clothes. "My gun?" he asked, and Smolin produced the ASP from the table, together with the spare magazines and the baton. As he dismantled and reassembled the weapon, Bond surreptitiously checked the more secret parts of his clothing, to make sure that certain other items had been left in their hiding places. "We agreed, then? We make a run for it as soon as the chopper appears?"

The others nodded, but Smolin did not look altogether happy.

"Maxim?"

"Yes, it's the only way—or go now and risk their full firepower. I'd be happier if we'd had the time to take them out."

"You going to arm the girls?"

"He already has." Heather had certainly become more confident. Bond made a mental note to ask her why she had offered herself to him, so blatantly, at the Airport Hotel—but that was a question he would not put to her in front of Smolin, to whom he now turned. "And you have the BMW's keys?"

Smolin nodded.

"Then what're we waiting for? We should get down to the main doors. Maxim, when we go down, why don't you walk out to the car? That would be natural enough. Play around with it, and give us a yell as soon as the chopper appears."

They went down the stairs, and the castle suddenly seemed very cold and cheerless. Outside there was still plenty of light, though the sky was just starting to redden in the West; but the flagstoned hall retained an almost ghostly chill.

"Going to be a lovely sunset." Bond smiled cheerfully, mainly to keep the girls in good spirits. He knew from Smolin's face that escape from this place was not going to be easy.

At the door Maxim asked how they should sit when they reached the BMW. "Okay if Irma—sorry, Heather—comes in front with me? You, James, in the back with Ebbie. I suspect we should all keep as low as possible once it's started."

"That's fine by me." Ebbie grinned happily at Bond, who suggested that all the windows should be opened—"In case we have to return fire."

"Right." Smolin gave a curt nod. "I think that would be most wise. None of this is going to be easy."

"You've made the point, Maxim. But I really don't fancy swimming into Kolya Chernov's shark-infested waters at the moment. Now, a private word with you." He took Smolin's arm and pulled him to one side, away from the girls. "If we *do* get clear, where do you think we should head for?"

"Out of this country, for a start. But there's no hiding place from Chernov—not in the long run."

"You got any ideas about Jungle and your colleague—Susanne, is it? Where they might be?"

"You know where they were last sighted?"

"Yes, and you?"

"The Canary Islands."

"That's what I had, but I should imagine it's old news by now."

"It was a week old when M gave it to you. I think they'll have moved on, but once we're clear—and that's no foregone conclusion—I'll have burned my boats. We'll have to try to follow their spoor, and that will mean doing it alone. No help from my people—"

"And very little from mine, if we're sticking to M's rules."

"Chernov'll expect us to head for Dublin, Shannon, or one of the ports—Rosslare or Dun Laoghaire."

"Which we'll have to do eventually, if we're going to get out."

Smolin gave him a fast sideways glance. "Not necessarily. I still have some contacts we can use. Come to that, so do you. But I could get us out quietly."

It was Bond's turn to look anxious. "I can't go into the North, you do know that? Even if M's sticking to the brief he laid down about denying me, I still daren't go into the North. Off-limits to my department. Strictly MI5 territory. We've had too many internal battles about that one already. I would *really* be persona non grata if I turned up there. 'Five' are very touchy about it."

Smolin made pushing movements with the flat of his palms. "I'm not thinking about the North. Again, *if* we do get out, we'll have to pull some kind of deception. Make them think we're heading for Dublin, then double back. I want to get us into West Cork. From there I know how we can be moved out with the minimum fuss. Okay?"

Bond nodded. "You'll be at the wheel, so you lead."

Smolin gave his first cheerful smile for some time. "At least I know where we can switch cars," he said with some glee, as though he had only just thought of it. "I also know a nice quiet hotel where they're unlikely to come looking for us."

"Well," Bond began, then changed his mind. "How many telephones have they got in this place?" he asked, as though suddenly struck with another idea.

"One here, in the hall." Smolin pointed to a small table set under the stairs. "There's one in the control room—the door to the left, on the gallery at the top of the stairs—and one in the main bedroom, that's the next door along."

"They're all linked to the same number?"

"Yes." He recited the number, which Bond instantly committed to memory. "The line in is the one in the control room, where they keep the communications equipment. The others—in the hall and main bedroom—are extensions. Why?"

"Just a little idea. Keep the girls happy. Get them outside with you. It'll only take ten minutes."

Smolin raised his eyebrows. "If we've got ten minutes. This is necessary?"

"I believe so, yes." Bond gave a cheerful smile and turned away, taking the stairs as quickly as he could. The arm did not hurt so much, but he still felt weak.

The control room was small, with most of the space taken up by great banks of radio equipment, tape machines, and a large computer, all of which were ranged against the longest wall, on professional wood and metal desks, each with a high-backed office chair. On the desks were scratch pads, blotters, calculators, and the like. The telephone stood on the center desk, in front of the main radio gear.

Almost before he was in the room, Bond had unclasped his belt to seek out and remove the ingeniously hidden miniature tool kit, put together by Q'ute some time ago. It contained an assortment of compact tools, detonators, picklocks, wire, and fuses, and folded into an almost flat leather container.

From what was at his disposal, Bond took a small plastic cylinder, removing the top to display several different screwdriver heads. He selected one that would easily fit the screws on the underside of a standard telephone, and slid the driver into the other end of the tiny cylinder, which became a handle. Thus equipped, he removed the four screws at the base of the instrument.

Once he had opened up the phone, he took out his wallet and extracted a small packet—given to him by Q'ute just before he had left the headquarters building and was starting off for Heather's beauty salon, Dare to Be Chic.

The packet contained what appeared to be six black grains of wheat, each with two tiny wires trailing from it. Again he changed the screwdriver head, this time using the size normally associated with jewelers.

Each of the wheatgrain-like objects was, in fact, the latest advance in what at one time was known as a harmonica bug—small now being beautiful in the eyes of all concerned with surveillance and sound-stealing devices.

It took Bond less than two minutes to attach one of the bugs to the requisite terminals within the telephone, and another two to close the whole thing up. He breathed a silent thank-you for these skills, which he had learned many years ago at the hands of Q Branch's special telephone instructor—a perky cockney called Philip, known to all at the Regent's Park HQ as Phil the Phone.

He then went to the main bedroom, quickly located the telephone, and inserted another of the tiny—well-nigh undetectable—devices.

Downstairs again, he went through the same routine with the third telephone. Smolin and the girls were outside, watching for Chernov's arrival, which could now be any minute, for the sun was quickly sinking and the light had started to go.

He had hardly completed the work on the last telephone when Smolin reopened the door, calling out, "I'm going to the car, James. He should be here by now. Right?" He squared his shoulders, pushed at the heavy front doors, and walked slowly toward the BMW, playing around with the boot for a while before going to the interior of the car, activating the windows to open, and climbing behind the wheel.

They heard the first sound of the helicopter's engine in the distance. Smolin started the BMW, leaning over and opening the passenger door, shouting for them to come on.

Hardly had they reached the car—with the helicopter clearly visible, an insect against the blood glow of the sky—when the first shots came down, from the rim of overlooking hills. They were warnings, smacking against the hard tar of the turning circle, well away from the car.

Inside there was heavy breathing, Maxim Smolin crouched over the wheel and the others as near to the floor as they could get; Ebbie, close to Bond, tensing as a second strike of bullets hit the ground nearby.

Smolin took off like a racing driver, weaving as he went, building up speed to take the bumps along the rough track that led, some two miles on, to the main entrance.

The helicopter had turned away from its run in, as though alerted by the gunfire, circled low, and, as Bond had hoped, came between them and at least some of the marksmen. He could now see that it was a version of the big twin-finned, double-rotored KA-25, and that it carried civil markings—the Hormone, as NATO dubbed it.

"If we do get out," Heather shouted, "where're we heading for?"

"*If* we make it!" Smolin yelled, and at that moment they heard the roar of the helicopter just over the roof, and the sudden rattle of automatic fire, kicking up the dust and stones to their right. Bond raised his head and watched as the squat, cumbersome-looking machine turned on its own axis and started to run in again, toward them—its two huge rotors whirling fore and aft.

Bond had the ASP clasped in his right hand, and felt the downdraft of the Hormone battering at the car like a gale. It was low, and chopping in alongside them, one man half out of the rear sliding door, manning a machine pistol. The ASP kicked and banged twice, and the marksman was cut straight out of the door, while a small amount of the helicopter's fuselage went with him. Bond steadied his hands, lifted the weapon slightly, and loosed off another two rounds, aimed at the lower rotor blades.

The Hormone faltered and began to fall away—the forward rotors whining as a hunk of one blade was torn off by a Glazer impact.

Smolin let out a gust of laughter. "You got the bastards," he shouted, "the stinking, rotten bastards! There they go . . ."

Bond glanced back through the rear window to see the helicopter put down heavily, with a jolt that almost crushed one of the wheels of its undercarriage, sending it into the fuselage. "They won't get that fixed in a hurry at the handy local garage," he muttered. Then the bullets started to come down around them again and he had to fold himself flat on the floor, so close to Ebbie that he could smell the scent of her hair. It reminded him of summer in the fields of Kent.

"Let's get the hell out of here," Smolin called. "Hang on! Hang on, tight! I'm going to take a short-cut."

12

Strange Meeting

The car lurched—first right, then left as Smolin dragged it around rough grass. At one point there was a thump and bang, which knocked the vehicle precariously to one side, so that the girls screamed, and for a second even Bond thought they were going to turn over—he knew it was the impact of a heavy-caliber bullet, and what *that* was capable of doing.

Dusk was rapidly turning to night, but the grounded helicopter had its forward lights on, a glaring immobile cone that lit the main track toward the entrance, barring exit there, unless Smolin decided on a suicide dash along the beam.

But he heaved the BMW away from the track, swinging it over the uneven rutted meadow, moving closer to the rising ground as he did so. The castle was to their left now, and the helicopter a long way behind—to the far left of the building.

Another three shots came down around them, one hitting the front passenger side door, passing through but appearing to do no damage. The long-range snipers were almost certainly using night scopes.

"Should we try it on foot?" Bond shouted to Smolin above the noise.

"On foot they'd get us. There used to be a gap along this side—overgrown, but not properly sealed off." He sounded perfectly calm as another shot, from somewhere above them, ricocheted past. "It's about our only chance."

He drove without lights, craning forward to peer into the darkness, the engine whining under stress and the whole car bumping and grinding, slewing like a small boat in very choppy water.

"There!" Smolin's voice was full of glee. "Now we pray." The car slowed as he began to change down, pumping at the brakes. They were moving right, wheels protesting and the back swinging violently.

"Ever done any rallying?" Bond called casually, as though to take the girls' minds off the alarming experience.

"No!" Smolin laughed. "But I've done the GRU course—*Scheiss!*" It looked as though they were now hurtling toward an impenetrable wall of trees.

"Down! Hang on!" Bond shouted.

The car struck and there was a grinding noise as the underside hit the hard roots of bushes and undergrowth, followed by the whisper of branches and foliage parting against the vehicle.

There were no solid trees, however, and, while the dense growth had slowed them, the car did not stop. It crunched, bounced, and made some impressively terrifying noises, but kept going to the point where Smolin had to change right down to first, with his foot hard on the accelerator. Then, as suddenly as they had struck the barrier, they were through, but with a heavy pole and barbed-wire fence facing them, towering a good seven feet above the ground.

"Keep praying." Smolin's voice dropped a shade as he changed up, accelerated, and rammed the fence head-on. This time the impact was more dramatic—Smolin and Heather were thrown against their seat belts, while Bond catapulted hard against Smolin's seat back.

Ebbie came off best, having stayed on the floor, though she reacted with touching concern as Bond gave a small cry of pain as his injured arm banged against the driver's seat—"James? Are you—*ouch*"—as she was rolled back by the jolt.

The car kept going, then, tangled in wire, spluttered and stopped, halfway onto the road ahead of them.

Smolin forced his door open, pushing it against the broken wire to get it free. "Get out—if you can!" he yelled, and Bond tried the door on his side. It opened halfway, then became trapped in the wire, so, following Smolin, he shoved hard until both of the men were out, scrambling around the car, grappling at the wire with bare hands, which in moments were cut and bleeding from the vicious barbs.

Each cursed in his respective language, under panting breath, as the car was slowly cleared of the tentacles that seemed almost alive, springing up and waving about as each new strand was loosened.

"Where now?" Bond breathed heavily.

"Dump this car, and get another one." Smolin

ducked to avoid a snake of wire that shot up, missing his face by inches as he freed it from the back wheels.

"Where?"

"I have a good British-made Rover Vitesse stashed away—that is correct, yes? Stashed?"

"Yes." Bond tugged the last piece of wire from around the rear bumper. "You've certainly got this country sewn up, Maxim—cars stashed away, covert routes in and out."

Smolin was heading back for the driving seat. "Not just me. I'm sure Chernov has more transport near at hand. We'll be running another gauntlet."

They were both back in the BMW with Smolin twisting the ignition key in a vain attempt to start again. The engine coughed and died several times, then—to everyone's relief—fired. As though nothing had happened, Smolin slammed the gears and edged the car onto the road, driving with no lights, turning left—which, Bond recalled, would take them to the Dublin–Wicklow road.

"They'll send the Mercedes after us first, and probably organize another couple of teams," Smolin continued. "But our switch in cars should help. This one I kept up my sleeve. It's private, *nobody* knows I have it. Did the whole thing alone."

"Far?" Bond asked, thinking of other things. Personally he badly wanted a telephone.

"Fifteen minutes as the crow flies—but have you noticed how many crows there are in this country? And they don't seem to fly. They litter the roads and walk out of our way." At long last, he switched on the headlights, while still treating the car, road, and his passengers in an unnervingly cavalier fashion.

They were moving swiftly through lanes that appeared to have been constructed from several sets of leftover S-bends, overhung by bushes and hedges. Nobody spoke, though Ebbie's hand stole softly into Bond's palm, then was snatched back again as she peered in the half-light at the blood flowing from what seemed to be hundreds of cuts and gashes.

Without a word she reached down, lifted her skirt, exposing a generous segment of thigh—unmistakably white against the semidarkness—and started to tear at her slip. When she had a sizable piece of light-colored silk, she put it to her mouth, biting to rip it into two pieces, which she then tenderly bound around both of Bond's damaged hands. "Poor you," she whispered. "I'll kiss them better." So saying, she bent her head and ran her lips over the exposed part of his fingers. First one hand, then the other, her tongue licking the flesh and her lips closing over the middle finger of one hand.

"I don't think anyone's ever made love to my hands before," Bond whispered. "Thank you, Ebbie."

Breaking the spell, she looked up at him, her eyes wide with innocence. "Hope your tetanus shots are up-to-date," she murmured—and even that sounded stimulating.

After a couple of miles they turned off, abruptly and with no warning, onto another narrow road that led into a forest of some size. The night had closed in fully now, and the trees on either side lost their color in the headlights. Every few hundred yards, timber was stacked neatly on wooden bunkers by the roadside, and half a mile on they turned again, straight onto a track leading into the trees, ignoring a notice that plainly said, NO MOTOR VEHICLES. PEDESTRIANS ONLY.

"You see that, Maxim?" Bond asked with no trace of criticism.

"We're in Ireland, James. Notices like that don't mean what they say. Anyway, I figured out it would be best to hide a car where no cars drive."

"And no birds sing," Bond muttered reflectively. "The GRU teach you that as well?"

"I suppose so. But I'm pretty certain that, for all their clever ways, Chernov's lads'll be out looking single-mindedly for this BMW, not for the pretty lady over here." He flung the car sideways on, almost brushing against the thick trunks of two fir trees, then another, and a third pair before the headlights revealed a small clearing containing what seemed to be a mound of branches.

"Okay, everybody out. Uncover that car, then use the stuff to hide this one. I must look to my maps."

It took less than ten minutes, and when it was done, a dusty but patently new black Rover Vitesse stood in the clearing, while the pile of branches covered the BMW.

Smolin, ever cautious, paced out a number of steps from the nearside front wheel of the Rover, dug in the moss and bracken, and retrieved a small package containing two sets of keys. Bond, standing over him, spoke in a low voice. "Get the girls into the car, Maxim. We need to talk."

Smolin nodded, carefully ushering Heather into the front and Ebbie to the back. Then he walked over to Bond, a short distance from the Rover, where the girls could not hear them.

"First"—Bond moved very close to him—"when you were in Berlin, did you have a sidekick called Mischa? Because if you didn't, Maxim, you should look to your lady."

Smolin nodded. "Yes, Mischa was around, but he was KGB plant on me. You should know, James, that nothing can ever be straightforward between KGB and GRU. We are up to our ears in suspicion concerning one another. You ask about Mischa because he's one of Chernov's killing party. He was in London, yes?"

Bond nodded. "Okay. Now, further plans. I just about trust you, Maxim, but I need to know what we're up to. You mentioned throwing them off the scent and getting to West Cork."

Smolin smiled in the gloom. "You have special contacts, James. I also. I run two people in Skibbereen. They have a light aircraft. By night we can fly very low—escape all detection and land quietly, and without anyone knowing, in a field—glorious Devon. I have done it several times."

It was feasible, Bond knew it. Hadn't Special Branch and "Five" suspected illegal entry by light aircraft for some years now? Nobody could ever pinpoint places, yet they knew it was done by the lads from the North and, they thought, other interlopers.

"Right." Bond knew what he needed from this situation. "Chernov wants us, the girls, and, presumably, Jungle together with his lady friend, Dietrich. If we drive to Skibbereen now we won't make it until the very small hours. That'll mean holing up close to our departure point, not the best thing. I agree that—given the KGB's form—they'll be looking for four people in a BMW. So, using the Rover we've partially thrown them."

"Completely thrown them." Smolin was firm.

"You, of all people, Maxim, should know better than that. The girls—and, I suspect, ourselves—need some rest. There are also things I have to do. The telephones at the castle, you follow?"

He saw Smolin's head move.

"Why don't we drive partway tonight"—he peered at his watch—"it's eight-thirty now. We could be in Kilkenny by ten o'clock. Stay overnight, then continue the journey tomorrow—late afternoon. You can get hold of your people by telephone, and they're contained, I presume?"

"How contained?"

"From KGB doubling."

"KGB cannot know of them. They're personal. Mine alone. This will be the first time I've taken anyone in with me, okay?"

"Okay. They won't be looking for a black Rover, but they will be on the trail of four people. Once we're on the road we could telephone ahead—"

"If we find an unvandalized telephone, yes."

"Book in at two different hotels. You can drop Ebbie and myself off near one, and take the car to whichever watering hole you choose. We can make contact and arrange a meeting for the morning."

He saw Smolin nod like a wise owl. "That seems good. Also, I have two cases in the boot—sorry we did not have time to pick up yours, James. There's nothing that will fit you, but it will make the right impression, yes? The girls can shop in Kilkenny tomorrow, as long as they're careful. Ebbie has some stuff in that big shoulder bag, so she may be okay for a day or two."

"What kind of papers you carrying, Maxim?"

"British passport. International driver's license. Credit cards."

"Are they good?"

"The best forgeries ever to come out of Knamensky Street. My name is Palmerston. Henry J. Temple Palmerston. You like it?"

"Oh yes." Bond's voice was heavy with sarcasm. "You just pray that no passport control officer is a student of nineteenth-century British politics."

"Correct." He could feel Smolin's broad smile in the dark. "They are mainly people whose interests lie elsewhere—airplane modeling, railway trains, the novels of Dick Francis and Wilbur Smith. Very few of them graduate to Margaret Drabble or Kingsley Amis. We ran a thorough check—through the mail. Simple questions, but effective. Eighty-five percent filled in our little forms. We said it was for market research and offered a prize of five thousand pounds sterling. A man working at Heathrow won the lucky draw, and all others got small consolation prizes—Walkmans, pens, diaries. You know the kind of thing."

Bond sighed. At least the Soviets were sometimes thorough. "Well, Mr. Palmerston, don't you think we should get going?"

"If you say so—Mr. Boldman."

They arranged that Smolin and Heather should not stay in Kilkenny, but at The Clonmel Arms

Hotel—thirty minutes away. "It will be best to be completely separated," was Smolin's judgment. They had, to everyone's surprise, come across an unvandalized white and green booth marked TELEFON only fifteen minutes after leaving the dense wood.

Bond and Ebbie were booked into The Newpark, near to the famous castle, in Kilkenny. "You can have the bed," he told her. "I'll sit up and keep watch."

"Let's wait and see." Ebbie's hand slid into his again. "I do know you're a gentleman, James. But perhaps I don't want a gentleman."

"And I have certain professional duties," he replied calmly.

Ebbie grinned. "Duties, I might like. I'm sure you do everything like a professional."

Arrangements were made between the two men concerning contact by telephone, simple code phrases and the like. They arrived in Kilkenny just before ten and Smolin passed The Newpark, stopping a hundred yards or so further on. He got out, unlocked the boot, and hauled out a black travel bag. "A few clothes of mine, and there is a razor and toothbrush." He smiled. Ebbie had a large shoulder bag that she had carted with her from The Ashford Castle Hotel to what she imagined was to be sanctuary at The Three Sisters Castle. "It's got warpaint, another shirt, and some jeans in it," she explained, somewhat archly, opening her eyes widely and adding that it also contained *Unterkleidung*, as though this was a very daring admission. "Very small." She giggled, holding her hands close together with forefingers extended, about two inches apart.

As Mr. and Mrs. Boldman, they were greeted

with great friendliness at the hotel, told that the restaurant was closed, but the chef could "knock you up anything you might fancy, so."

Bond suddenly realized he was ravenous, while Ebbie also reacted to the idea of food rather in the manner of someone who is starving but wishes to be polite—"Well, a little something," she said. "Steak, perhaps, with potatoes and a green salad. Possibly some mousse, or profiteroles to follow—oh, and coffee, bread, maybe some wine."

"Anything at all, madam." The receptionist smiled. "Anything, so long as it's Escalope Holstein, French fries, green salad, and fruit salad."

"That'll do nicely," Ebbie said quickly. Bond nodded agreement, also choosing a white Burgundy of vague vintage and dubious nomenclature.

Ebbie also asked for, and got, some bandages and disinfectant—"We had a small trouble with the car, and my husband burned his hands." All in all, Bond decided, Ms. Ebbie Heritage was a treasure.

Treasure or not, he could not wait to get to the telephone once they were shown to their room: pleasant, if somewhat lacking in originality—no surprise, for the hotel's foyer was decorated adobe style, with a distinct Spanish influence.

"I must do those hands," Ebbie pleaded, "and, James, they'll be here with the food any minute."

Bond quietened her, reached up to the top button of his Oscar Jacobson jacket, and, using a thumbnail, prised off a thin strip of gray plastic—around an inch in length and a quarter of an inch thick.

He dialed for an outside line, and then the number of Three Sisters Castle, committed to memory when Smolin had given it to him.

As he heard the automatic exchange click through, a second before the ringing tone, Bond put the piece of plastic to the mouthpiece and pressed hard. For two seconds it emitted a tiny, piercing beep not unlike the sound of a muted harmonica. The earpiece of the phone gave a small beep back, meaning that the black grains of plastic wheat he had planted in the castle telephones reacted to the tone and grew ears. With the tiny harmonica bugs coming to life it was now possible for him to listen in, not just to telephone conversations, but to any speech or noise within thirty feet of each bug. He could have been far away—in Australia or South Africa—and the same thing would happen. These powerful tiny transmitters, if not detected, can be activated from thousands of miles away, making the telephone in which one has been implanted into a live, ever-ready microphone. Theoretically, you could obtain infinite intelligence. But now, even though the tone had reassured him that the transmitters were active, Bond could hear nothing at the other end but odd noises, far away, probably from one of the many other rooms that contained no phone.

Softly, Bond put down the receiver, glancing at his watch, knowing he must go on activating the bugs again and again until he got a result.

Ebbie had been hovering, looking perplexed, her hands clasping bandages and the disinfectant. "James, will you let me do your hands? Please."

Bond nodded, his face grave as he debated whether he should telephone Smolin now. Somebody would certainly be in the castle, if only to tend the injured Ingrid. But the fact that he could pick up nothing else meant one thing only—Chernov had every available man, including himself, scouring the countryside for them.

"Yes, okay, Ebbie. Do your worst." He sighed.

She in fact did her best. Soothing, soft, gentle, and very disconcerting. In the middle of her ministrations the food arrived, and they set to eating once she had finished.

"I shall bathe after this." She spoke with her mouth half full. "I'm sorry, but I was so hungry."

"That's all right, Ebbie. You've been very kind."

She looked across the little table that had been brought in for them. Her head was bowed, but she lifted her eyes, half-hooded, then opening wide. "I want to show you every kindness, James. You were wonderful back at that awful castle."

"I don't need payment, my dear."

"Oh, I liked you all those years ago—on the submarine. You've bugged the phones at the castle, yes?"

"You're very astute, Ebbie."

"Astute? What's astute? Is it sexy? I find you very . . ."

"It means you're very shrewd—clever at spotting things."

"But it was obvious, what you were doing just now—we were taught about it when we prepared for . . . for *Cream Cake*—that is such a stupid name. But you have listening devices in the castle, yes?"

"Of course I have."

"Then you're a very clever little bugger, James, to be able to listen to things in the castle from this telephone."

"I think you have the wrong word, Ebbie, but no matter." He smiled, and her face lit up.

"James, dear man, I hope you don't have to listen to them all night?"

"It depends. At the moment there's nobody there."

"I hope you don't. Oh, I do hope you don't."

"We shall see. I must keep trying."

They finished eating and Ebbie disappeared into the bathroom, while Bond wheeled the debris-cluttered room service table into the corridor. He was about to dial the castle again when Ebbie came out of the bathroom, dressed only in what she would have called her *Unterkleidung*, and very fetching she looked as she grinned unselfconsciously, gathered up her bag, and disappeared again.

He tried the castle once more, and this time caught a short conversation—a man talking in Russian to the obviously weak Ingrid. It amounted to nothing, and he waited for fifteen minutes, but there was no other sound.

At last, he put down the telephone and lay back on the bed, feeling tired and now very aware of the pain in both arm and hands.

Closing his eyes, he wondered what the next move would be. Like it or not, he would have to reactivate the bugs at regular intervals, and his experience told him that within a few hours they should all be on the move if there was no further news from the sound-stealing devices. If they got back to England in one piece he could park the girls in one of his *own* safe houses—which hc kept well hidden from the Service—and report to M with Smolin. At least two-thirds of the mission would have been accomplished.

At the moment he started composing his apologia to M, Ebbie returned to the bedroom, hair glistening and her body only partially covered by an oyster satin negligé.

"The bathroom's free now, James." She allowed the negligé to slip from her shoulders. "Unless you have something better to do."

Bond looked at the young fresh body, which held for him that same urgent attraction of innocence he had felt earlier. Slowly, he moved from the bed and into her arms. Their first kiss lasted about a minute, though it seemed like a lifetime, or a departure from one kind of life to another. His hands slid down to the neat silky little buttocks, and he felt his mind shrinking to one great need as Ebbie returned his kiss, her tongue darting and reaching hard into his mouth.

He pulled away, looked into the wide-open blue eyes. "With these bandages on, it might be difficult for me to take a bath," he said, his throat dry. "I wonder if you could . . ."

"Why don't we have a bath together?" Ebbie's firm hand closed around his wrist and she led him, unprotesting, into the bathroom.

She drew the bath and Bond allowed her to undress him. When he was lying in the warm water she stood over him, naked, to soap his body—her hands and fingers exploring him as she did so. When he was washed clean she stepped into the narrow tub, sliding onto her side and lifting one leg over his so that he took her beneath the warm water.

When it was over, Ebbie dried him with a rough towel, and redressed his hands. This time, he led her back to the bedroom. With all her innocent looks, she was like a woman who had just discovered the secret joys of life for the first time. It was soon obvious, however, that she was far from innocent, for she showed not only great stamina, but also imagination and invention. Through that night they made love three more times, once with a stormy wildness, then with passion—Ebbie above him, reciting a sensuous poem to the rhythm of her own body.

Between the lovemaking, when she left him to visit the bathroom, or lay back happy and panting on the bed—Bond tried the castle several times. Still with no result. In the end he gave up, drifting to sleep with Ebbie twined around him.

He woke with a start, realizing that, while it was still dark, dawn was not far away. Gently, Bond disentangled himself from the smoothness of Ebbie's body and looked at his watch. Five-thirty in the morning.

Sliding from the bed, he quietly padded to the bathroom. His hands felt better, though the arm mangled by Fafie still throbbed. Washing was easier than he expected, and by six o'clock, with dim light starting to show outside, Bond was dressed and equipped with the ASP, baton, and other hidden items.

Ebbie still lay supine in a deep sleep, her fair hair ragged on the pillow, her face tranquil with content. She might need all the rest she could get that day, so Bond pocketed the room key and went silently into the corridor.

The room service table had gone, and the whole hotel seemed wrapped in silence. As he made his way down to the main lobby the calm was broken by occasional sounds of movement from below, as the kitchen staff prepared breakfast.

Nobody appeared to be on duty at Reception, so he quickly made his way to the coin-operated telephone, dragging a pile of Irish change from his pocket.

A decidedly sleepy and disgruntled voice answered from The Clonmel Arms Hotel, and he had to repeat his request to be put through to "Mr. and Mrs. Palmerston."

There was an unduly long wait for any response and, finally, the operator came back on the line. "I'm sorry, sir, but they've checked out."

"When?" Alarm bells sounded in his head.

"I've just come on duty myself, sir. But some friends of theirs arrived unexpectedly, so I'm told. Mr. and Mrs. Palmerston left around a half hour ago."

Bond's nerve ends shrieked as he quickly thanked the operator and hung up. What friends? His Service, alerted from afar, or Blackfriar? The queries in Bond's mind were rhetorical, for he already knew the answer—Blackfriar. General Chernov had caught up with Smolin, and, if that had occurred, it would not be long before they reached Ebbie and himself. He might have half an hour or ten minutes, yet in that time it was essential he take some action to put himself back in control of the situation.

Within seconds he was dialing a Dublin number that rang and rang before the voice answered sharply, "Murray."

"Jacko B. There're problems. I have to make this official."

"Where are you?" Norman Murray sounded on edge.

"Kilkenny. Newpark Hotel. I think your friend—and mine—Basilisk's been lifted, with the girl you saw at the airport. The rumor about the other one, who I'd bet you already know as Blackfriar, is true. There's a place called Three Sisters Castle . . ."

"We know all about Three Sisters. No jurisdiction. It's Embassy property. Bit of a fracas there, Jacko, was that you, now?"

"Some, but I'm here with the girl from The Ashford Castle Hotel, got me?"

"Right. The girl with the romantic name."

"We're also due to be lifted. If you can—"

But Murray was way ahead of him—"I know all about Basilisk, and it's a lash-up. I'll do what I can, Jacko. Watch your back. Official now, you say?"

"Very official, and *very* dangerous."

"I doubt it, but get out and head for Dublin. We don't have orders to lift *you*."

"What d'you mean?"

"We were lifting Basilisk, and it's gone sour. Now, will you get going."

"No transport."

"Well, you'll have to steal something, Jacko. I hear you're good at that kind of thing." Murray gave a quick laugh and closed the line, leaving Bond looking at the dead telephone in his hand.

Ebbie, he thought. Get her out, even if we have to hide in the hedgerows. Yet, as he turned, another thought struck him. One more try for the harmonicas in the castle. He peeled the activator from its button, dialed the number, and bleeped the tiny plastic gizmo into the telephone. Suddenly the earpiece was filled with a confusion of noise—several people talking in different parts of the castle. What he could hear made him tighten his grip on the phone.

"They've lost the traitor Smolin, and his girl—shit . . ." Spoken in Russian.

A laugh, undoubtedly the sinister Ingrid. "The General's going to be very happy."

Then, clear, probably from the control room.

"Yes, message received and understood," this in German. "Hans," the voice shouted loudly, and an answer came from far away, and then close. "Hans, the team in Rome have tracked them down at last—Dietrich and the man Belzinger. Took a flight out last night. Can you get the Chief?"

"He's trying to locate the other pair—radio silence."

"Break it. Dietrich and Belzinger are headed for Hong Kong."

"Christ, I don't believe it."

"Neither will the General, but get him. Get him quickly."

Hong Kong, Bond thought. Jungle and his lady Captain were really distancing themselves from Europe. The sooner he got Ebbie out, the better it would be for all of them. He turned and took the stairs at a run, reaching their room, unlocking the door, and heading straight for the bed.

"Ebbie! Ebbie, wake up . . . !" His voice trailed off, for the bedclothes were pulled back and Ebbie was gone.

The alarm bells sounded again, but before he could react to the prickle of danger a voice whispered close to his ear. "Don't even think about going for the gun, Mr. Bond. You are of little use to me and I'd blow you away, now, in this room, if I had to. Hands on your head and turn around slowly."

He had heard the voice once before, on tape, so knew as he turned that he would be gazing into a face seldom seen in the West—the clean-cut, almost French-looking features of General Konstantin Nikolaevich Chernov, Chief Investigating Officer of Department 8 of Directorate S, KGB: Blackfriar himself.

"A strange meeting, Mr. Bond, eh? After following each other in office paper chases all this time." Chernov had a smile on his face and a large automatic pistol in his hand, while behind him three big men crowded in, like hounds gathered for the kill.

13

Blackfriar

"Well"—Bond looked straight into Chernov's green-flecked eyes—"you're out of your usual territory, Comrade General. It must be odd to be away from your comfortable office in the Square, or have they moved Department Eight out to that modern monstrosity off the ring road—the so-called Scientific Research Center?"

A wisp of a smile appeared on Chernov's lips. Anyone, Bond thought, could have taken him for an influential, wealthy businessman: the powerful body under a beautifully cut gray suit; the tanned, slim, and undeniably good-looking features; the personal magnetism of the man combined with his height—he was well over six feet tall—to make him a particularly commanding personality. It was easy to see how this man had become the Chief Investigating Officer of what had at one time been SMERSH.

"You read the right books, Comrade Bond. If I may say so, the right kind of fiction." He lowered the pistol, a heavy Stetchkin, turning his head in a slightly diffident manner to give a crisp instruction to one of the men behind him. "I'm sorry." He smiled again, as though he genuinely liked Bond. "I'm sorry, but your reputation goes ahead of you. I've asked my people to remove any obvious toys you might be carrying." His free hand went up to brush one of the graying, thick wings of hair that Headquarters always pointed to as one of his principal identification marks—*the hair is thick, graying at the temples, unusually long for members of the Russian Service, but always well groomed, and distinguished by the wings that almost cover his ears. It is swept straight back, with no parting.* Bond knew most of the senior KGB and GRU officers' profiles by heart.

One of Chernov's men, obeying the order, caught hold of Bond's shoulders, turning him around roughly and ordering him—in cumbersome English—to place his palms on the bedroom wall.

Chernov snapped another command, then, "I'm sorry, Mr. Bond, he was instructed to handle you more gently." His accent could easily have been acquired at one of the older British universities, the whole manner near to being deferential—the voice, usually quiet and calm: a trait that made him even more sinister.

The man conducting the body search was all too thorough—first the ASP and Concealable Security Baton; then the more devious tricks of the trade: pen, wallet, and the precious belt that contained so many secrets. He felt the lining of Bond's clothes and then his shoes, one at a time, each removed, examined, and returned. Within a matter of minutes Bond was left only with the tiny harmonica beeper still attached to the top button of his jacket.

Everything else of any value to him had been taken.

"It's interesting, isn't it?" Chernov said in his near-languorous tones. "Interesting how our masters are always dreaming up new little pieces of technology for us?"

"With respect, you're one of the masters." Bond willed himself to show equal calmness, for Chernov would be like an animal who could scent fear at fifty paces.

"So I am." He laughed, low-pitched.

"One to be admired, so we are told."

"Really." He did not sound flattered.

"Isn't it true that you are practically the only senior officer to survive the 1971 purge, after Lyalin's defection?"

Chernov shrugged. "Who knows about Lyalin? Some say that was a put-up job to get rid of us altogether."

"But you *did* survive, and helped to build the Phoenix out of the ashes of your department. You're to be admired." This was not mere flattery on Bond's part, for a man with Chernov's track record would never fall for flattery.

"Thank you, Mr. Bond. The feeling is mutual. You have also been resurrected against much criticism, I gather." He sighed. "What a difficult thing our job is. You realize what must be done?"

"The price on my head?"

"There's no price—not this time." He chuckled. "However, you *are* on a list. Therefore, I would be failing in my duty if I did not see that your execution was carried out. Preferably at the Lubyanka, following some question-and-answer sessions." He shrugged again. "But I suppose that could prove difficult. To dispose of you will not be a problem; yet my career demands that justice must be seen to be done. Your death has to be public rather than in the privacy of the Lubyanka cellars."

Bond nodded, knowing the longer he kept the man talking, here in the hotel, the more chance Murray would have to be the US Fifth Cavalry and ride in, at the eleventh hour, to his rescue. Official or not, Murray would certainly do all that was possible—did he not owe Bond his own life?

"I'm glad you are philosophical about it, Mr. Bond. You say you admire me, and it would be unjust if I did not admit to holding you, your ingenuity, speed, and resourcefulness, in some awe. As the American criminal fraternity would say, you must understand that there will be nothing personal about your death. It's just business."

"Of course." Bond hesitated for a moment. "Might I ask what has happened to the lady?"

"Don't worry about the lady." He smiled, inclining his head to one side in a condescending gesture. "Eventually she must also pay a penalty—together with the turncoat Smolin and his whore—not to mention our other traitor Fräulein Captain Dietrich, and *her* gigolo, Belzinger—or Baisley, as he now likes to be called. My duty is to see justice done to them. You are a most delightful bonus." He looked around him, at his lieutenants. "We should be on our way. There is much to be done."

"I'm ready when you are." Bond realized that he must have sounded a shade too confident, and saw his error in the worm that stirred deep in Kolya Chernov's eyes.

For a second the General looked at him suspiciously, then turned on his heel, flicking his hand in a gesture that was itself an order for his people to follow with Bond.

They took him along the corridor, away from the main exit, and down two flights of stairs that were meant for emergencies only. Behind the hotel stood two cars—a Renault of some kind, and a sleek black, official-looking Jaguar with customized darkened windows.

Chernov walked straight toward the latter vehicle, and Bond's captors pushed him in the same direction. The Renault was obviously either the trail or scout car. Bond was to travel in the comparative luxury of Chernov's Jaguar. A man detached himself from the driving seat and strolled over to open the rear door. He wore a black turtleneck and his head was bandaged. Even from a distance, Bond recognized Mischa, the killer who had made the abortive attempt on Heather's life in London. The bandages made him look more piratical than ever, and he stared at Bond as a jackal might view his cornered victim.

General Chernov ducked his head and climbed into the rear of the Jaguar, while the others pushed Bond around to the far side. There was no sign of Ebbie.

Another man climbed from the offside door, standing to one side as Bond was bundled in next to Chernov.

Chernov sighed. "The ride will not be that comfortable; it's a shade cramped with three people in the back."

The guard climbed in after Bond so that he was sandwiched between him and Blackfriar. Mischa returned to the driving seat, while one of the other men took the front passenger seat: riding shotgun.

Being a realist, Bond did not think about what might happen if Murray missed his cue.

Mischa started the engine, and the Renault pulled away in front of them—a forward scout, Bond thought. It was exactly how he would have played it.

Within minutes it became obvious that they were taking the road to Dublin. In a matter of hours they would be back at Three Sisters Castle.

Mischa drove with almost exaggerated care, keeping around a steady thirty yards behind the Renault. He did not look back at Bond, though you could feel the malevolence coming from him like static. The hood next to Bond kept onc hand inside his jacket and occasionally Bond could glimpse the butt of a pistol grasped firmly in his paw. The General dozed, but the fellow riding shotgun remained alert, occasionally turning round, or watching the rear from the vanity mirror set in the sun visor, which he had pulled down.

Time dragged, and Bond tired of the views of lush greenery, and the untidy towns and villages through which they passed. His mind ranged through every possibility. There was no way he could escape from the car in one piece—that was sure: certain death, even on the main roads of the Republic of Ireland. Murray, he kept thinking, if only Murray would turn up there might be a way. For the present the ball was out of his court, and he had lost control over the situation.

But they covered the miles without incident, finally passing through the narrow streets of Arklow.

About three miles on, the Renault turned off to the left, up a very narrow road bordered by high trees and hedges, and with barely space for two cars to pass comfortably. Bond had a sense of déjà vu, knowing that this was the road leading to the main castle entrance.

Chernov—Blackfriar—stretched and woke, telling Mischa he had done well, sharing a joke with him in Russian. Ahead, the Renault turned a sharp bend, and as the Jaguar followed, Mischa let out an obscenity. On the other side of the bend, the Renault had been forced to pull up sharply. There were two Garda cars angled across the road, and as Mischa applied the brakes, Bond glanced behind to see an unmarked saloon slewing to their rear.

"Stay calm. No weapons!" Chernov ordered, his voice cracking like a whip. "No shooting. Understand!"

Half a dozen uniformed Gardi were surrounding the Renault, and another four now approached the Jaguar.

With a slow insolence, Mischa activated the window, and a uniformed officer bent to speak with him.

"Gentlemen, I'm afraid this road is closed to all but the diplomatic traffic. You'll have to get the car turned around."

"What appears to be the trouble, officer?" Chernov leaned forward, and Bond noticed that both he and his guard, in the rear, had placed themselves in a vain attempt to hide their passenger's face.

"It's diplomatic trouble, sir. Nothing serious. There

were some complaints last night, so we're having to keep the road well shut down for a while."

"What kind of diplomatic trouble? I carry a diplomatic passport, as do my fellow passengers. We're heading for the Russian Embassy property at Three Sisters Castle."

"Ah, well, that makes a difference, then." The man took a step back. Already, Bond could see the cars ahead of them had been moved slightly, to let the Renault through. He was also aware of men in civilian clothes close to the car. One of them now leaned forward to the rear window that Mischa had been forced to open. Bond did not recognize him, but he had the roving, relaxed eyes of an SB man.

"There were reports of shooting around here last night. You'll understand that people get a bit nervous of that kind of thing. So I'll have to see your credentials, sir, if you'd care to—"

"Certainly." Chernov fumbled in his coat and pulled out a wedge of documents, including his passport. The Irish SB man took them, examining the passport carefully.

"Ah!" He looked hard at Chernov. "We knew you had arrived, Mr. Talanov. It's your Foreign Ministry you're from, is it not?"

"I am Inspector of Embassies, yes. Here on the usual annual visit."

"Now, it wasn't you who came last time, though, was it, Mr. Talanov? If I recall correctly, it was a short man, now didn't he have a beard or something? Yes, a beard and glasses. Name of . . . God love me, I'll forget my own name next, so I will."

"Zuyenko," Chernov supplied. "Yuri Fedeevich Zuyenko."

"That's the fella, now. Zuyenko. He's not coming this year then, Mr. Talanov?"

"He is not coming anywhere." Bond detected a slight edge. Chernov, with his experience, would know by now that the garrulous Special Branch man was playing for time. He obviously was already irritated by it. "Yuri Fedeevich died. Suddenly. Last summer."

"Lord rest his soul, poor man. Suddenly, last summer, eh? Did you ever see that filum, sir? It had the lovely Katharine Hepburn in it, and Miss Taylor—you know she has a cottage hereabouts, did you know that?"

"I really think we should be moving. Especially if there has been trouble up the road—at Three Sisters?"

"Bit of something and nothing, I should think, Mr. Talanov. But, before you go . . ."

"Yes?" Stern, his eyes glittering with more than a hint of anger.

"Well, sir. We do have to check *all* diplomatic credentials."

"Nonsense. I vouch for all in the car. All are under my care."

As Chernov spoke, Bond felt the hard metal of the guard's pistol in his side. He could not yell or make a fuss—though, heaven knew, Chernov would not want a killing incident on his hands out in the open.

Another face replaced the one who had been speaking to Chernov. "I'm very sorry, Mr. Talanov, as you call yourself, but we'll be taking that gentleman there." Norman Murray pointed at Bond. "You're keeping bad company, sir. This man's wanted for questioning, and I think you'll agree he's not a Russian citizen, and certainly no diplomat. Am I right, so?"

"Well . . ." Chernov started.

"I think you'd better let him come quietly. Out of the car, you!" Murray reached in across the guard and took hold of Bond's jacket. "You'll come quietly, won't you, me boyo? Then the other gentlemen can get on their way."

"Quits now, Norman?" Bond did not smile at the Special Branch man. He could see that something had gone seriously wrong—had seen it as soon as Norman Murray led the way to his private car, and nodded for Bond to get in, before taking the wheel, leaving the other Gardi and SB officers to see Chernov's car through to the castle.

"More than quits, Jacko. I'll be for the high jump tomorrow, no doubt about that. There's little I can do for you. I doubt if I could walk the length of my shadow for you, and that's a fact. Though there's some very funny business going on, I'll tell you."

"What's happened?" Bond knew Murray well enough to see the man was engulfed in a strange mixture of anger, frustration and concern.

"It's what didn't happen. First, I was wakened before dawn with a message about your man Basilisk. Your friends across the water wanted him pulled in and delivered to them on the quiet, right, and seeing as how we do favors for one another, a couple of cars were dispatched to The Clonmel Arms where, we were reliably informed, Basilisk was staying with your young woman—the one I met at the hotel in Dublin."

"You didn't say anything when I telephoned you."

"Because you said they had been lifted. I thought it'd be a nice surprise for you to know *we* had lifted him."

"You took the girl as well?"

"Didn't get either of them. They weren't there. I had a call five minutes after you got in touch. The people at the hotel were like the proverbial clams—said friends had picked them up. But later they changed their tune. It appears that Basilisk made a large number of telephone calls during the night. Then he and Heather came down around three-thirty in the morning, paid the bill, and left."

"What about the girl I was with?"

"Neither hide nor hair. There really were complaints about shooting and explosions at Three Sisters, and one of our people spotted you being brought out of the hotel. But it's a great chance I've been taking meddling with the fella you were with."

"None of this is good." Bond felt foolish at his understatement.

Murray laughed. "You've yet to hear the really bad news, Jacko. Your Service refused to make you official."

"Damn!"

"You're on leave. No sanction for you to be in the Republic, operational. That's what I got. On no account are you to give this officer assistance. On *no* account, Jacko. That's what they said."

In the event of anything going wrong we will deny you—even to our own police forces. He heard M's voice, gruff as it was when he first said the words as they walked through the park. "Our own police forces" implied everyone else's forces as well. But why? M had held out on the turning of Basilisk—Smolin—though that had, in some measure, been explained. There had been contact between M and Smolin, using the offices of the Irish Special Branch, probably through Murray, who was the most pliable Irish SB man the Service had on tap. Already Bond had run Smolin and two of the girls to earth. Why in heaven's name would the old man go on denying him?

"Norman, you realize who that was in the car?"

"I know exactly who it was, Jacko."

"Then why didn't you—?"

"Hands off. Those were the instructions from *my* people, and I gather they liaised with your own folk across the water. Take in Basilisk and deliver him to us, but don't touch Blackfriar. That's what was asked of us. Well, Basilisk's disappeared, and—"

"And the girls as well. The girls were my real collateral, Norman."

"I don't want to know."

"You're not going to know. Except that I have to find those girls, and someone else."

"Well, you won't be finding them here, not in the Republic. I'm to get you to a secure place we have at the airport and move you on—with a giant boot up the backside."

"What?"

"You heard, Jacko. We don't want you here. So off you go. Even your Embassy doesn't want you here."

Bond's mind reeled with the queries that gnawed at him. "If we come to a phone, will you stop for a minute, Norman?"

"Why should I?"

"Old times' sake."

"We're square."

"Please," he said with gravity. Smolin and Heather had disappeared off the face of the earth. Ebbie had vanished in minutes from their room and her place taken by Chernov. Nasty question marks, and even nastier answers, were starting to form in his head.

Slowly Murray nodded, and a couple of hundred yards along the road they came to a telephone booth and he pulled over. "Quickly as you can, Jacko. And no stupidity, we've enough trouble and duplicity without you going walkabout."

Bond already had the plastic harmonica bleeper unpeeled from the button before he even got to the box, which—praise heaven—was unvandalized. By now, Blackfriar should be back in the castle, and Bond reckoned the General would immediately have the phones checked. In many ways he was surprised it had not already been done, for Chernov was obviously scrupulously careful in the field.

But, no. The bugs grew their ears again, bringing the usual chaotic commixture of voices into the earpiece. He could make out very little, and was about to replace the instrument when he suddenly heard Chernov's voice, very clear, as though he stood over one of the activated phones—"I want every man we have on the streets of Dublin." His tone was calm, but laced with authority and threat. "The man Bond—and Colonel Smolin—*must* be found, and soon. I want them both. Understand? They took him from under my nose. We've also got the added trouble of those two German whores, the damned *Cream Cake* business. What have I done to deserve such idiots?"

"Comrade General, you had no option. It just couldn't be helped." The conversation was in Russian. "Your orders have been obeyed to the letter. Everyone knows who, when, and why. Once we run everyone to earth it will be simple. But the firefight, last night, has caused almost a diplomatic incident."

"Diplomatic nincompoop!" Chernov all but snarled.

Now there was another voice, close to Chernov. "We've just had a message from one of our Hong Kong people, Comrade General."

"Yes?"

"They've tracked Belzinger and the traitor, Dietrich. She's opened up the house on Cheung Chau Island. The GRU house."

"Has she, by Lenin. I always thought Dietrich was an overconfident bitch. We shall have to move fast. Get a message to Hong Kong. Tell them to watch at a distance. I don't want anyone going in there until I arrive."

The line began to break up, and another thought stole into Bond's mind. Now, above all else, it was essential for him to take the initiative. Delving into his pocket, he pulled out the few Irish coins that Chernov's man had left him. Closing the line he reopened it again, dialing the castle number, letting it ring without activating the harmonicas.

When it was picked up, he spoke quickly in Russian, asking for General Chernov by name, saying it was urgent—"Most urgent! A life-and-death matter."

Chernov was on in a few seconds, quietly cursing and talking about secure lines. "We don't need a secure line, Comrade General," Bond said in English. "You recognize the voice?"

There was a short pause. Then, cold as Siberia, "I recognize."

"Just wanted to say that I look forward to meeting you again, Blackfriar. Catch me if you can. North, South, West, or *East.*" He put the accent on East, goading Chernov. After replacing the instrument, Bond left the box, walking rapidly to the car. Chernov would know Bond was calling him—like a man playing poker. He would also be aware that Bond had an edge, and some knowledge of Chernov's likely movements. M would probably have said the call was an insane move, but M was also playing a devious game.

"For a minute there I thought you were after playing games with me, Jacko. They've been on to me from Dublin. What country do you want?"

"What d'you mean, what country?"

"You're being deported, Jacko. Your own folk in London have said we can send you to the moon as far as they care. Even your old boss—who, as you know, I have dealings with—says you're to take the rest of your leave elsewhere."

"He used those words?"

"Those exact words. 'Tell the renegade to take the rest of his leave elsewhere. Tell him to be missing.' That's what the auld divil said. So where's it to be, Jacko? Spain? Portugal? A couple of weeks on the Canary Islands?"

Bond glanced at him, but Murray showed no sign of any particular knowledge concerning the Canaries—where they had thought Jungle to be before he had stolen the latest news, fresh from the presses at Three Sisters Castle, via the tiny transmitters.

"Let me think for a minute or two, Norman. Wherever I choose, you can get me out really quietly?"

"As the grave. You'll go so still that not even the Dublin airport controllers'll know."

"Give me a minute, then." Already he knew exactly where he wanted to go, but first Bond needed to turn his mind to the whys and wherefores of M's attitude. All controls worked on the basis of need-to-know, so why had M decided—from the outset—that Bond should be told he was on his own? And why, when M must know two of the girls had been found, and then disappeared, was he still denying Bond had any rights in the field? Bond was never supposed to meet Smolin, so he did not need to know about him. Was this a case of Bond *not* needing to know something else?

He tried to be logical, going through the events and then turning back to elementary trade and fieldcraft. When did a control deliberately withhold some piece of vital information from his agent—even when it might put his man at a grave disadvantage? There was only one set of circumstances that allowed this kind of risk, and already there had been a hint of it in the conversation overheard through the harmonicas. You withhold one kind of information only—that a trusted person might well be a double. You withhold that when you do not know which person could be guilty. Bring them all back, M had told him. *All.* Which meant Ebbie, Heather, or Jungle could be doubles. It had to be the only answer—one of the *Cream Cake* team had been turned, and, knowing the ingenious way M's mind worked, Bond had to include Smolin and Dietrich among the suspects.

They reached the outskirts of Dublin, sashaying their way through the heavy traffic. Why deny him? Simple. Deny a field agent only when the Foreign Office and their political masters would be gravely embarrassed; or deny him when his targets *know* he is getting no assistance. Damn M, Bond thought, he's playing it very long indeed—long and dangerous. Any other officer would have called it a day, gone back into London with his spoils, and laid them, like a gun dog, at M's feet. But not Bond. M was putting all his money on Bond seeing it through until the end; risking his man like a gambler, knowing the stakes had risen dramatically once Blackfriar had shown himself.

"Is there a secure telephone at this place you have at the airport, Norm?"

"I told you not to be calling me Norm." Murray sounded annoyed.

"Well, is there?"

"Safe as you can get." He glanced toward Bond, giving a large smile. "We might even let you use it, if you've decided where you want to go."

"Can you get me into France—as near to Paris as possible?"

Murray laughed, loudly. "You're asking for miracles, so. You know what the DST is like, non-bloody-cooperative."

"You live in a country of miracles, Norman. Me, I'd rather be going back across the water to the good life—you know, click of the willow against a villain's head; the roar of the riot, the smell of tear gas; the scent of new-mown grass snakes."

"Lord love you, but you're turning poetical, Jacko. Thank heaven the blessed St. Patrick rid us of snakes."

"Did he?" Bond returned the grin, knowing he was about to have all his requests fulfilled.

The secure quarters were inside the airport itself, in an area well away from any possible prying eyes. A small walled compound hid any cars or their passengers from possible surveillance teams, and, when they reached the approach road, Bond realized there were more than the usual number of Garda patrols around.

On the face of it, Dublin has one of the most open airports in Europe. In fact, it boasts discreet and powerful security, the bulk of which is hidden from public view.

Inside there was a comfortable waiting room—with armchairs and magazines. Bond thought of dentists. There were also a couple of plainclothes men who showed a certain amount of deference to Norman Murray.

"There's a soundproof booth over there. One of the most secure telephones in Ireland." The Special Branch man pointed. "Use it now while I set everything else up."

"Not until I'm certain you can get me into France,

and that I can be in Paris by tonight." Bond looked at him as though calling a bluff.

"It's as good as done, Jacko. You do your telephoning. You'll be on your way with nobody the wiser within the hour."

Bond nodded. Norman Murray was a very convincing officer.

Inside the booth, Bond dialed a London number. The female who answered asked straightaway if they were scrambled, and he said probably, but it was totally secure.

Q'ute had made the offer of help when he last saw her. Bond had known then that it was no idle remark. Q'ute was primed when, just before he left on this unofficial mission, she said, *If you want anything from here—if you* need *anything—just call and I'll bring it to you myself.*

He was calling now, with a longish shopping list and an almost impossible delivery time and place, but Q'ute took it in her stride. When he finished talking she merely said, "It'll be there. Good luck," and closed the line.

Murray was waiting for him, a set of white overalls in his hand. "You put these on"—it was a command—"and you listen carefully."

Bond did not argue, and Murray continued. "The passage through that door leads to the flying club. You're going on a spot of cross-country with an instructor. The flight plan is filed. Permission has been given for you to overfly Northern France—they do it all the time, here. This time, you'll have a small problem. Engine trouble near Rennes, which is your turning point. You won't be able to make an airfield, so your instructor'll put out a Mayday and you'll glide into a field—not any old field, but a particular one. There'll be a car and someone to take your place in the aircraft for when the gendarmes and customs arrive. It's got to go like clockwork. Do as you're told and it should be okay. But, if you're asked, I had no hand in this—you follow?"

Climbing into his white flying suit, Bond nodded. "Thanks, Norm."

"And don't you be calling me Norm. The aircraft's directly in front of the building, with engine running and cleared to taxi. A nice little Cessna 182. Take four at a pinch. Good luck, Jacko."

Bond took the firm hand and shook it, thanking his old Irish colleague and knowing that, somehow, M was still with him, for a reason best known to the old man himself.

The aircraft was drawn up very close to the buildings, and Bond kept his head well down as he walked quickly toward it, ducking under the wing and climbing up beside the instructor—a young, happy-looking Irishman who grinned at him, shouting that it was about time.

He had hardly strapped himself into the pupil's position to the instructor's left before the Cessna was taxiing away, quite quickly, toward the short runway on the far side of the field.

They waited for a few minutes as an Aer Lingus 737 came in from London, then the instructor opened up the engine and the light plane took to the air almost of her own accord.

They turned out to sea, and began to climb. At two thousand feet the instructor leveled out. "There we are," he shouted, "all set for the fun and games. I'll be turning onto course in five minutes." He moved his head. "You okay back there?"

"Fine."

Bond turned to see Ebbie's face peering over the back of his seat, where she had been hiding. "Hello, James. Pleased to see me?" She planted a kiss on his cheek.

14

Dinner in Paris

Every field agent worth his salt has his own special left-behind sources—a bank account in Berlin; weapons cached in Rome; passport blanks in a strongbox in Madrid. With James Bond it was a safe house in Paris—not really a house, but a small apartment owned by good friends who were willing to leave their home at a moment's notice and with no questions asked.

The apartment was on the fourth floor of one of those old buildings off the Boulevard Saint-Michel—the Boul' Mich—on the Rive Gauche.

They arrived just after six in the evening, following a series of events that had gone almost too smoothly for Bond's peace of mind.

The instructor had piloted the Cessna all the way, and Bond noticed that, once over the French coast, he allowed their flying height to become erratic, to a point where the Paris ATC people were constantly calling him up to remind him of the altitude he was allowed to maintain.

The RV itself had been well picked, a lonely spot

west of Rennes over which they circled for fifteen minutes, gradually losing height until their pilot was certain his contact was in place.

He's done this before, Bond thought, wondering when and in what circumstances. Maybe Murray had something on the man—smuggling, or even a tricksy business concerning the lads, as the Provos are always referred to in the Republic.

Whatever the circumstances, it went like clockwork. ATC called up again, anxious about loss of height. The pilot waited for around four minutes as he turned, bleeping his engine, positioning himself for a landing, then began his Mayday call, giving a heading and fix that was around ten miles out, so that the authorities would take longer to reach them.

"When we're down, you've got around five minutes to get going," he shouted at Bond, cutting the engine, then giving it another burst. "A bit of realism for the paying customers," he said, grinning. "Only I hope there aren't any paying customers."

They drifted over some flat farmland with no sign of life for five or six miles, and touched down to taxi toward a clump of trees and a ribbon-straight road lined with poplars.

A battered elderly Volkswagen was parked near the trees, almost out of sight from the road, and a figure, wearing a white coverall identical to the one Bond had been given, detached itself from the trees, arriving at the Cessna just as the engine stopped.

"Go! God be with you." The pilot had already begun to climb out.

Bond helped Ebbie down into the field, stripped off the overalls, and looked at the man who had joined them.

The replacement merely nodded, inclined his head toward the VW, handed over the keys, and said there were maps in the car.

Taking Ebbie by the hand, Bond set off at a trot. The last they saw of the two intrepid flyers was from the car. They had part of the cowling off and were fiddling with the engine. But by this time, the VW was already on the road, heading for Paris.

"Right, young lady." Bond allowed himself time to get used to the car before he spoke. "How, and why, did you turn up again?" It had been impossible to carry on any detailed conversation on the aircraft, and he was now vastly suspicious of Ebbie's dramatic reappearance—even if it did have Norman Murray's blessing.

"That nice policeman thought it would be a good surprise for you, darling James."

"Yes, but what happened to you at The Newpark—in Kilkenny?"

"He didn't tell you?"

"Who?"

"The inspector. Murray."

"Not a word. What happened?"

"At the hotel?"

"Well, I'm not talking about your daring escape from Germany, Ebbie," he replied with a certain crustiness.

"I woke up." As though that explained it all.

"Yes?" he coaxed.

"It was early, very early, and you weren't there, James."

"Go on."

"I was frightened. Got out of bed and went into the passage. Nobody was there, so I went along to the stairs. You were using the telephone. Down in the lobby. I heard your voice, then other things—people coming in at the other end of the passage. I was very embarrassed."

"Embarrassed!"

"I only had—only little . . ." She indicated what she had been wearing. "And nothing up here at all. So, there was a cupboard—is that right? A closet, where they keep cleaning things."

Bond nodded, and she continued. "I hid. It was dark and not nice. But I hid for a long time. I heard other voices and people walking along the passage. When it was silent I came out again. You had disappeared."

He nodded again. It could just be true, and she was convincing enough.

"I dressed." She gave him a small, uncomfortable look. "Then the policemen came and I told them. They used the radio in their car and told me there were orders. Then they brought me to the airport—James, I have no clothes. Only what I stand up in, and my shoulder bag."

"Did Murray—the inspector—tell you what would be happening?"

"It was a risk for me to stay, he said. For me to remain in Ireland. He said I should go with you, but to give you a surprise. He has a sense of humor. Very funny man, the inspector."

"Yes, exceptionally droll. Hilarious."

Now, as they arrived at his safe apartment, which he had telephoned from a service area on the A-11 Autoroute, Bond still had no way of knowing whether to believe her or not. In these circumstances there was only one course of action he could take—stick with her, keeping her in the dark as much as possible, and behave normally.

There was food in the large fridge, two bottles of a good-vintage Krug, and clean linen on the double bed. No notes or messages. That was always the way—the quick telephone call, giving time and possible duration of the stay, and his friends would be gone by the time Bond arrived. He did not ask where they went, nor did they ever question him: the husband was an old Service hand anyway, but the trade had never been mentioned by either side. In eight years the routine rarely changed. Everything was invariably ready, and this time—in spite of the very short notice—was no exception.

"James, what a beautiful little apartment!" Ebbie appeared genuinely enthusiastic. "This is all yours?"

"When I'm in Paris, and when my friend is away." He had not allowed her to be privy to the telephone call. In the main room he went to the desk, opened the top drawer, and removed the false interior, under which he always kept a float of around a thousand francs.

"Look, there is steak." She was exploring the kitchen. "I cook us a meal, yes?"

"Later." He looked at the stainless-steel Rolex. It would take him the best part of half an hour—given a favorable wind—to get to the RV arranged with Ms. Ann Reilly, better known by her nickname, Q'ute. "Thank heaven there are shops that stay open late in Paris. Ebbie, I want you to make a list of the absolutely necessary clothing you need, and your sizes."

"We are going shopping?" She gave a little jump, like a small child looking forward to a sudden treat.

"*I* am going shopping," he said with great firmness.

"Oh. But, James, there are some things you cannot get. Personal items . . ."

"Just make the list, Ebbie. A lady will get the personal things."

"What lady?" She bridled. Ms. Ebbie Heritage was either one hell of a good actress, or a really jealous woman. Bond would have sworn the latter, for her cheeks had gone scarlet and her eyes were brimming. "You are seeing another woman?" A small stamp of the foot.

"We haven't known each other for long, Ebbie."

"That's got nothing to do with it. You have been with me. We are lovers. Yet, as soon as we come to France . . ."

"Whoa. Hold on. Yes, I am going to see another lady. But I'm seeing her for strictly business reasons."

"*Ja*—Yes, I know. The funny-business reasons."

"Nothing like that. Now, calm down, Ebbie. I want you to listen to me." He realized he was talking to her as he would speak to a child. "This is very important. I must go out. I shall take your list with me. You must *on no account* answer the door or the telephone. You keep the door locked until I return. I shall give a special knock, like so." He demonstrated: three quick raps, pause, another three, pause, then two harder raps. "Got it?"

"Yes." Almost sullen.

"Then show me."

She gave a small shrug and repeated the pattern of knocks.

"Right. Now the telephone. Do not touch it unless

it rings three times, goes silent, and then starts ringing again." The codes were as simple as lovers' signals, but they were equally easy to remember.

Bond went through it again, then sat her down at the table with pen and paper while he went round the apartment closing shutters and drawing curtains. By the time he had finished, she held up the completed list.

"How long will you be gone?" she asked in a very small voice.

"With luck, about two hours. Not much longer."

She pulled herself up very straight. "Two hours, and I shall smell this other woman's scent on you if you are making love with her. You be on time, James. Dinner will be here—on this table in two hours exactly. Understand?"

"Yes, ma'am"—he gave her a winning smile—"and don't forget what I told you—the door and the telephone. *You* understand?"

She lifted her face, hands behind her back, raising herself on tiptoe, and turning her cheek toward him.

"Don't I rate a proper kiss?"

"When you come back in time for dinner we'll see."

He nodded, kissed her cheek, and let himself out, walking down the four flights of stone stairs to street level. He always avoided elevators in Paris; in these old apartment blocks, nine times out of ten the lifts were on the blink.

He took a taxi to Les Invalides, then went on foot back to the Quai d'Orsay, crossing the Seine and walking toward the Tuileries Gardens. Only when he was certain he had not picked up a tail did Bond flag down another cab, which he ordered back to the Boul' Mich.

Ann Reilly was sitting in the corner of the small, crowded bistro he had named, only a ten-minute walk from the apartment where Ebbie was, he presumed, cooking dinner.

Bond went straight to the bar, ordered a *fine,* and crossed to Q'ute's table. It did not look as though they were being watched, but he spoke low. "Okay?"

"Everything you ordered. In the briefcase. It's just by your right foot, and it's safe. Nothing will show on the X-ray machines, but I'd unpack and put the whole lot in your suitcase."

Bond nodded. "How are things back at the buildings?"

"Hectic. There's some kind of flap on. M's been closeted in his office for three days now. He's like a general under siege. The powdervine says he's sleeping there and they're taking crates full of microfilm to him. The main computer's been barred to everyone else and the Chief of Staff's been with him all the time. Moneypenny hasn't been out, either. I think she's lying across his door with a shotgun."

"That figures," he muttered. "Look, love, I've a favor to ask." He passed over Ebbie's list. "There's a supermarket one block down, on the corner. Just do your best, eh?"

"I use my own money?"

"Put it on expenses. When I get back I'll fix."

Q'ute looked at the list and smirked. "What's her taste in—?" she began.

"Sophisticated," Bond cut in quickly.

"I'll do my best, being a plain and simple girl myself."

"That'll be the day. I'll set up a drink for you—oh, and get a cheap case, will you."

"Sophisticated *and* cheap?" Ann Reilly left the bistro, hips moving almost suggestively. Bond made a mental note to buy her dinner once this was over and he was back in London.

She took just under half an hour, coming in with a flurry. "I've got a cab waiting outside. I can catch the last Air France back to LHR if I get a shift on. The case is in the cab. Give you a lift?"

Bond was on his feet, following her to the door and telling her to drop him off a couple of blocks away. She kissed him full on the mouth, whispering good luck when he left, carrying the suitcase and briefcase.

He took forty minutes of back-doubling, riding the Métro, walking, and using another cab, before he got back to the apartment, within ten minutes of Ebbie's childish little deadline, and a lot of Q'ute's lipstick on his handkerchief.

Ebbie sniffed him suspiciously, but could only smell the brandy and so softened slightly—particularly when he gave her the suitcase and told her to open it. Once more there was a chirping of ooh's and ah's as she examined Q'ute's purchases, giving Bond time to check his own clothes—always kept in a particular part of the bedroom wardrobe. A case was no problem, there was always a spare in the flat. He could pack, and repack the items from the briefcase later, at leisure.

"The dinner will be ready in five minutes," Ebbie sang from the kitchen.

"One phone call and I'll be with you." He used the extension in the bedroom, dialing the Cathay

Pacific desk at Orly. Yes, they had two first-class seats on their flight to Hong Kong tomorrow. Certainly they would reserve them in the name of Boldman—he gave them his Amex number. "Thank you, Mr. Boldman, that'll be fine. Just pick the tickets up at the desk by ten-fifteen. Have a nice flight."

He peeped inside the briefcase, checking that Q'ute had not forgotten the small rubber stamp with which he could doctor their passports. A sudden horror struck him. "Ebbie!" he called. "Ebbie, you have got a passport with you, yes?"

"Of course. I never travel without it."

He went into the main living room. The table was set for an intimate dinner for two—candles, the lot. "You've been a busy girl, Ebbie."

"Yes, are we going somewhere?"

"Not until the morning. Tonight it's a romantic dinner in Paris."

"Good, but in the morning where are we going?"

"Tomorrow," he said quietly, "we're off to the mystic East."

15

The Mystic East

The Cathay Pacific 747—Flight CX 290, ex Paris/Orly—located the primary ILS, bringing it onto a heading descending over Lantao Island toward the mainland of the New Territories. There the great jet began its almost one-hundred-degree turn to the final-approach ILS taking it right across Kowloon and so down onto Kai Tak, Hong Kong's International Airport, with its long finger of runway thrusting out into the sea.

As the engines whined, giving the machine the last ounce of extra thrust to carry it over the rooftops, James Bond peered out of the window, craning to see the Island of Hong Kong below, with the Peak shrouded in cloud.

They would be low over Kowloon Tong now, and he thought of its translation—Pool of Nine Dragons—and the story that the late Bruce Lee had consulted a fortune teller before buying an apartment in this exclusive district. The young Kung Fu film star had been told that, should he buy the flat, he would have only bad joss, because his name meant little dragon, and nothing good could come of a little dragon going to live in a pool with nine dragons. Nevertheless, Bruce Lee bought the apartment, and within the year he was dead. Bad joss.

The Boeing touched down, the reverse thrust coming on with a huge roar, flaps fully extended as the speed bled off, and it slowly rolled to a halt at the far end of the runway—buildings towering to the left, and boat-littered water stretching out to the right between the mainland and Hong Kong Island—Fragrant Harbor.

They had arrived in the mystic East, though there was little mystic about it these days.

Within twenty minutes of landing, Bond found himself standing, with Ebbie clutching at his hand, in the somewhat garagelike surroundings of Passport Control, where serious, and scrupulous, Chinese officers scrutinized documents.

From the moment they had left the aircraft, he had done his best to try to spot likely watchers in the airport buildings, but in the sea of faces—European, Chinese, and Eurasian—*everybody* was a potential lookout.

A large Chinese in slacks and a white shirt held a board that announced that he waited for MR. BOLDMAN. Taking Ebbie's arm, Bond steered her forward.

"I'm Mr. Boldman."

"Ah, good. I take you Mandarin Hotel." The Chinese grinned widely, showing what appeared to be several sets of independently working teeth, most of them filled with gold. "Car here. Inside please, never mind." The driver ushered them toward a limousine, opening the door. "My name is David," he supplied.

"Thank you, David," Ebbie said prettily, and they climbed in.

Bond glanced out of the rear as they moved away, to see if he could spot any other car positioning itself behind them. The search was fruitless, for cars left the airport arrivals rank all the time, and most seemed to have just picked up passengers. What he was looking for was some nondescript vehicle with two people up front . . . He caught himself in time—that was what he would have looked for in Europe; in Asia things were different. He recalled an old China hand once saying, "As for watchers, they're most likely to be the people you least expect. East of Suez they watch in plain sight, and they're a bugger to spot."

There were no positive signs as they entered the cross-harbor tunnel, which was jammed with the usual traffic—a whole dictionary, in fact, of transport: cars, trucks, both ancient and modern, and those open 15 cwt. trucks that seem beloved of the Hongkongese, some with tattered awnings, flapping and displaying Chinese characters.

Nowadays you only have to return to Hong Kong after an absence of a few weeks to notice changes. It was a couple of years since Bond had been in the Territory—few refer to it as the Crown Colony since the agreement with China for its return in 1997—so he saw huge differences as they came into Connaught Road, in that part of the island known as Central. Whatever the changes, flying into Asia always causes a subtle culture shock, which often does not make itself felt quickly, but comes as a gradual revelation.

Ahead, to their right, the massive Connaught Centre rose with its hundreds of portholelike windows, making it look as though it had been designed by an optician; and behind that the almost completed glass triple towers of Exchange Square. The traffic was still as heavy as the heat outside, while the sidewalks and futuristic linking bridges over the main roads were crammed with scurrying people. On the left he caught a glimpse—through Chater Square, with its very English War Memorial—of the new huge and unusual Hongkong and Shanghai Bank Building, erected like a large Lego kit on four great, tall cylinders.

Then they were pulling up in front of the main doors of The Mandarin, which, next to the high-rise opulence, appeared quite insignificant. But this feeling vanished, as it always did, when they stepped through the glass doors into the main lobby and a world of crystal chandeliers—one seeming to literally drip from the high ceiling—Italian marble, onyx, and the luster of the past reflected in one wall encrusted with highly detailed golden wood carvings.

Ebbie's eyes, which had been alive and full of wonder all the way from the airport, widened like a child's. "This is really fantastic, James," she began, then took in a sharp breath.

Bond, who had been steering her toward the black-suited Chinese gentlemen at Reception, saw her eyes narrow as she peered across the marbled floor at the concierge's desk.

"What is it?" he asked quietly.

"Swift," she breathed. "Swift's here. I just saw him."

"Where?" They had almost reached the main reception desk.

"Over there." She nodded toward the far end of the lobby. "He was there. Typical of him. He was always a—how do you say it? will-o'-the-wisp?"

Bond nodded—a good name for Swift, he thought, starting to complete the hotel's check-in form. Swift had always been a will-o'-the-wisp; a tortured soul trapped between heaven and hell who led people to destruction with his little lights of burning coal. Swift's expertise in the handling of agents in the field had led many members of opposition intelligence services to destruction.

In a fraction of time all the contradictions and hidden secrets of *Cream Cake* rushed through Bond's mind yet again. M had asked him to take on a job that, because of its delicacy, could not be an official operation. Yet there were things official about it. Already, the conclusion that he was there because someone within the *Cream Cake* setup had been turned had hardened in his mind. But for the two luckless girls who were now dead it could be anyone, and M, like Bond, had no idea of the traitor—Heather? the already doubled Maxim Smolin? Jungle Baisley, whom Bond had yet to meet? Baisley's target, Susanne Dietrich? Even Ebbie. Damn, he now thought, signing the check-in card, why had he been foolish enough to allow Ebbie to come with him to Hong Kong? By all the rules she should have been popped into some form of safety, yet he—James Bond—had not thought twice about her coming with him. Intuition, or merely his growing affection for Ebbie? How stupid could a man be, when led by emotions? But then, he had not been led by anything. Ebbie had, in a manner of speaking, been foisted on him. And now there was Swift. Could Swift be the key? Hardly.

"If you will follow me, Mr. Boldman, Mrs. Boldman."

Bond realized that the under manager at Reception was repeating his courteous words.

"Sorry. Of course." He snapped out of the confusion of thoughts, and, taking Ebbie's arm, followed the man, who was armed with papers and a key.

They went toward the far end of the lobby past the concierge's desk, turning left to the banks of elevators. "Tell me if you spot him again," Bond whispered, and Ebbie nodded.

Around them the hotel was functioning with a disciplined ease and efficiency—gold-jacketed page boys moved swiftly, with fixed smiles; one of them, wearing a form of skullcap that set him apart from the rest, marched through the lobby bearing a bell-hung tinkling board displaying the fact that he was looking for a Mrs. David Davies. An American couple argued softly near the elevators—"Whaddya want, then? We're in a hotel—you want we should move to a different hotel?"

The elevator lifted Bond and Ebbie imperceptibly to the twenty-first floor, to a light and airy room, the balcony of which looked out upon the thousand eyes of the Connaught Centre building and a very large slice of the harbor over which ferries, motorized junks, and sampans plied their way.

The under manager hovered, making certain the

room was to their liking, until the room boy arrived with the luggage, asking if he could unpack for them—an offer they both declined.

"You're sure it was Swift?" Bond stood close to Ebbie once they were alone.

"Certain. God, I'm tired, but it *was* Swift." She opened the balcony windows, letting in the sound of Hong Kong's traffic, deafeningly loud even from the twenty-first floor.

Bond joined her on the balcony, feeling the blast of heat as he passed through the doorway. Below, the traffic streamed unendingly; the water of the harbor twinkled in the morning haze; the white wakes of churning propellers, now joined by the long, creamy trail of a hydrofoil sweeping west, and the muddy bow waves of three towed barges, low in the water, weighed down by piles of containers—chugging toward one of the world's largest container ports.

To the left, across the road, everything was dwarfed by the high-rise Connaught Centre and the even larger Exchange Square building—the complex connected to The Mandarin side of the street by an elegant tubular pedestrian overpass. In the foreground, and to the right, the most fabled view in the world—Kowloon, Hong Kong, and the water between—the Fragrant Harbor—dazzled the eye. A pair of helicopters swept down, low, inland—one hovering while the other chopped in to land at Fenwick Pier, below Bond and Ebbie and to their right. The entire scene—buildings, ships, vehicles, helicopters—had a futuristic look about it, almost like a huge set for a twenty-first-century movie. As he gazed, Bond suddenly realized that the elusive familiarity he always felt in Hong Kong came from images of the distant past, when he saw Fritz Lang's *Metropolis*—that classic film made, incredibly, in the 1920s.

"Come on"—he touched Ebbie's arm—"we've got work to do." The air smelled moist, with traces of salt, spices, dust, fish, pork, and money.

"We have to go out?"—excited at the prospect.

"Just wear something casual." Bond smiled, but she did not understand he was joking, and rushed to her suitcase. "Jeans and a T-shirt'll be great," he quickly added, standing by the bedside telephone, delving into that memory bank of telephone numbers that he carried constantly in his head. Even in Asia he had contacts outside the normal Service channels, and this one was important.

Picking up the handset, he quickly punched in the numbers. The call was picked up on the fourth ring.

"Weyyy?"

"Mr. Chang?" he asked.

"Who wants him, *heya?*" The voice was deep, almost gruff.

"An old friend. A friend called Predator."

"Ayeeya! Welcome back, old friend. What can I do for you, *heya?*"

"I wish to see you."

"Come, then. I am in my usual place. You come now, *heya?*"

"Fifteen minutes, never mind." Bond smiled. "I shall have very pretty lady with me."

"So, times never change. My people have saying, *When man visits a friend once with woman, he seldom returns alone.*"

"Very profound." Bond smiled again. "Is that an old saying?"

"About thirty second. I just make it up. Come quickly, *heya?*"

In another part of Hong Kong's Central District, Big Thumb Chang put down the telephone and looked up at the man standing beside him.

"He comes now, just as you predict; he also brings a beautiful woman, though if she is European I fail to see how she can be beautiful. You want I should do something special with him?"

"Just do as he asks," the other said. He had a slow, calculating voice. "I shall be near. It is essential that I speak with him in private."

Big Thumb Chang grinned, nodding like a toy with a spring in its neck.

16

Swift

Big Thumb Chang was so called because of a deformity to his right hand. The thumb was almost as long, and twice as thick, as his index finger. Enemies said it had grown like this from counting the large sums of paper money that came his way from many, and varied, business deals.

He could usually be found—when there was money involved—at a small ground-floor hovel, consisting of two rooms off one of the many dauntingly steep streets that step upward at a thigh-aching angle from Queen's Road.

Bond took Ebbie by the scenic route. They rode the elevator down to the mezzanine floor, walking through the sumptuous hotel's shopping arcade, over the pedestrian bridge, from which they viewed the gaudily decorated trams cramming Des Voeux Road, and on into the opulent Prince's Building and through another walkway into Gloucester House and The Landmark—one of Central's most splendid shopping malls.

Ebbie—who had already been gasping with

amazement at the glittering shops and the near Swiss-like cleanliness of the buildings—gave a hoot of joy as they entered The Landmark on its fourth tier. Indeed, the hundreds of shops and restaurants around the square, the escalator-linked terraces, combined with fountains, decorative plants, and airy space made London's Bond Street look downmarket, and the famed Los Angeles malls seem ordinary by comparison.

Below them, by the big circular fountain, a jazz combo was playing "Do You Know What It Means to Miss New Orleans?"

They went down to the ground floor, pausing only for Bond to make a quick purchase—a holdall with a long shoulder strap—before taking the exit to Pedder Street, and so into the noisy, crowded sidewalks of Queen's Road.

It took all of fifteen minutes to reach Big Thumb Chang's door, which was open; Chang himself was seated behind a table within the small dark room, which smelled of sweat and old cooking odors, relieved only marginally by the joss sticks burning before a small shrine to a household god in the far corner.

"Ah, old friend." The fat little Chinese gave a grin that displayed discolored teeth. "Many years since your shadow crossed my miserable door. Please enter my slum of a home."

Bond saw Ebbie wrinkle her nose with disgust.

"You forget, most honorable Chang, that I know your real home is as rich as any Emperor's palace." Bond's eyebrows lifted. "So it is I who am humbled by coming to your office."

Chang waved a hand toward two hard and not

very clean chairs. "Welcome, beautiful lady"—he grinned at Ebbie—"welcome to both of you. Sit. Can I offer you tea?"

"You are most kind. We do not deserve such lordly treatment." Bond observed the complex rules of negotiation as Chang clapped his hands and a thin, young girl in black pajamas materialized from the street behind them. Chang jabbered instructions to her, and she bowed and left.

"My second daughter by third wife," Chang explained. "She is a lazy, good-for-nothing girl, but out of my duty and good nature I allow her to do small jobs for me. Life is difficult. Never mind."

"We have come to do business," Bond began.

"Everyone wishes to do business." Chang gave him a weary look. "But seldom is this profitable, with so many to support, and gossiping wives and children always wanting more than I can give."

"Well, we need your help." Bond looked equally grave. "It must indeed be hard to live as you do, honorable Chang."

Big Thumb Chang gave a protracted sigh, and the girl reappeared with a tray bearing bowls and a teapot, placing it in front of Chang, receiving his directions to pour the tea, which she did, making heavy weather of it, as though she also was bowed down with care and fatigue.

"Your kindness surpasses our miserable needs." Bond smiled—tapping twice on the table with his fingers to signify thanks to the girl—before sipping the bitter tea: hoping that Ebbie would drink it without comment or any facial expression of dislike.

"It is good to see you again, Mr. Bond. How can I be of service to you and this wondrous lady?"

Bond was surprised that Chang had come to the point so quickly. It was not unusual to spend an hour or more in pleasantries before getting down to business. The fast response put him on his guard.

"It is probably impossible," he said slowly. "But you have done such favors for me in the past."

"So?"

"I am in need of two revolvers and ammunition."

"*Ayeeyah!* You wish to see me imprisoned? Taken away in chains and kept for the bureaucrats of Beijing who will come in 1997 anyway, never mind?" Already, in Hong Kong they were using the true Chinese name for Peking—Beijing—as the year approached for power to be transferred back to the People's Republic. It was ironic that the street hawkers were now selling green caps, emblazoned with the red star, among their usual tourist junk.

"Respectfully," Bond lowered his voice, still playing the game expected of him, "this has never bothered you in the past. Big Thumb Chang's name is well known in my profession. It is held in great reverence, for it is a password to obtaining certain items forbidden in the Territory."

"Certainly it is forbidden to import arms, and in recent years the penalties for such things have been great."

"But you can still put your hands on them?"

"*Ayeeyah!* With the greatest of difficulty. One revolver and a few miserable rounds of ammunition I might *just* be able to find—and that at great cost—but two! Ah, that would be miraculous, and the cost truly exorbitant."

"Let's pretend you *could* lay your hands on two

good revolvers—say a pair of very old Enfield .38s—with ammunition, of course . . ."

"This is impossible."

"Yes, but if you could get them. . . ." He paused, watching the Chinese shake his head in what appeared to be not only a negative reaction, but also the sign of one who wonders about the sanity of the person with whom he is dealing. "If you *could* get them, how much would it cost?"

"A veritable fortune. An Emperor's ransom."

"How much?" Bond pressed. "How much in cash?"

"One thousand Hongkong for each weapon—the size not counting—and another two thousand Hongkong for fifty ammunition, making four thousand Hongkong dolla."

"Two thousand, for the lot." Bond smiled.

"*Ayeeyah!* You wish my wives and children to go naked in the streets? You wish my rice bowl empty for all time?"

"Two thousand," Bond repeated. "Two thousand and the weapons returned to you before I leave, with an extra thousand HK on top."

"How long you here, never mind?"

"A few days only. Two, three at the most."

"You will see me beggared. I shall have to send my best daughters onto the streets as common whores."

"Two of them were already making good money on the streets the last time I was here."

"Two thousand dolla, with two thousand when guns are returned."

"Two thousand, and one more on return," Bond said firmly. There were two reasons he asked for revolvers. First, parted from his ASP 9mm, he would not trust an automatic pistol begged, borrowed, hired, or stolen, even from Big Thumb Chang. Second, he knew that Chang could supply only basic weapons.

"Two, with *two* thousand when you return."

"Two and one. That's my last and only offer."

Big Thumb Chang threw up his hands. "You will see me begging in Wan Chai, like No Nose Wu or Footless Lee." He paused, eyes pleading for a higher bid. None was forthcoming. "Two thousand, then. And one when you return the weapons, but you will have to leave five hundred HK as deposit in case you do not come back."

"I've always come back."

"There is the first time. Man always comes back until the first time. What else will you steal from me, Mr. Bond? You wish to sleep with my most beautiful daughter?"

"Take heed." Bond gave him a withering look. "I have a lady with me."

"A thousand pardons." Chang realized that he had gone too far. "When you wish to collect the items?"

"How about now? You used to keep an arsenal under the floor in your back room."

"And many dolla it cost me to keep away the police."

"I don't think so, Chang. You forget that I know exactly how you work."

Big Thumb Chang gave a sigh. "One moment. Excuse, please." He rose and waddled through the bead curtain that separated the rooms.

Ebbie started to speak, but Bond shook his head,

mouthing, "Later." It was dangerous enough to have her there at all, now he had made up his mind that *anyone* from the old *Cream Cake* team was suspect.

They heard the Chinese rooting about in the other room, then, quite unexpectedly, the bead curtain parted and, instead of Chang, another man appeared—a European, dressed in slacks and a white shirt; a tall, slim man in his late fifties, but with iron-gray hair and eyes to match. The eyes twinkled brightly as Ebbie breathed, "Swift!"

"Good day to you both." The voice was English, flat and unaccented.

Bond moved quickly, standing and placing himself between Ebbie and the newcomer, who held up his hand. "I come in peace, bearing messages," Swift said softly. "Our mutual Chief told me I would probably make contact with you here. If that happened, I was to say, *Nine people were killed in Cambridge and an oil fire started at Canvey Island.* That mean anything to you?" He paused, the gray eyes holding Bond's face, unblinking.

Unless they had old M tied up in some safe house, and pumped to the eyebrows with sodium pentothal, Swift was truly Swift—a noted member of Service, who had indeed received orders directly from M. By mutual arrangement, Bond always carried in his head some meaningless identification code from his Chief. Anyone repeating the code to him would be genuine, as it was always concocted in ultrasafe conditions. The one running at the moment—unchanged for six months—had been given to Bond in M's office, without a word passing between the two of them.

"Then I am to reply that the sentence comes from

Volume VI of Gilbert's excellent biography of Winston Churchill." Bond put out his hand. "Page 573. Okay?"

Swift nodded. He had a firm grip. "We must speak alone." He clicked his fingers, and the girl—Chang's second daughter by his third wife—appeared behind him.

"Ebbie." Bond smiled at her convincingly. "Ebbie, I wonder if you would go with this girl. Just for a few minutes, while we have some man's talk."

"Why should I?" she bridled.

"Why should you not, Ebbie?" Swift's eyes commanded her. She held out for around fifteen seconds, and then meekly followed the girl. Swift glanced back through the curtain. "Good, they have all gone out. We have ten minutes or so. I am here as M's personal messenger boy."

"Demoted?" Bond asked lightly.

"No, only because I know all the participants. First, M apologizes for having put you in such an intolerable position."

"Good of him. I *am* getting a little tired of playing the odd man out. I didn't even know about Smolin."

"Yes, so he told me. M has asked me to find out how much you *do* know first, and then how much you have put together."

"First, I trust nobody—not even you, Swift—but I'll talk because it's unlikely you could get that personal code phrase from anyone but M. What I now know, or at least suspect, is that there was something terribly wrong about *Cream Cake*. So wrong that it had to be taken care of when two of its former agents were murdered. I can only presume that the truth lies in one or more of those left living. One, or more, have been turned."

Swift nodded again. "Almost correct. One or more was always a double. That became all too apparent after Smolin was left in place; and, yes, the Head of Service has no idea which one. But there's a good deal more to it than that."

"Go on."

"M is being leaned on very heavily. So heavily, in fact, that certain people in the Foreign Office are calling for his resignation. A lot of things have gone wrong for him, and when the *Cream Cake* business resurfaced he saw yet another debacle heading toward him like an avalanche. He put a plan up to the Foreign Service mandarins and they turned it down flat—too dangerous, and nonproductive. So he had to go it alone. He chose you, underbriefed you, even withheld a large wedge of intelligence from you, because he believed that you—his most experienced operator—would eventually put two and two together."

That sounded like M at bay. No wonder the old boy was so firm about the operation not having his blessing. He remembered Q'ute's description of the situation, in Paris—*M's been closeted in his office for three days now. He's like a general under siege.*

As though reading his mind, Swift continued, "M is still under siege. In fact, I'm surprised that he even talked to me—which he did under tremendous security precautions. But he won't last another scandal. He stands no chance of weathering the storm if another double is found within his house, or even near to it. You follow?"

"Does, say, Chernov—Blackfriar—know this?"

"Quite possibly. What you haven't figured out yet, I am supposed to tell you. He's pleased with what you've done so far—M, I mean. But now you have a need to know two things." He paused, as though on the brink of disclosing the most secret thing ever known to him. "First, the double within *Cream Cake* has to be eliminated—with no comebacks. Understand?"

Bond nodded. This was not an order M could have given to him directly. Under the relatively new Foreign Office and Government instructions, assassination was never to be used. It had been the end of the old Double-Oh Section, though M maintained that he always thought of Bond as 007. Now he was being told to kill for the Service—and, in particular, to save M's neck. "That means I've first got to finger the double." He felt quite calm about it, for Swift's disclosure had given him a new impetus. M was a shrewd and tough old devil. He was also quite ruthless. His head was on the block, and Bond had been chosen as the one to save his neck. M knew that, of all his people, James Bond would fight shoulder to shoulder with him right up to the end.

"Right"—Swift gave a fast nod—"and I can't help you there, as I haven't a clue, either."

It could be any one of them, or all of them, Bond thought once more—Smolin, Heather, Ebbie, Baisley or Dietrich, both of whom he had yet to meet. "Good Lord!" he said aloud.

"What?" Swift took a step toward him.

"Nothing." Bond closed up like a clam, for he suddenly realized there was yet another contestant.

It could be one of them, or all of them, or . . . He did not even allow himself to think of the ramifications of the idea that had just sprung into his head.

"You sure it was nothing?" Swift pressed.

"Certain."

"Good, because there's something else—someone else. To add weight to his position as Head of SIS, M requires a coup. The *Cream Cake* investigation provided the man and the means. He wants Blackfriar, and he wants him alive."

"We could've taken him in Ireland."

"And risked one devil of an incident on foreign soil? True, the Irish Special Branch, in the Republic, are most cooperative, but I don't think even they would have been *that* cooperative. No, we have to take him here, on what is still British territory. Here we have rights. That's another reason M sent *you* into the field, James. As soon as he discovered Blackfriar had been tempted to leave Soviet territory to follow up on *Cream Cake,* he baited the trap with you."

"Because I'm on his department's hit list?"

"Exactly."

That also made sense. M was never squeamish in putting men like Bond into dangerous situations.

"And to help things on their way, I was told to instruct Jungle to head East. Chernov's a determined devil, and he's fallen for it."

"You mean *I* fell for it." Bond looked at him coldly.

"I suppose that also. If you hadn't got out, James, I would probably be dealing with this alone, because General Chernov's already here."

"On Cheung Chau Island?"

Swift gave him a quick, surprised look. "You're very well briefed. I thought that would be my little surprise."

"When did he get in?"

"Last night. But there have been a number of arrivals in the past twenty-four hours. Some came in via China—in all, Blackfriar's got quite an army here. He has also taken prisoners. Even brought some—Smolin and Heather. By now I should imagine he has Jungle and his German girl under lock and key out on the island. It's up to us, James. We're very much on our own, so I suggest we meet at around ten-thirty tonight—in the lobby of The Mandarin? Okay?"

"If you say so."

"I'll organize a way to get us out to Cheung Chau—they call it Long Island, or Dumbbell Island, here—it's roughly shaped like a dumbbell. The house is on the eastern side of the island, perched on a promontory at the northern end of Tung Wan Bay. It's very well situated and custom-built for the GRU, so Chernov's probably laughing his head off now he's there—at least, I presume he's there."

"Ten-thirty, then." Bond glanced at his watch. "I have one or two surprises for Blackfriar."

"You're also willing to give your life for M, aren't you?" Swift was not smiling.

"Yes, and damn him, he knows it."

"Thought so." Swift gave a bleak smile, turned his head, and called loudly through the bead curtain. At the back of the building, a door opened.

Ebbie was the first to return. "And how's life been treating you, Emilie—I'm sorry, I should say Ebbie?" Swift greeted her.

"Like always. Danger. I feel that the Soviets have a revenge with me. Is that right, a revenge?"

"A vengeance," said Bond, and at that moment Big Thumb Chang came back into the room carrying several items wrapped in oilskin, which Bond immediately began to transfer to the holdall.

"You not examine the weapons, never mind?" Chang looked momentarily shocked.

Bond tossed several packets of notes onto the table—money had been only a small part of his shopping list to Q'ute. He gave the Chinese a twisted, cruel smile. "Between trusted friends it is not necessary to count the money—*very* old Chinese proverb, as you well know, Big Thumb Chang. Now, please leave us in peace."

The Chinese cackled, scooping up the notes and backing into the inner room.

"When we leave, I suggest you and Ebbie go first." Swift's voice had been very soft throughout his conversation with Bond. Now it became almost soporifically calm. The voice was recognizable from his file (*Always calm and usually speaks quietly*, it read), for Bond had seen this agent's profile and followed his fingerprints over many an East German operation.

Bond moved to the beaded curtain, glancing into the inner room to make sure that Chang had retreated through the rear exit. Satisfied, he spoke rapidly. "Ten-thirty, then?"

"Count on it." With an almost imperious nod of the head, Swift sent them on their way, back down the steep steps flanked by the stalls of street traders and dim-sum sellers.

"Swift," said Ebbie, pronouncing it Svift and almost running to keep up with Bond.

"Yes?"

"That is where Heather and I got the idea for names, for using fishes and birds."

"From Swift?" Bond turned his head away from a dim-sum stall. The food was probably wonderful, but to his sensitive nostrils it smelled too pungent.

"*Ja.* Yes, Swift is a bird and Heather said we should use code names like animals and birds. In the end, birds and fishes."

Bond grunted, quickening his pace so that Ebbie clung to his arm, struggling to keep up with his fast, long, and purposeful strides. They took no short-cuts, going straight back along Pedder Street, dodging the traffic into Icehouse Street, and so to The Mandarin. During the whole walk, Bond's eyes roved the crush of Chinese in the streets, feeling a million watchers around them, a thousand imperceptible signals passing between them.

Back in the hotel, Bond went straight to the elevators, almost dragging Ebbie with him.

"Wait by the door," he ordered when they reached their room. It took less than four minutes for him to transfer the main items provided by Q'ute from his suitcase to the canvas holdall. Then they were off back to the elevators and the hotel foyer. He strode to the main desk, Ebbie panting in his wake. A pretty Chinese girl who looked all of fifteen years old glanced up from a computer keyboard and asked if she could help him.

"I hope so, is there a ferry to Cheung Chau?" Bond asked of the girl.

"Each hour, sir. Yaumati Ferry Company. From Outlying Districts Services Pier." She gestured with her hands.

Bond nodded and thanked her. "We must go. Go now." Turning to Ebbie.

"Why? We are to meet Swift. You arranged . . . ?"

"I'm sorry, yes, I did arrange. Just come. You should know that I've ceased to trust anybody, Ebbie. Even Swift—and even you." He became vaguely aware of police sirens close at hand, and, as they reached the main doors of the hotel, a knot of people was already gathering across the road in the decorative square that surrounded the Connaught Centre.

Dodging traffic at great risk, they dashed toward the crowd just as two police cars and an ambulance drew up.

Pushing through the throng, Bond managed to get sight of the trouble. A man lay spread-eagled on his back, blood seeping onto the paving stones. There was a terrible stillness about him and the gray eyes looked steady and sightless into the sky above.

The cause of Swift's death was not immediately apparent, but the killers could not be far away.

Backing from the crowd, Bond caught Ebbie by the forearm, propelling her away and to the left, in the direction of the Outlying Districts Pier.

17

Letter from the Dead

The sampan smelled strongly of dried fish and human sweat. Lying close together for'ard, looking back toward the toothless old lady who sprawled across the tiller, and the twinkling stars that were the lights of Hong Kong behind her, Bond and Ebbie could feel the fatigue and tension emanating from each other.

The afternoon, with its sudden violent changes, seemed far away, as did the sight of Swift's body in front of the Connaught Centre building.

After the shock of seeing the man lying dead, Bond's thoughts had been unusually imprecise and jumbled. He was certain of only one thing—that unless Chernov had shown monstrous cunning, Swift had been straight. There were moments during the conversation at Big Thumb Chang's when he had doubted. But there were other people he also doubted. All things were possible. Now he was on his own, and the one chance of fingering the *Cream Cake* double, and getting Chernov alive, lay in putting himself on offer—a living lure.

His first instinct was to give chase, to head for the island by the quickest possible means. He was in fact halfway toward the Ferry Terminal when he realized that this was just what Chernov might want.

He slowed his walk, keeping the holdall close to his left side, and Ebbie fast by the arm to his right. She had not seen the body and thus kept asking what was wrong, and where were they going. Angrily, Bond continued to drag her along until the moment when his fragmented thoughts came together, and a certain peace reigned within his mind.

"Swift," he said, surprised at the calmness of his own voice. "It was Swift. He looked very dead."

Ebbie gave a little gasp and asked, in a small voice, if he was sure. He told her what he had seen, not being kind, in a way wanting the picture he drew to be shocking.

Her reaction had been unexpectedly good. After a lengthy silence, as they almost strolled along the waterfront—picturesque, with little arbors and a pyramid fountain below them—she merely muttered, "Poor Swift. He was so good to us—all of us." Then, as though the full implication had struck her, "And poor James. You needed his help, didn't you?"

"We all needed his help."

"Will they come for us also?"

"They'll come for me, Ebbie, but I don't know about you. Depends which side you're working for."

"You know which side I'm on. Were they not trying to kill me at the hotel, The Ashford Castle

Hotel, when I was lending my coat and scarf to the other girl?"

She had a point. Even Chernov would not be so stupid as to kill an innocent bystander in the Irish Republic. Bond had to put trust in at least one other human being. Ebbie was apparently straight—had been from the outset. So, with some reluctance, he would have to accept her.

"All right. I believe you, Ebbie." He swallowed, and then went on to tell her the briefest details—of how Chernov was certainly on the island, with others; that he was holding Heather and Maxim Smolin prisoner, and almost surely Jungle and the Dietrich woman as well. "We're probably under some form of surveillance now. They might even expect us to go charging over to Cheung Chau straightaway. I'll say this for the KGB, they've got quite classy lately when it comes to psychological pressure." He went on to explain that *they* were being put under stress at their weakest physical and mental moment. "We're both tired, disoriented, jet-lagged. They'll expect us to make moves automatically. We need time—time to rest, organize, and work out some more logical way."

But where to go? What to do? In this place, even though the crowds were constant, you could not get lost, for you could never be quite certain who was watching. He had no safe house at his disposal. Only his own experience, the weapons, and other items in the holdall; and Ebbie Heritage, whose form in the field he did not know.

The only possible chance would be to go through the complex business of throwing a tail—even though he could not spot one. After that, well, it would be a matter of luck—another hotel, possibly. At least they could try it.

He pulled Ebbie closer to him, leaning on the wall and looking out over the harbor. Three low barges were being towed across the center of the bay; the usual junks and sampans plowed and turned; one of the high double-decked car ferries was nosing out to their left, while two of the Star Ferry boats, which ran every ten minutes between Hong Kong and Kowloon, hooted as they passed one another in the center of the harbor.

Asking Ebbie to stand still for a moment and keep quiet, Bond went through the various means of running the back-doubles in Hong Kong. The Mandarin was out as a resting place, for they were certain to have watchers back there. Kowloonside seemed the best idea.

Very carefully, he explained to Ebbie what they must do. Then he went over it a second time, for luck. Smiling down at her, he asked if she was up to it.

She nodded. "Oh yes, we'll show the devils. I have scores to settle with them, James. At least two—three, if you count the poor Irish girl to whom I loaned my scarf and coat." She gave a little smile back. "We will win, won't we?"

"No contest." He tried to make it sound casual, though his mind told him that to win, here in Asia, against the kind of people Kolya Chernov had at his disposal—and with at least one of the *Cream Cake* team as his ally—would take very good joss indeed.

Together they started to walk back along the harbor front, dodging up the open stairs near the central post office to get onto the covered overpass that brought them out on The Mandarin Hotel's side of Connaught Road. The offices were closing, and the crowds had thickened, yet—even among so many people—there was a strange orderliness.

"Keep your eyes open. Watch shoes more than faces," Bond advised her, though now that they were actually doing it he realized how many people wore trainers. A Chinese team would almost certainly be wearing them.

At the hotel they turned right, into Icehouse Street again, but this time they were heading for the smart, red-brick, ivy-covered entrance to the Mass Transit Railway station, less than a hundred yards behind the hotel—to the right, in Chater Road, behind Swire House. It was the Hongkongside, end-of-the-line station, known as Central.

The MTR is, rightly, Hong Kong's pride and joy, and the envy of many cities, for in efficiency and cleanliness there are few underground railways in the world that compare with it. Certainly Moscow has its huge baroque stations; Paris its fabled Louvre station with the objets d'art on view; London has its somewhat dingy charm; and New York its blatant air of danger. But Hong Kong has bright, shiny trains, air-conditioned, with a sense of order and cleanliness—ranging from the electronic turnstiles to the passengers themselves.

They dodged down the steps from the street into the high-ceilinged modern complex. Bond went straight to the booking booth, flashed his Boldman passport, and purchased two special Tourist Tickets, slapping down the HK$30 and receiving a pair of colored-plastic smart cards in return. All tickets are the size of credit cards, but they contain electronic strips recognized by the turnstiles when each journey has been completed, and swallowed up so that they can be reissued, creating a saving of thousands of dollars a year. The Tourist Tickets, however—each with a printed view of the harbor—allow unlimited travel for a certain period, and so save much time. There are high penalties for damaging the plastic smart cards—as there are for smoking, or bringing food and drink into the hallowed, cool atmosphere of the MTR system, hence the scrupulous cleanliness.

Still keeping both the holdall and Ebbie close to him, Bond headed toward the trains—down more stairs, and onto a platform. A train heading for Kowloonside hissed in.

They just made it, settling themselves on the somewhat spartan seats and studying the simple map that Bond had picked up when purchasing the tickets. Now he pointed a finger to the station at which they would get out, and set about casually looking around. Few people took any notice of them as the train pulled into Admiralty station, and then out again to start the crossing, directly under the harbor to Tsim Sha Tsui, a short way up the famous wide Nathan Road. This was where they planned the first jump-off and, when it came to it, the point where Bond spotted at least one pair of watchers.

The trains traveling over to Kowloon followed the same route until the split in the line at Mong Kok or Prince Edward—at the southern side of Kowloon, where the railway branched to the Tsuen Wan line, to the West up the coast, or to the Kwun

Tong line, which followed a great curve to the Northeast. The one on which they traveled was bound for this third line, which would take them too far from the center of things. Bond reasoned that, if he could contain matters within a relatively small area, life would be easier.

As they alighted, he noticed, bunched among the crowd of passengers, two well-dressed young Chinese, their eyes undisguisedly averted from Bond and Ebbie, yet somehow appearing to follow their progress. He turned left, as though to make for the exit, the Chinese duo getting closer.

"Back on again, at the last minute," he whispered as they came abreast of a set of carriage doors. It was an old trick, but it could still work. As the doors began to close, he pushed the girl in, following her quickly and seeing, to his frustration, the two Chinese do the same thing, one carriage down.

He told Ebbie to get off at Jordan, the next station, but to leave it until the last moment. When they did so, it took but a few moments in the scurrying crowd to realize that the two men were still there, keeping pace with them, and too close for comfort.

Both watchers wore light gray suits, neat collars, and ties, even in the afternoon heat. They could easily have been taken for two businessmen returning to the office. But to Bond's practiced eyes, they worked with a precision that gave him not only cause for alarm, but also the feeling that another team was at work—possibly in front of them.

They came out of Jordan station and went right, into the noisy, bustling Nathan Road, Bond edging

Ebbie to take the harbor direction. Smiling, he quietly told her that they were being followed and that there could be a team somewhere ahead of them. “Stay casual,” he said. “Stop and look in the shop windows, move slowly. At the bottom end of the road we come to The Peninsula Hotel. We’ll try to lose them there.”

The sidewalks were tight with people, more Chinese and Indians than European, for Nathan Road seemed to be a strange cultural meeting place. Garish banners overhung the street; on ground level modern shopfronts squeezed together, yet above them there could still be seen the old ramshackle buildings dating back to the 1930s or even ’20s. Neon and paper signs hung drunkenly at angles, sprouting out to catch the eye, while the omnipresent food stalls added an amalgam of smells. There were more camera and electronics shops here on Kowloonside, so Bond and Ebbie were able to stop regularly, as though comparing prices, while they watched for the watchers.

Ying and Yang, as Bond had mentally christened the two surveillance men, kept pace with a cunning that bespoke good and thorough training. But, within five minutes, Bond thought he had latched on to the team in front—a girl and boy, around eighteen or nineteen, seemingly wrapped in each other’s company but always stopping when Ebbie and Bond stopped. The boy wore a long, loose shirt outside his jeans, enough cover for a weapon. Ying and Yang, in their tailored gray suits, had plenty of hiding places for handguns. The thought crossed Bond’s mind that they could just as well be an execution squad—had it not already been done to Swift? No, he reasoned. Chernov would wish to be present at the end. There should be witnesses from within Moscow Center.

At last they reached The Peninsula, entering by one of the side doors that led into a bright shopping arcade.

As they turned to climb the stairs to the main lobby, so Ying and Yang followed them in. Doubtless the younger pair had made for the front of the hotel to complete the box. "Go ahead," Bond muttered to Ebbie. "Take the armory with you," he added, handing her the holdall. "Make for the loo. I'll be in the lobby as soon as I've dealt with this." At least this would be a thorough test for Ebbie's loyalty, and he nodded to her, smiling and relaxed as he reached for his cigarettes, placed one between his lips, and began to pat his pockets for matches or lighter.

Ying and Yang looked slightly startled as they saw him stop, but, being committed, came on, paying no attention until Bond stepped in front of them and, in English, asked if they had a light.

Close to, they looked like twins—jet short hair, round faces, but with darting, cruel eyes. For a second they paused, and Ying muttered something as his hand went up to reach inside the unbuttoned jacket. When the arm was almost level with his lapel, Bond grabbed the wrist, twisted hard, then pulled down, his right knee coming up with all his strength behind it.

He could almost feel the man's pain as the knee smashed into his groin; he certainly heard the gasp of agony, but, almost before that came, Bond had spun the man around and jerked him forward toward Yang, propelling him downward so that the top of his skull caught Yang's face—head-on. Bond heard the crunch and felt Ying's body go limp in his grip.

By the time anyone came out of the shops along the arcade, both Ying and Yang lay only partially conscious—Ying doubled in pain from both groin and head; Yang's face looking as though he had met a heavy lump of concrete: there was blood pouring from a broken nose, and possibly a cheekbone had been cracked.

Loudly Bond shouted for someone to get the police. "These men tried to rob me!" he shouted, and there was a jabber of Chinese and English.

He bent down, reaching inside each man's jacket. Sure enough, they were armed, with neat, stubby-looking .38 revolvers, easy to conceal and twice as lethal as larger guns. "Look!" he said loudly. "Somebody get security, these men are bandits."

The outraged noises from the small crowd gathered around them told Bond that they were most certainly on his side. He edged back into this growing circle, dropped one of the weapons, slid the other into his belt, inside the short Oscar Jacobson jacket he wore over shirt and slacks, and slipped away up the stairs. "Down there," he said to the two security men who were descending, almost bumping into him. "Couple of brigands just tried to rob my friend."

Ebbie waited inside the doors, in the corner of the vast, gilded hotel foyer where waiters scurried around tables, serving late tea, watched over by a silver-haired maître d' while a four-piece orchestra—seated high up in what looked like a royal box—played selections from musicals, old and new. Mainly old.

He took the holdall, muttered that they should move fast, and headed toward the main doors, his eyes swiveling around to spot the young couple whom he had fingered as the backup team. But there was no sign of them, either in the lobby or outside in the forecourt.

They crossed the road when the heavy traffic allowed, heading toward the harbor front, among the many building sites giving Kowloon a constant face-lift, Bond's eyes still restlessly moving to try to spot the other team.

"I think maybe we've thrown them." He squeezed Ebbie's arm. "Come on, keep going left. The least we can do is treat ourselves to a decent hotel for a few hours, and The Regent's just along here—great brick blockhouse of a place, but I'm told it's a strong rival to The Mandarin."

The view to The Regent was blotted out by vast hoardings enclosing building works, but as they reached the end of these they saw the hotel, with its driveway sweeping upward, and the forecourt awash with Rolls-Royces and Cadillacs. It was not the only thing that came into view. As they turned the corner, the young man and his girlfriend stepped out directly in front of them.

Bond grasped the revolver butt and was about to draw the weapon when the young man spoke—his hands clearly empty and the girl obviously watching his back.

"Mr. Bond?" he asked.

Bond took one step back, ready for the next move. "Yes." He nodded.

"Do not be alarmed, sir. Mr. Swift said that, should any ill befall him, I was to give you this, never mind." Slowly his hand went to his pocket, from which he drew an envelope. "You might already know that Mr. Swift had serious accident this afternoon. My name is Han. Richard Han. I worked for Mr. Swift. All arrangements are made. I presume you dealt with the two no-good coolie hoodlums who were following you—we heard large commotion . . ."

"Yes," said Bond, still a shade wary.

"Good. There will be a walla walla down by Ocean Terminal at ten-forty-five. I will be there to see you both aboard. Ten-forty-five, near the Ocean Terminal. Okay, *heya?*"

Bond nodded, and the young couple smiled, linked arms, and turned away.

"What's a walla walla?" Ebbie asked later as they lay resting naked in a room high up in The Regent.

"Motorized sampan." Bond chuckled. "Some people'll tell you they're called walla wallas because of the noise of the engines. Others say it's because the very first one was owned by a guy from Washington, D.C."

"You are clever." Ebbie snuggled up to him. "How do you learn all these things, James?"

"From the official Hong Kong Guide. I read it while you spent all that time in the bathroom."

They had encountered no difficulty in getting a room at The Regent—especially when Bond flashed his Amex Platinum Card in the name of Boldman, and said that price was no object.

Nobody even queried the lack of luggage, though Bond supplied a story about it coming on from the airport later, casually showing the holdall—which he refused to let anyone else carry for him.

After ringing room service—ordering a relatively simple three-course European dinner for two—he opened the envelope. Inside was a single sheet of paper that contained a short message and a map of Cheung Chau Island.

In case anything happens, I have given this to a young colleague. Richard Han will assist in any way he can. I have arranged transport to Cheung Chau. The woman will drop you at the harbor, which is to the west of the island. You want a white villa that stands almost opposite The Warwick Hotel on the eastern side—ten minutes' walk over the narrow isthmus. Take the lane through the houses just right of the ferry landing stage. The villa is well placed, high up on the northern side of the bay of Tung Wan, looking out across a rather beautiful stretch of sea and sand—needless to say, The Warwick is on the southern side. To my knowledge there are no warning devices, but the place is always well guarded when anyone's in residence. It has at least one telephone, and the local number is 720302. Remember the nine killed in Cambridge, and the fires started at Canvey Island. If you get this, I will not be there to wish you luck, but you have it anyway.

Swift.

Bond had no alternative but to accept the note, the map, and the person of Richard Han as being genuine. At least this was a way of getting to Cheung Chau and finding the house. After that, who knew?

Before the food arrived, he went into the bathroom, checked the weapons and equipment in the holdall, and decided to arm Ebbie with one of the .38s. He would keep the similar weapon taken from Ying and Yang. The rest could be carried in the holdall. Once the villa was located, he knew what should be done. You could not take further chances with a man like Chernov. He went back to the bedroom, ate a hearty meal, waited for Ebbie to use the bathroom, then stripped and took a shower. They had no change of clothes, but at least they were both refreshed and clean. Bond stretched out on the bed, where, in spite of their tiredness, Ms. Heritage displayed a great deal of inventiveness in the practice of body language.

Now, after a short doze, Bond went over the essentials for the rest of the night. "You understand?" he asked at the end of this little briefing. "You will stay where I tell you until my return. After that, we play it by ear." He gave her a light kiss on each ear, as though to underline the point.

They dressed, armed themselves (he was pleased to note that she handled the revolver and spare ammunition professionally), and left the hotel just after ten o'clock.

On the dot of ten forty-five, Richard Han met them by the large and sprawling shopping mall, hard by the Star Ferry, known as Ocean Terminal. He led them away from the normal piers, down a path to the harbor, where the toothless old woman in black pajamas waited with her sampan.

"She knows where to take us?" Bond asked.

Han nodded. "And you must give her no money," he said. "She has already been paid enough. The trip will take the best part of three hours. I'm sorry, it's only one hour on the ferry, but this is the best way."

In the event, it took nearly four hours, the woman not speaking a word to them but leaning back, relaxed, at the tiller.

So it was that around three in the chill morning that James Bond and Ebbie Heritage were landed on Cheung Chau Island, around seven and a half miles west of Hong Kong. The sampan had bucked and rolled in the sea, but, once it neared the harbor, the old woman cut the engine, working an oar to bring them noiselessly in through a throng of junks and sampans, some lashed together, others riding at anchor. At last they reached the harbor wall, and the woman whispered something the meaning of which was obvious. Together, they scrambled up onto the wide stretch of concrete that fronted the harbor, Bond lifting an arm in farewell to the woman.

18

Tung Wan Bay

The island, as Bond had already seen from the map, *was* shaped roughly like a dumbbell—the south side much wider than the north, with a short spit of land, less than a mile wide, that ran between the two main areas.

Their eyes had adjusted to the dark long before landing, so Bond could make out the buildings ahead. He took Ebbie's hand, made certain that she had her revolver ready, and guided her toward the first dark gap, leading to a narrow lane. As they drew near, he could make out the shape of a clear-glass telephone booth, which he considered using once he had carried out the reconnaissance on the villa.

"You stay here. Don't move, and make sure nobody sees you," he whispered. "I'll be back within the hour." Through the darkness he saw her nod. Ebbie was certainly proving to be less nervous than he had any right to expect. Squeezing her hand, Bond set off up the lane, feeling very closed in by the buildings—shops by day—that made up the sides of this gulch. After a couple of hundred yards, the lane narrowed even more.

There was a large tree to the right, and Bond became conscious of someone near at hand. He stopped, moving only when he realized that it was an old Chinese, flat on his back, snoring under the tree.

In all, it took around twelve minutes before the buildings gave way to a wide strand of pale sand, with the sea, soft and shimmering, directly in front of him. Tung Wan Bay.

Keeping to the cover of the buildings, he edged forward. To his right a glitter of lights indicated The Warwick Hotel. He waited, peering around the bay and up to the promontory on his left. High up, he could see a small splash of gray with two lights burning—certainly the villa Swift had marked with an X.

Staying in dark cover and praying that nobody was using infrared night glasses from the villa, Bond slowly made his way along the buildings to his left until he reached open ground. The sand stretched out, white in the blackness, toward the promontory, the villa still in view.

He guessed that roughly seventy yards of open sand separated him from the shadows to the foot of the bluff—fifty yards of which could be viewed from the villa. Taking a deep breath, Bond sprinted forward, slowing down to a walk once he was in dead ground. The sand petered out, turning to a steep climb on short, spiky grass. Settling the hold-all's strap more comfortably on his shoulder, he began the climb. The grass had no sweet smell to it, the roughness scratched at his hands, and occasionally he felt a softness beneath it, as though the whole promontory was nothing but an overgrown sandbank. It took a good ten minutes of hard work before the angle of the climb gave way. He was now on flat, rising ground—still dead to the villa, which did not come into sight for a good thirty yards, and as soon as the first outlines of the building appeared against the lighter sky, Bond dropped onto his belly, adopting a crawl for the next ten yards or so.

He was now quite close—the building being only a few strides away. He lay for five minutes examining the target. It seemed to be a low white bungalow, with a terracotta roof and a series of arches running along the side, making it look more Spanish than Chinese. It also appeared to be set in a circular garden, surrounded by a small wall—some four or five bricks in height.

As he continued to watch, it became apparent that the arches were a kind of cloister that seemed to run round all four sides of the villa. The lights he had seen from below came from a large pair of what looked like sliding glass doors on the side overlooking the bay. There was movement behind the glass, and he thought he could make out Chernov himself, walking to and fro, speaking with somebody hidden from view.

Bond lay there for some time, judging distances and impressing the whole setting on his mind. To the left the ground ran upward—that had been clear when viewing the skyline from the beach below. Recalling the map, he knew that, should he choose to go in that direction, he would eventually find himself on a path that led back, round to the harbor, passing the temple for which the island was well known.

He worked out that if a man moved from the villa toward where he lay at this moment, it would take around fifteen long strides before he could disappear below the skyline—fifteen or sixteen yards, then he would have to slow and stop, as a headlong dash would bring him to the steeply angled ground, and probably a long, unpleasant fall down the slope to the beach below.

If Bond was to outwit Chernov, he needed to take precautions now, in the hope of being able to make use of them later. Carefully he crawled back until he was well hidden from the villa, and in the darkness his hands moved around, seeking soft earth. Eventually the palm of his left hand touched a stone. He shifted until he was lying directly behind it—a rough, circular stone about two feet across and a foot high, with an irregular surface.

Unslinging the holdall, he quietly opened it, removing a small oilskin package—a carefully prepared parcel of goodies made up by Q'ute and delivered to him in Paris. Most of what it contained was backup material—sophisticated lethal extras, all mirroring equipment already hidden in a duplicate belt around his waist, or posing as everyday items spread through his clothing. Digging into the sandy earth behind the rock, he deposited the oilskin package, secured with wraparound tapes. Covering this emergency pack with loose earth, Bond now eased himself forward again, taking mental bearings, hammering them into his head so that, should he have need of it, he could locate the package quickly in relation to the house. Only when he was certain of angles and distances did he retreat again, making the slow descent to the beach.

Some twenty minutes later he was back with Ebbie, whom he found well hidden in the shadows of the buildings fronting the harbor.

"All set," he whispered, adding no explanation. The less she knew, the better it would be.

"Are they there?" she asked, her voice just audible.

"Well, Chernov's there, and where he is I suspect we'll find the others." He had one of the revolvers in his belt, the barrel slanting to one side. Softly, indicating that Ebbie should stay where she was, he padded over to the harbor wall and dumped the holdall into the sea. They were now both armed, with ammunition to spare.

"We're going to show ourselves," he told Ebbie. "Just let ourselves be seen, and avoid actual contact for the time being—Swift's way: like a will-o'-the-wisp. Our job is to draw Chernov out. The house is quite small, but difficult to assault. If he's got a few good men there it would be madness for us to attempt any kind of attack. The ground around it is too exposed, so it would be suicidal."

"Should we not send for the police? This is British territory. Couldn't you have that terrible man arrested?"

"Not quite yet." He did not want her to know that before Chernov was nailed for them someone had to die—whoever was the traitor within *Cream Cake* needed to be disposed of, even if it looked like an accident. That had been implicit in Swift's briefing. The double could not be publicly exposed if M was to be brought into safe waters again. What was it

Swift had said? *M is still under siege. . . . He won't last another scandal. He stands no chance of weathering the storm if another double is found within his house, or even near to it.* And now Bond's only way of proving the *Cream Cake* traitor's identity was to offer himself—and Ebbie—on a plate.

"We'll go in a minute." He put his finger to his lips and headed for the glass telephone booth noted on their arrival. Digging in his pocket for the silver cash he required, Bond carefully dialed the number given in Swift's note—720302. The ringing started, and the distant instrument was picked up. Nobody spoke. He slowly counted to six and then, in Russian, he asked for General Chernov. It was Blackfriar himself who had answered.

Very softly, Bond hissed into the phone, "I'm close. Catch me if you can," and immediately cradled the instrument.

Returning to Ebbie he led her back along the lane that would take them onto the beach of Tung Wan Bay. This time, he did not bother to take any precautions. Instead of keeping well in shadow, Bond steered Ebbie onto the beach itself, and then to the left, slowly walking toward the promontory, and finally starting the upward climb—but this time much further to the right than before. Unless they had accidentally spotted him on the first reconnaissance, he wanted to keep Chernov's people well away from the area he had already covered. But it would be necessary to take risks in order to draw them from the villa, and so deal with them well in the open.

Eventually, they reached the flatter ground, crawling together toward the house and stopping only a few yards from the low wall, just hidden from view.

All the lights were on now, and the sky in the east had already started to lighten. In a matter of minutes, daylight would make them completely visible.

Turning on his side, Bond said he thought they should work their way around to the back.

"We should do this soon, I believe." Ebbie's eyes were clouded with concern. "The ground is very open here. I think they could see us easily from the house if they are awake and looking."

The voice came from behind them—"We seldom sleep for long, here on Tung Wan Bay. How nice of you to join us. Now I have the full set."

Bond rolled, the revolver up and ready to fire.

There were three of them: Mischa and one of the thugs who had been with Blackfriar when they picked Bond up at The Newpark. The third, dressed neatly in well-fitting cavalry twill trousers, shirt, and a dark jacket, was of course General Kolya Chernov himself, smiling at his triumph—and pointing an automatic pistol straight at Bond's head. "You invited me to catch you, Mr. Bond; and I have cordially accepted your invitation."

19

Meet the Robinsons

Like many a safe house in Europe, this villa—set on its promontory and presumably worth hundreds of thousands for the view alone—was spartan once you passed inside. Certainly there were the usual signs of soundproofing—heavy unnatural-looking wallpaper decorating the main living room, which they entered through the large sliding doors that Bond had first observed during his reconnaissance. The rest was functional—chairs made of bamboo, one table of some very solid wood. No pictures adorned the walls. No birds sang.

Bond had dropped the revolver as soon as he knew the odds. He had also turned to Ebbie, signaling with his eyes that on no account should she open up and say anything that mattered. When he spoke at last, it was to Ebbie—"Ms. Heritage, the gentleman pointing the gun at us has what we call star quality. May I introduce you to General Konstantin Nikolaevich Chernov, Hero of the Soviet Union, Order of Lenin—the list of decorations is very long, but he is at present Chief Investigating

Officer of Department Eight, Directorate S of the KGB. The Department that was, at one time, known as SMERSH. I suspect the General would prefer it to be still called by that emotive name."

Chernov gave him a pleasant smile, nodding to Ebbie even as in two words he instructed the men to take them into the villa. Now, inside, he spoke to Bond. "I cannot tell you how glad I am to see you again." Then, switching his attention to Ebbie, "I've also been looking forward to meeting you. By some stupid oversight we missed you in Ireland, Miss Heritage—or should I rightly call you Fräulein Nikolas?"

"Heritage," she answered calmly.

Chernov shrugged. "As you like. However, I am also *very* pleased to see you—the last piece of the ludicrous *Cream Cake* business. All the chickens have come home to roost—and make their final payments, eh?"

Bond had already decided on his strategy. He cleared his throat, coughed, and said, "General, I am empowered to negotiate."

"Really?" The shrewd eyes met Bond with an amused glitter. "You have bargaining powers?"

"Within certain parameters, yes," he lied. "Certain exchanges can be offered for those you hold here—for Ms. Dare, Ms. Heritage, Maxim Smolin, Mr. Baisley, and Fräulein Dietrich. I'm sure you would like some of your own people back, we have quite a number in stock."

Mischa laughed, a quiet, evil sound, while Chernov gave a throaty chuckle. "Everyone connected with *Cream Cake,* eh? All of those under sentence of death."

"Yes."

Mischa laughed again, then spoke—"So, what do we do first, Comrade General? Deal with the traitors and spies, or put your tame puppets to the test?"

"Well, there's plenty of time, Mischa. Relax, this is a pleasant place. Today will be hot. When the sun goes down we'll put the puppets to work. When that is finished, there'll be time to perform the little ritual you seem to long for. With all of them confined here we can be lazy about it. They deserve to go slowly. Really, they wanted us to take Smolin and Dietrich back to Moscow; however, we could be a little pressed for that." He sighed, then looked slyly at Ebbie. "Now, the Nikolas girl here could well provide me with a morsel of pleasure before we extract her tongue and dispatch her with a shade more speed." He turned to Bond. "Don't you agree?"

"I wouldn't know what I'm agreeing to."

"Really? Let's have some coffee and rolls. I can explain while we're eating." He asked Mischa if the Chinese amah had yet arrived with the day's provisions. He nodded, yes—"But I've sent her away again," he added. "Today I felt we had no need for outsiders."

"Quite right, Mischa. Some coffee, then? rolls? preserves?"

"You should have brought your servant, General."

"Perhaps. One of these idiots will help you." He nodded to the man who stood impassive by the door. And at another who seemed to have materialized near the window. Both held machine pistols at the ready. Mischa tapped the arm of the one by the door, and spoke to him in Russian. The man shouldered his pistol by its strap, and was about to follow Mischa out when Chernov intervened. "He can help, but first I think the young lady should join her companions. They probably have a lot to talk about. You should make the most of it." He smiled at Ebbie—this time there was a horrible chill around the eyes—as Mischa called her over and the guard prodded at her with his pistol.

Ebbie nodded, uncurled herself from the chair in which she had been sitting, looked first at Bond, then at Chernov, paused, and went up close to the General, spitting full into his face. He reeled back in disgust, then moved so quickly that even Bond did not see his hand come up to slap Ebbie's left cheek and backhand her right.

The little blonde hardly made a sound, riding with the blows, not even putting her hand to her face. Both the hoods sprang forward, but she merely turned and meekly followed the frowning Mischa from the room, one man behind her, the other returning to his place by the sliding doors. Chernov was wiping the spittle from his face.

"Foolish girl," he muttered. "I could have made the inevitable a little easier for her."

"For all your veneer of sophistication, you're really a cold-blooded bastard, Chernov, aren't you?" The man's dossier and profile at the Regent's Park Headquarters adequately described his devious ruthlessness, but the words did little to reflect the degenerate nature of the man who, for all his cunning intellect, could well have been equated with the most callous and perverted KGB head of all time—the infamous Lavrenti Pavlovich Beria.

"Me?" Chernov's eyebrows shot up. "Me, cold-blooded? Don't be stupid, Bond. These little girls were used by your own cold-blooded Operations Planners, so presumably it was explained to them what risks they were taking." He gave a snort. "You and I know what *Cream Cake* was about—it was about securing the defection of two highly trained and experienced officers, Smolin and Dietrich. To muddy the waters, your people added an extra pair of targets for makeweight, to confuse the issue if need be. Well, it worked! But now, the operation is about to be canceled out. We—KGB *and* GRU—just cannot leave the matter there. Surely you understand that justice must be seen to be done. Two of the girls have been disposed of. It would be greatly unfair to let the rest off with a caution. The intelligence communities of all countries must see that we will not stand by and allow people to get away with this kind of thing." He gave another of his shrugs. "In any case, I have direct orders from my Chairman to carry out summary executions—the bodies left as a warning, with special marks: a kind of ritual. You understand?"

Chernov spoke in a calm, rational tone, as though the murders of Heather, Ebbie, Jungle, Dietrich, and Maxim Smolin—together with the horrors that would take place, such as the ripping out of their tongues, probably while they were still alive—were of as much consequence as imposing a fine on a luckless driver for exceeding the speed limit.

"We cannot negotiate, then?"

"You cannot negotiate with dead people."

"What of me, General?"

"Ah!" He turned, the finger of his right hand raised pointing at Bond, but before he could say more there came a tap on the door, which opened to the hood carrying a large tray, heavy with a coffee pot, cups, a basket of bread rolls, and some large jars of jams and preserves. He was followed by Mischa, who held the man's machine pistol, demonstrating that he was not going to act as butler for anybody, not even General Chernov.

The finger came down. "Ah!" Chernov repeated. "Breakfast."

Mischa left with the other man, and Bond saw that the big fellow who stood guard at the window eyed the food with some envy. "You were saying, General?"

"Oh, after we've eaten, my dear Bond. Enjoy my hospitality while you can." And with that, he refused to enter into any further conversation. In fact, it was the last he was to say about Bond's future for many hours, for as soon as they had eaten, Chernov rapped out several commands. The other hood came back into the room and, with no warning, both men took Bond by the arms and hauled him into the passage outside, and from there down two flights of stone steps. Finally they opened a stout, heavy door, and threw him into a small cell that was completely bare but for a light recessed in the ceiling and covered by a thick metal grille—no windows, no furniture: just an empty room with unpainted block walls and ceiling, and about enough space for a man to stand and spread out his arms.

Mischa appeared in the doorway. "Mr. Bond." For the first time, Mischa displayed an effeminate lisp. He clutched at a bundle of clothes, which he then threw onto the cell floor—a pair of dark blue overalls, nylon socks, underwear, and a pair of cheap moccasins. "They're your size, Mr. Bond. We checked with Moscow. The General would like you to strip and put these on." He gave a toothy smile. "You have a reputation as a bit of a magician—things up your sleeves and that kind of thing. So the General felt it would be safer this way. Just change now, please."

There was no option. As slowly as possible, Bond discarded his own clothes—together with the precious equipment concealed in them—and climbed into the overalls, which made him feel foolish. Mischa and the guards took his clothes and slammed the door. He heard a heavy deadlock clunk into place.

For a while, he took stock. There was a tiny hole, no larger than a pencil, set over the door, so he knew from experience that he was almost certainly being observed by a monitoring system, using minute fiber-optic lenses. The cell was obviously located deep in the ground, under the villa. There was no chance of escape from this place. Now his only hope was that, by some means, he could get to the backup equipment hidden in the earth outside the house. He had hoped this would not be necessary, but at least it was there, and he thanked whatever fate looked after people of his profession for giving him the foresight to have Q'ute bring in the stuff to Paris. Then, once he had accepted that even the equipment hidden outside might be of no use to him, Bond crossed his legs and sat, impassively, emptying his mind of all thoughts and anxieties of what might come; and mentally preparing himself by centering his whole being on nothingness.

He did not know how much time had passed before they came again—the two guards, with more food, which he refused. The men accepted this with ill grace but withdrew.

Time passed, and Bond controlled both body and mind, knowing that, whatever trial the General had in store for him, he would need all his experience and all his mental and physical attributes to combat it—even turn it to his advantage, if he was to save the *Cream Cake* team, and himself, from the certain death that awaited them. All, of course, except the unknown traitor.

In his bones he felt the waning of the day, and at last the door was unlocked and the same men dragged him out and up the stairs to the main room where he had last sat with Chernov.

This time the place appeared smaller, and it was full of people. Outside he glimpsed the long slash of white sand being turned red by the blood from the day's dying sun.

Looking around him, Bond saw Chernov sitting on a bamboo chair in the center of the room. The others—guards apart—were chained together, and he realized there were two new faces. It took Bond almost a full thirty seconds to recognize the man as Franz Wald Belzinger—otherwise Jungle Baisley. The face was certainly the one he had studied on photographs during that first fatal afternoon, following the lunch with M at Blades. The surprise came when he saw that Baisley was a huge man—Bond reckoned over six feet tall, and broad in the shoulders. He looked even younger than his twenty-seven years, possibly because of a shock of red hair that, even though well combed, seemed to be impossible for him to rule. He grinned broadly at Bond, as though welcoming him.

"I think you know everybody, except Fräulein Dietrich and Mr. Baisley, as he likes to be called."

Susanne Dietrich was a slim woman, older than he expected and with light-colored, untidy hair. She gave Bond a frightened look, while Jungle tried to rise and grinned an American coed's grin. "Hi, Mr. Bond. I have been hearing much about you." The voice had German undertones, but more to do with syntax than accent, and he certainly was not going to let anyone know he had an ounce of fear in him.

Bond nodded and smiled, trying to be reassuring. He looked along the line, at Maxim Smolin, Heather, and Ebbie. Heather smiled back; Smolin winked; and Ebbie blew him a kiss. It was good for him to know the trio were obviously going to face their fate with a great deal of dignity. He asked if they were okay. They said nothing, but each nodded resignedly.

"So, I call this meeting to order." Chernov laughed, as though this was the joke of the decade. "Or should I call it a court, rather than a meeting?" he added.

Nobody spoke, so, with a wry smile Chernov continued. "The five prisoners here already know what is to happen to them. They have been informed of their guilt and the reason they are to die. They also know the method of their deaths, which will take place at dawn tomorrow." He paused, savoring the thought. Then—"As for this officer, for we must dignify him with that title, Commander James Bond, Royal Navy, Secret Intelligence Service, as for him—well, the department I represent has had an execution order out on him for many years now. Do you understand that, Commander Bond?"

Bond nodded, thinking of the many times he had outwitted and damaged that part of the Soviet Service sometimes referred to as the black heart of the KGB, and once known as SMERSH.

"Let us not be hypocritical about Commander Bond." Chernov's face was revealed in its serious mode. "He has proved himself a valiant enemy. Resourceful, highly efficient, and brave. It would, therefore, not be in keeping with the principles of the department I represent if we simply dispatched him with bullet, knife, a cyanide spray, or an injection of Racin, the drug our Bulgarian cousins favor. As in a bullfight, Commander Bond should, I believe, be given a fighting—if outclassed—chance." He turned his eyes, and the sinister smile, onto Bond's face. "Commander Bond, do you know what a 'puppet' is—in an operational sense, I mean?"

"One who is easy to control?" Bond tried.

Chernov laughed aloud. "I am not being fair to you, James Bond. It is the Red Army's Special Forces, the Spetsnaz—which we believe to be the equivalent to your SAS, or the Americans' Delta Force—who use the word 'puppet.' Puppets are of great assistance during their training. The puppets, or their equivalent, have been used in the USSR to great effect for more than fifty years now. In the beginning, our noble ancestors, the Cheka, called them gladiators; then the NKVD spoke of them as volunteers—though they are hardly that. SMERSH, under all its different guises, has always called them by an English name, which is strange, eh? We call them Robinsons, Commander Bond. You might be more familiar with them under that appellation. So, I ask you again, do you know what Robinsons are?"

"I've heard rumors." He felt a tightening of his stomach at the thought.

"And you believed the rumors?"

"I think so, yes."

"You would be right to believe them. Let me explain. When somebody is sentenced to death in the Soviet Union, it depends upon his usefulness to the community whether he dies quickly, or if his death can serve the state." Again, the grim and chilling smile lit Chernov's eyes with black ice. "Unlike the decadent and sloppy British, who are so neatly delivering themselves into our hands by their self-indulgence, their laxity, their failure to see how we will finally take complete control of their politics"—his voice rose to a slightly higher pitch—"unlike the British, who are too squeamish to use the death penalty anymore, we use it to advantage. True, old men and women are executed almost immediately. Others go to medical centers; some to assist in the building and running of our nuclear reactors—to do the dangerous jobs. The stronger, fitter, and younger men become puppets, or come to us as Robinsons. It provides good training for our men. Until a soldier has proved he can kill another human being, one cannot be certain of him."

"That's what I'd heard." Bond's face felt frozen, as though injected by a dentist. "We are told that they provide living targets on exercises . . ."

"Not simply targets, Commander Bond. They can fight back—naturally, we keep them under great control. They know that, should they try to escape, or turn their weapons on the wrong people, they will be cut down like wheat. They are, for the time of one exercise, real, live opponents. They kill and get killed. If they are really good, they can survive for some time."

"Three exercises and they are reprieved?"

Chernov smiled. "An old wives' tale, I fear. Robinsons never survive forever. They know they are under sentence, so they fight harder if they *think* a reprieve will come after being put up against our people for only three times." He looked closely at his fingernails, as though inspecting them for some deformities.

The room seemed charged with tension. Chernov turned, nodding to the pair of hoods who went out, carefully closing the door behind them.

"When we heard that you—a man on our death list—had been attached to the clearing up of *Cream Cake,* I made a request to Moscow Center. I asked for some Robinsons. Some very good men. Ones who had lasted for two exercises and imagined they had only one more to win before reprieve. I asked for young men. Mr. Bond, you should feel honored, this is the first time our people have allowed Robinsons to operate outside the Soviet Union. Tonight, from midnight until dawn, you will be out on this little island, with our four best Robinsons intent on killing you. They will be armed, and we are allowing you a small weapon also. But for six hours, in the dark and on ground that you do not know—and, incidentally, they do—you will be hunted. James Bond, I would like you to meet your Robinsons." He shouted a command and the door was opened by one of the men outside.

20

Zero Hour

At first sight, the four Robinsons looked docile enough. They were not shackled or under any form of restraint—apart from the two guards with their machine pistols.

"Come in," Chernov beckoned, speaking Russian.

If he had expected shuffling cowed prisoners, Bond would have been disappointed. The quartet marched into the room, their bearing military, eyes fixed ahead.

All four were dressed in loose black garments—lightweight trousers and shirts. They even wore black trainers, and Bond reckoned that their faces would also be blackened before the night was over. There had been no moon last night, and there would be none tonight. The Robinsons would become invisible out in the darkness of the island.

"You see, Commander Bond, they are a good little team. They have worked together before, and to good effect—once against a Spetsnaz group of six trained soldiers: five are dead, and the sixth will not walk again. Their second mission was with KGB trainees. Man to man, four to four." He gave his now constant shrug. "KGB are four trainees less. Need I say more?"

Bond stared at the men, sizing them up. All were well built, alert, and clear-eyed, but one stood out from the rest, mainly because of his height—around six-five, towering over the others who were closer to six feet. "What were their crimes?" He tried to make the question sound casual, as though he was a racehorse dealer checking on pedigree.

Chernov smiled. Until this moment, Bond had simply recognized that smile as being somehow humorless and sinister. Now, he realized why. The smile reminded him of the famous *Mona Lisa.* Art experts raved about the look of that painting's lips and eyes—describing them as enigmatic, beautiful, and secretive. Certainly he agreed with the last of these descriptions, but to Bond it had always been something else, as though the lady was smiling at a secret so hideous and appalling that it could never be translated into words. He hated that painting, and knew, instinctively, that it was probably some deep reaction to his own kind of work that caused this particular loathing.

"I have to think," Chernov said, his eyes running along the line of men who stood, statue-still, in front of them. "The big fellow, Yakov, was condemned for six offenses of rape: all very young women, girls almost. He also strangled his victims after using them. Then we have Bogdan—also a killer, though not a rapist. Young men were his specialty. Bogdan broke their necks and tried to dispose of them by cutting up the bodies and spreading the pieces in woodland near his home. He's a peasant, but strong and with no moral sense where death is concerned."

Bond stopped himself from blurting out the obvious—"Like you, Kolya. Just like you."

Chernov continued down the line. "Pavl and Semen are less complex. Pavl, the one with the bulbous nose, was an army officer who took to converting military funds for his own use. Five of his comrades discovered the truth, over a period of two years. Four have never been found. The fifth managed to pass on the information. As for Semen, he is a straightforward murderer—three counts: his lady friend, her lover, and her mother. Very good with a meat cleaver, that's Semen."

"All part of life's rich pattern." Bond knew the only way to fight Chernov was to make light of these four monsters who, in a matter of hours, would be out to kill him. "You say they will be armed?"

"Of course. Two will carry handguns—Lugers, if you want the details. One will be equipped with a knife—a killing knife, similar to the Sykes-Fairbairn Commando dagger, which we know is familiar to you. And one will be given a weapon that he likes, a type of short mace, similar to the old Chinese fighting irons, a spiked steel ball hanging from a rather sharp blade, attached to the end of a two-foot handle. Unpleasant."

"And what about me?"

"You, my dear Bond? Well, we wish to be fair. You'll have a Luger pistol. A Parabellum. In good condition, I assure you."

Eight rounds, Bond thought. Eight chances to kill, if he could put himself in the right position.

Chernov was still speaking. "We have provided you with one magazine—half full. Four 9mm bullets. One for each of the Robinsons, should you be lucky enough to get within range before one of them comes screaming out of the night at you. As I have already implied, this team has been given a walk over the ground. As far as I know, you have not."

"What if they decide to make a run for it? Grab themselves a boat—a sampan—and clear off?"

Again the tantalizing smile. "You still do not understand, do you, Commander Bond? These men are trained and have nothing to lose but their lives—which they keep once you are dead."

"They *think* they'll keep their lives."

"Oh, Bond, don't try to spread dissension. It will *not* work, my friend. They cannot be turned; they will not run; nor will they believe any stories you might try to tell them—in any case, they won't give you the time."

And you know I won't run, either, Bond thought. You think you know me inside out, Comrade General. You know I won't run because, if I can possibly outwit your deadly foursome, I shall return here and try to save the others. Mentally he sighed, thinking that Chernov *did* know him, for that was exactly what he would do. He wondered if Chernov also knew he would try to return in order to unmask the traitor among the other prisoners?

Chernov gave a signal, and the Robinsons were marched out, each one meeting Bond's gaze upon turning toward the door. Was it imagination, or did he detect a bleak hatred in those four pairs of eyes?

"You have a couple of hours to rest before the ordeal." Chernov rose. "I suggest you make your peace with the world." One of the hoods came back into the room, ready to lead Bond away, but Chernov took a step forward. "Let me say something else, just to make certain you are familiar with the rules of this drama. Do not try to be clever. It is possible that you have thought of the obvious scheme. To leave and drop below that little wall that encircles the house, then pick off the Robinsons as they come out—we know you are an excellent marksman. Please, do not even think of trying that. When you are given the order to run, then you run. Any other little tricks and my two guards will cut you to ribbons. Should you, by luck or skill, manage to avoid, or kill, my Robinsons, I would advise you to go on running, James Bond. To run as far as you can. We will kill you tonight, I am certain of that, but if I am wrong, the time will come again and I, personally, will kill you. My department will never rest. Understand?"

Bond nodded, curtly, and left with dignity.

Back in the cell, he began to go over his assets. For a while, up there with the deadly Robinsons, he had almost allowed despair to reach him. Now, alone again, he began to plan.

They were giving him a Luger Parabellum with four rounds of ammunition. Well, that was a start. But there was more, if he could get to the already hidden backup package.

The package, worked on by Q'ute and other members of the Service, was for use only in the event of absolute necessity, in the field and almost certainly only in wartime, for it consisted mainly of killing devices.

Constructed on the principle of the old-fashioned Royal Navy "housewife"—always pronounced "hussif"—the COAP, Covert Operations Accessory Pack, was basically a thick oilskin oblong, measuring one foot three inches by eight inches, with two long tapes running out from the left-hand side.

When laid out flat, the COAP contained five pockets, each made to an exact size to fit the object it contained. On the far left were two objects that, unless examined under laboratory conditions, looked like a pair of squat, stubby HP11 batteries. One of these was in fact a powerful flare to be held firmly in the hand, at arm's length, and activated by pressing the little button that looked like the battery's positive nipple. It would shoot a pure white-light flare to around twenty feet. Anything within a quarter of a mile radius was illuminated like daylight. Fired at the right trajectory, the flare could also have a blinding effect.

The second battery was operated like the first, though you did not hang on to it, for within seven seconds the thing exploded with almost twice the power of the old Mills hand grenade.

Both batteries contained the plastique substances that so concerned antiterrorist organizations in these troubled times, for the plastique could not be detected in any conventional way—by X ray or sniffers, either electronic or canine.

Moving on to the third pocket, one came to a six-inch knife blade—again, undetectable by airport security because it was fashioned from toughened polycarbon. The blade was protected by a scabbard that, when removed, could be screwed to the blade, thereby producing a killing knife.

The fourth pocket was almost flat, containing a saw-toothed garroting wire; the last pocket held probably the most deadly weapon of all—a pen. Not an ordinary pen, but one made in Italy that also had security men worried. With one quick twist, the pen became a small projectile-firing gun. It was operated by compressed air, and could be used only three times to fire toughened steel needles—each the size of a ballpoint, every one a killer if it entered the brain, throat, lung, or heart from around ten paces.

When rolled up, the COAP was tied with the tapes, using a quick-release knot, and now—in his mind—Bond rehearsed where each of these items could be found in the open sheet, remembering the many times he had trained in the dark, handling and using all the items by feel alone, and comforted by the fact that he knew he could have everything stowed away on his person, or in use, within less than a minute. There was nothing like the threat of death, he considered—as many had done before him—to concentrate the mind.

Having gone through the positions in the COAP several times, he could now do no more but prepare himself mentally for the test. So he sat as before—legs crossed, eyes closed—but, this time, going over his memories of the map Richard Han had passed on from Swift. He knew where the house lay in relation to the remaining terrain, and, within the hour, he knew what he would do. If luck and his expertise were with him, there was a chance—a slim chance—that, before the night was over, he would have won.

They told him that it was eleven-thirty when they came for him. The hoods spoke no English, but while one covered him with the machine pistol, the other raised his arm, grinning proudly at his brand-new eight-function digital watch.

Chernov was waiting alone in the main room. The doors had been opened, and a few lights twinkled from the cluster of houses around the center and above the beach of Tung Wan Bay. Across the water, on the southern promontory, The Warwick Hotel had a lot of lights gleaming.

"Come and listen." Chernov beckoned him toward the doors, and the two men stepped outside into the warm night air. Bond thought, Why not kill him now with your bare hands, and be done with it? But that would serve no purpose. He would follow Chernov quickly to the grave, cut down by the man who had stayed in the room behind them.

"Listen," Chernov repeated. "Hardly a sound. You realize that around forty thousand people still live on this little island—most of them on the junks and sampans in the harbor—yet after midnight few people stir. There is little nightlife on Cheung Chau."

As Chernov spoke, Bond took his bearings—reciprocal bearings. Directly in front of them the ground slid away flatly to the place where he had hidden the COAP during his first reconnaissance. He could, thank heaven, pinpoint exactly where he should cross the low wall. Below, the strand circled the bay, while to the right the ground sloped sharply upward. He knew that, once over that rise, it was only a few hundred yards to a rough road that weaved downward toward the central isthmus where the main village was built—its harbor and most of its buildings being on the western side. To reach it, the road swept down, passing the famous Pak Tai Temple onto the Praya, or waterfront, with its fish-processing factory and hundreds of fishing junks.

Chernov slapped him on the shoulder. "But we'll *give* them a little nightlife, eh, James Bond?" He glanced at his watch. "It is almost time." He turned, shepherding Bond inside again.

"Do I get a last request?"

Chernov looked at him, a worm of suspicion in his eyes. "That depends."

"I would like to say goodbye to my friends."

"I think not. It would be emotional for them. They are well controlled—particularly the women. I would not like to risk unbalancing that. You realize it is not a pleasant job I have to do in this place tomorrow. It will be best if those under sentence bear pain—and the inevitability of death—with fortitude. It will make the whole business easier for me. You understand?"

Yes, thought Bond, the last thing you want is for me to see them now, because, like as not, they are one short. The traitor will have been pulled out. Aloud, he said, "You're a butcher, Chernov. Let's get on with it."

Chernov nodded, looking solemn. "You have my word that a full five minutes will pass before the Robinsons are unleashed on you. Come, the weapons are here."

As though by magic, the table was now littered with the means of death—three Luger pistols, the long gunmetal dagger—perhaps an inch longer than the old Sykes-Fairbairn Commando knife—and the unpleasant fighting iron: a wooden haft, some two feet in length, with a reinforced handgrip at one end, and a sharp movable steel blade at the other. The blade was flat at its far end, to which a short length of chain was attached. From the chain dangled a mace, twice the size of a man's fist and covered with sharp spikes. Chernov touched the mace and laughed. "You know what they used to call these?"

"Morning stars, as I recall."

"Yes, morning stars, and"— he chuckled mirthlessly—"and holy-water sprinklers. I prefer holy-water sprinklers." His hand hovered over the weapons, coming to rest on one of the Lugers. "Yours, I believe." He slipped the magazine out before handing it to Bond. "Please make certain the action is in working order, and that the firing pin has not been removed."

Bond checked the weapon. It was well oiled and in good condition. Chernov held out the magazine. "Count the four rounds. Reload the magazine yourself. I insist on fair play."

Bond did as he was bidden, aware that the thug with the machine pistol had stiffened in readiness, and that the Robinsons were being brought into the room behind him. He also knew that the whole setup was designed to add tension to the drama. Chernov was a good stage director, and all this byplay had a point.

"You may load the weapon and put the safety on."

Bond did so, holding the automatic loosely in his right hand as Chernov completed his speech. "When we are ready, I shall stand you by the doors and count down, from ten to zero. At zero the lights will be switched off, and you will begin your run. Do not forget what I've already told you about tricks, James Bond. They will do you no good. I do promise you again, though, on my word as an officer, that the Robinsons will not be unleashed for a full five minutes. I should make the most of your time. You are ready?"

Bond nodded, and, to his surprise, Chernov extended a hand for him to shake. Bond just looked at it, then turned to face the door. Chernov paused for a moment, as though hurt by his refusal, before he began to count. "Ten . . . nine . . . eight . . ." and so on to the final "zero!" The lights went out. Bond hurled himself forward into the sudden darkness.

21

Emperor of the Dark Heaven

Bond judged the leap over the wall with both skill and luck. Having done his calculations while standing outside with Chernov, he was able to count off the paces as he ran in what he knew to be the right direction.

In the event, he took it in his stride and went pelting straight across the flat scrub until he came to the slope. He went down, rolled rapidly about four times until he was sure his silhouette was well off the skyline. He was certain he had landed within a few feet of his goal, and so felt the ground around him with the palms of his hands. There were a couple of seconds of near panic, then his left hand touched the rock. He rolled toward it, scrabbling in the earth and dragging out the oilskin package.

On his feet again he turned left and began to pelt over the slope, aiming to get above the villa in record time, putting as much distance between himself and the safe house as possible.

Throughout the run he counted, using the old childhood recipe of "One Elephant . . . two Elephant . . ." to gauge the seconds. He had given himself two and a half minutes. Wherever he was at that point, he would stop.

He judged that the point reached in that time was around thirty yards above the villa, and it was there that he fell to the ground, placed the pistol where he knew he could grab it, threw the COAP onto the ground, slipped the tapes, and unrolled the oilskin . . .

By feel alone, in the darkness, he located each item, pulling them in turn from their holders, and distributing them around the pockets of his overalls—leaving the batterylike flare in his hand. Breathing heavily, Bond held out his arm, angled the little object toward the house, and pressed the firing button, and then reached for the Luger.

He judged the flare would explode at five minutes twenty seconds since he had left the house.

There was an open pocket on the right thigh of the overalls, and he jammed the Luger into it. Then, grabbing at the second battery—the small grenade—he waited.

The flare gave a thumping kick against his hand, then went up in a dazzling white flash of light. Bond closed his eyes as the projectile left his hand, then opened them immediately the moment the vivid first flash was over. It was as though someone had bathed the villa and its immediate surrounding area in a floodlight, just as he had intended. There, for anyone to see, were the Robinsons—one pair heading up the rise, toward him, the other two going down in the direction of the beach.

One of the men coming in Bond's direction threw up an arm to shield his eyes, but both kept going, like automatons. Bond could see clearly that the second pair were in no way deflected from their progress down toward the beach and isthmus.

Bond lay still and silent, clutching the tiny bomb. Already he could hear the men's heavy breathing as they came on toward him, their shapes visible in the dying moments of the flare's light.

This had to be judged to the second. It would be obvious tactics for one of each pair to be carrying a pistol, and, if the grenade did not explode at the right moment, taking out both men, he might be forced to use his own Luger—at least one precious shot that he could ill-afford to lose.

The panting and heavy footfalls grew nearer, and now he had only his own judgment to go by, for the flare had long gone. Bond prayed to heaven that he had their measure, pressed on the arming nipple, and aimed his throw in the precise path of the oncoming men.

He caught a quick glimpse of the pair—too close together for their own good—as the tiny cylinder packed with plastique exploded in the air directly in front of them. He ducked his head, feeling the burn and shock across his own scalp and the terrible ringing in his deafened ears. He thought a scream reached him through the explosion, but could not be certain. Stumbling to his feet, he half-walked, half-staggered forward until his foot hit something. He bent to feel a soft wetness he identified as body and blood.

On hands and knees, Bond carefully felt around in the scrubby grass, straining through his buzzing ears for any sound, and trying to condition that other sense of danger so necessary for men in his profession.

It was at least two minutes before he found the knife, and another two or three before locating the gun.

The charge had, as he hoped, exploded directly between the men, and very close to them. Before his hand closed on the Luger, it encountered unpleasant debris from the small bomb—Bond would never get used to the effects of explosions, particularly nowadays, when only a very small amount of modern plastique could do so much damage to human beings.

His head started to clear, and with his original pistol still tucked into the overall pocket—the other weapon clasped in his right hand—Bond began to race westward, heading for the road that would take him down to the Praya.

Chernov had made a point of telling him about the deadly experience of these four men—now there were only two, and it was reasonable to consider that, under discipline, the killers would stick to their route and then probably separate at the village, hoping to catch their prey in the open, or among the buildings running the length of the Praya.

Bond had his own plan of campaign. If he could make the Pak Tai Temple, which was a good vantage point, he would wait there. Let them come to him. It was far and away the best thing to do.

His ears still sang from the explosion, and he was aware that his clothes were stained with the blood of the two Robinsons who had died, but he reached the road without mishap, moving from the rough and stony surface—for it was not a road in the traditional sense—onto the softer grass at the side.

Bond stopped running now, trying to march at speed, taking great gulps of air in an attempt to regulate his breathing, as it had been a hard dash across undulating ground.

After ten minutes or so he thought he could make out the shapes of buildings ahead. Five minutes later he reached the edge of the village, cutting between dark bushes and feeling gently along a stone wall he knew must be the temple.

Working his way to the front of the building, Bond reflected on the fact that at least he had some gods he could pray to now, for Pak Tai is the Supreme Emperor of the Dark Heaven, and the temple in his honor also houses his martial gods—Thousand Mile Eye and Favorable Wind Ear. He could do with the help of all three tonight, for it was black as pitch, and he required the Emperor on his side with his colleagues to radar in on the last pair of Robinsons.

The temple fronted onto an open piece of land, and for the first time since the flare and explosion Bond felt his eyes adjusting to the dark. Within a few minutes he could make out the flat square and the shape of steps below him—the temple steps, guarded by traditional dragons.

Gently, he felt his way toward the top step, and, on reaching it, he retreated once more into the cloaked darkness of the temple doorway, moving to his right, sheltering at a vantage point behind one of the two great stone pillars. There he waited.

Minutes filtered slowly by, and he could but presume that the two other Robinsons were also taking their time, adjusting and moving slowly, silently through the night streets.

At least one hour passed. Then the best part of another. Self-discipline held him from even glancing at the luminous dial of his watch as he conducted a careful, regular search—from right to left, then left to right, moving his head and eyes very slowly, his body becoming cramped by standing so still for so long.

Finally, he broke the habit and looked at the Rolex. Ten to five in the morning. Just over an hour before the game was up and Chernov would be doing his butchery.

Bond's stomach turned over at the thought, and, as the horrific picture of Chernov at his work slid through his mind, so he caught movement, out of the corner of his eye. It came from the far right of the square, close to the houses—a fleeting figure, there for a second, a shadow against the lighter band that was the sea.

Slowly Bond moved, lifting the Luger, eyes riveted to the area where he had seen the shadow. For a moment or two he thought that he had imagined it. Then, there it was again, hard against the wall, moving at a snail's pace, using the full darkness.

He shifted position again, bringing the Luger up as the shadow detached itself from the wall and began to move nearer to the temple steps. It was then that, for all his training and experience, Bond made his first error of the night. Take him out now, part of his mind commanded. No, wait, where's the other bastard? It was this one second of mental confusion that brought about the next terrifying minutes.

Take him out now—his training overrode all else. He centered the Luger's sights on the advancing shadow. His finger took up the first pressure, then his sixth sense warned of closer danger.

He was standing in the classic side-on position, both arms raised in the two-handed grip, and the pain seared through his left arm as though someone had run a burning brand across it.

He heard his own scream of pain, feeling the gun drop from his right hand as he reached across to the injured arm. And, as he swiveled, he saw the Robinson with the fighting mace poised for a second blow.

The reaction was automatic, but everything seemed to go into slow motion through the blur of pain that was his shattered left arm. He could not recall the man's name, though for some obscure reason his mind wrestled with the problem. He thought it was Bogdan, the one who had broken young men's necks and then tried to dispose of them by cutting them up and spreading the pieces around the forest. He could hear Chernov's voice quite distinctly—*He's a peasant, but strong and with no moral sense where death is concerned.* And all the time Bond was looking into the man's eyes the mace was rising, very slowly, above his head. Then it started to come down, the big steel-spiked ball—the holy-water sprinkler—hard down toward Bond's skull. His right arm seemed to move very slowly, with the right leg going back, hand grabbing the butt of the Luger in the overall pocket, finger feeling for the safety catch. The spikes hissing through the air, nearer. The Luger sticking, then coming free, and his hand twisting, finger curling, and two sharp explosions—two shots, just as they were all trained—the scent of cordite and the sharp ting as spent cartridge cases clanged against the steps.

Then the slow motion ended, and things moved very fast indeed.

The two bullets lifted Bogdan off his feet, popping his arms into the air as though he was some obscene jack-in-the-box. The fighting iron was thrown back and Bogdan's body—the chest throwing blood toward Bond—bumped against the door of the temple.

At the same moment, the pain shrieked back into Bond's left arm, and with it another sound, a quick double crack and thump. Pieces of stone flew off the pillar near to where he had taken up his firing position. The other Robinson was firing from the square.

Bond doubled up with the pain, retching, vision blurring. As he almost keeled over, he saw the shape of the second Luger on the steps. He forced himself to turn—his gun, with two rounds still in the magazine, clutched in the right hand. As he went, so he found himself losing his balance, reeling like a drunk with shock and agony. A voice seemed to whisper, near to his ear, Get him. Take him out, now. Automatically, he squeezed the trigger, aware that the weapon was up, and his right arm straight. Two shots at a ghost, he thought. Drop the gun. Everything was in reflex and done by numbers. Drop the gun and pick up the other one. He went through the routine, and just as he ducked down another bullet whined over his head. His hand caught the

Luger's butt, and he couldn't straighten up, dropping onto one knee.

Bond raised his head and saw the other man standing over him taking careful aim, saying something in Russian, the Luger huge in Bond's vision.

Then the explosion and what Bond imagined was his own last cry echoed around the pillared entrance to the Temple of the Supreme Emperor of the Dark Heaven.

22

Death of a Double

If you are dead, Bond reasoned, you should not feel pain. His last memory was of the Robinson standing a couple of feet away from him, with the Luger pointing at his head, ready for the coup de grace, then the dull explosion. I saw, I heard, therefore I am dead. But he could sense the waves of nausea and the stunning pain in his left arm. He also knew that he could move, his eyelids were moving. He heard. A voice calling to him—"Mr. Bond? Mr. Bond? You okay, Mr. Bond?"

He allowed his eyes to open fully. The sheer blackness was giving way to the first light of day. He lay on his side and two things swam into vision—the soles of a pair of black trainers and a gray-black hump behind them, which he knew was a body; and the toes of another pair of trainers. He turned his head, eyes traveling upward from the shoes.

"You okay, Mr. Bond?"

From this angle he could not see the face properly; the figure went down on one knee. "Think we should get out of here pretty damn chop-chop."

The dark-haired Chinese boy grinned. "You remember me, Mr. Bond? Richard Han. Swift's man. Good thing I followed you. Mr. Swift say that, if anything happen, you might need much help, never mind. He said you would be here, Cheung Chau Island. Also I should watch your back."

"You killed the Robinson?" Apart from the excruciating pain in his left arm, Bond felt distinctly better.

"That his name? Robinson? Okay, yes, I kill him. You killed man with fighting iron. I shot this one." Han held a very large Colt .45 in his right hand. "It was correct that I kill him?"

"Too damn right it was correct. Hell!" Bond squirmed, shifting his head to squint down at his left wrist. The Rolex said five-fifteen. Forty-five minutes, or near enough, before Chernov would have the others in his killing jar.

Shakily, Bond pulled himself upward, testing his weight gingerly. All seemed well, except for the arm. "Give me that gun—the one on the ground."

Han reached out for the Luger.

"There should be another one." Bond peered into the gray light. His would-be killer's weapon lay to one side of the body. Han picked it up.

"Quickly," Bond urged him. "Take out the magazines and put all cartridges into one. Okay?"

"It's okay. Mr. Swift taught me much about guns. Said I was good shot."

"I agree with him. Look, Han, you know the house to the north of Tung Wan Bay? The house where they kept me?"

"No," the boy said blankly. "Swift say you will be here. I watch your back. So, I come here and nobody seen you. I stick around, then late I see these men behaving like they were looking for butterflies in the dark. Very strange. I think, Richard follow these, they are up to no good."

He would have gone on, but Bond stopped him. "Listen, Han, there is this house . . ." He explained exactly where it was. "Get the police. Tell them it is a security matter . . ."

"Swift give me a police number Hong Kong. He said it was special police."

"Special Branch?"

"Yes. I am stupid. I think first it is some kind of magic root. Then he explain."

"Okay. You can find a telephone on this island?"

"My father's fourth sister lives here. Has small shop with telephone. I shall wake her."

"Ring your number, but tell him to get local police to that house pretty damned fast—chop-chop. Okay."

"They be there very fast. You going?"

Bond took a deep breath. "While I've got the strength I'm going, yes. You get police there. Tell them to hold everyone." Han was already on his way, so Bond had to shout after him, "Tell them the people at the house are armed. They're very dangerous."

"Okay, I tell them, *heya?*" Han turned, one arm raised, and then, in the first light of dawn, the picture in front of Bond turned to one of carnage. Two heavy thumps, and Richard Han's head appeared to burst open, leaving a mist of blood above the body, which continued to run—three . . . four steps—before it hit the ground.

There was the sudden rattle of a machine pistol. Bullets were chipping and smashing into the temple wall around Bond. His reflexes and training came into automatic action. The muzzle flash was from quite near, to his right. Expecting yet another burst of fire any second, Bond wheeled, loosing off two rounds in the direction of the flash. There was a hideous scream, followed by the noise of someone going down: the crash of metal on stone, then a thud and a series of moans.

He dropped onto one knee, waiting, silent and still, head cocked to pick up any other noises, but only the moans continued. Slowly he raised his right hand, more conscious now of the acute pain in his other arm. Gritting his teeth. Listening.

The moaning had stopped, so, once more, Bond rose, taking a pace forward before he was stopped dead in his tracks by another, recognizable voice—"Move one more muscle and I'll blow your head off, Bond. Now drop the gun."

She was very close indeed. To his right.

"I said drop the gun!" Sharp. Commanding.

Bond opened his fingers, and heard the Luger hit the steps just as Heather Dare—originally Irma Wagen—stepped from the shadows.

"So?" Bond breathed, feeling the horror of her deception wash over him.

"Yes. So. I'm sorry, James, but you didn't really think the General was going to take any more chances. You did very well. *I* didn't think you'd be able to get the better of those men. But Chernov was worried. He seemed to sense the possibility."

"Bully for Kolya Chernov." He cursed himself for not having seen through it before. The white raincoat in London—*that* had worried him at the time, for nobody on the run, and with elementary training, would have worn such a garment. Then there was the offer to share her bed—that too had nagged, particularly when he saw her with Smolin, the two lovebirds. "No wonder the General was so well advised of our movements," he said aloud, hoping to bring her closer.

"I led him like a dancer—led you as well, James. Just as I managed to hook Smolin into revealing *his* treachery. We'd better get on with it, I think. My orders are to kill you here, though I hoped the precious Robinsons would have done the job for me."

"How long . . . ?" Bond began.

"Have I been KGB? A long time, James. Early teens. *Cream Cake* was blown from the start. When we all had to get out, the orders were to leave Maxim and Dietrich in place. They could have been taken out at any point, but Center thought London might use me once I was in England. They didn't, as you know, so it was decided to deal with all the others. *You* were a bonus. Chernov came out of safety just for you, James. You find that flattering?"

"Very."

"On your knees, then. We'll do it the Lubyanka way. A bullet in the back of the head."

He took a step forward, as though preparing himself. "And the attempt on your life in London was . . ."

"A small charade to help you trust me. Mischa underestimated you, though. He's very angry. Now he'll be pleased." She took another step closer to him, and Bond shrugged, the pain again angry, tearing at his arm.

"I'll lose my balance if I try to get down. That bastard's smashed my arm badly."

"Then just turn around, slowly." She was calmer than he expected, but she was coming even closer, as though drawn toward his voice.

He started to turn, mind reeling with the odds on him being able to take her with only one arm. Then, as she stepped in, right hand raised holding the pistol high, he moved.

Turn in. Always turn in toward the body but away from the weapon. It was what the experts taught, and if anyone was foolish enough to get that close with a pistol they deserved all they got. He wheeled right, knowing the position was good as he turned, like a ballroom dancer executing a complicated step.

It had to be very fast, and he knew his reactions were slightly impaired by the left arm, but he got it right. Her gun arm remained rigid for just the needed amount of time so that, when he came close to her the arm, and weapon, were to the right of his neck.

He brought his knee up hard. It was never as effective with a woman, but it still caused a lot of pain. He felt the breath go out of her, and could smell her, feel her body close against his.

As Heather doubled from his knee's impact, his right hand came up to grasp at her wrist. Even with one arm, he could execute a lot of force with the downward pull. She gave a little cry as he broke her arm against his knee—the pistol dropping to the ground, bouncing away down the steps.

Bond flicked his knee up again. She was off balance, in pain, and moving downward, so that her spine presented an ideal target. His knee caught her in the small of the back, so hard that he actually heard the spine go. Then she fell away, breath coming in little panting jerks. Though unconscious, she whimpered loudly.

He should have known that Heather was the obvious choice. The one who had taken the most prized target—Maxim Smolin. He should have seen it from the start.

Reaching out for the Luger, Bond did not hesitate. One bullet only. Straight to the lovely head. He felt no qualms about it. Death was sudden, and in a moment it was all over. What little nausea he felt came from the roaring pain in his left arm.

He slowly walked over to where he had hit the other man—the second half of Chernov's backup team. It was one of the two guards. He had hoped it would be Mischa. The man was dead, both bullets having caught him in the chest.

He looked at his watch again, and at the fast-lightening sky. Time was really running out now. He would be lucky to make it.

Taking another deep breath, Bond clenched his teeth. It was going to be one hell of a run, and Lord knew what he could do when he got to the villa. Yet part of the job was done—the traitor found and dealt with. The odds on him saving the others were small, but he *had* to try.

23

Chinese Takeaway

He thought his lungs were going to burst with the effort, for he ran faster than he had since leaving the house with the Robinsons at his heels. The pain in his lungs, combined with the increasing discomfort in his thighs and legs, helped, in a strange way, to take his mind off the agony of his torn and broken arm. Somehow he had managed to take hold of his left hand and secure the arm inside the overall. The good right hand held the Luger and he forced himself on, scuffing the stones and sending up dust from the road that would take him almost to the promontory and the villa.

He did not even try to calculate how much time had passed, but Bond knew he would be cutting it very close. Then, after what seemed an eternity, he crested the rise above the villa, sinking to his knees and sliding back from the skyline. Using his right shoulder as a prop, he pulled himself up to peer at the terracotta roof and that section of the front that was visible.

Only a few yards below were the remains of bodies, broken and strewn as though some willful child had dismembered a couple of dolls—the two Robinsons he had killed in the night.

He caught a movement from the front of the villa. The one guard Heather had left behind—machine pistol at the ready—was crouching near the front wall, circling, watching, and obviously very alert. Chernov must be edgy, Bond thought. They would know of the two Robinsons taken out close to the villa, and the other pair had not returned to report success. There would be itchy fingers down there, though he suspected they would be watching for Heather's return. The odds had been so heavily stacked against Bond that nobody in his right mind would have expected him to live.

Chernov would have Mischa inside with him, to help with the ritual killing.

Slowly and painfully, Bond started to work his way around to the rear of the house—aware of the time bomb that was ticking away inside the place. It must be very near to the moment of execution now.

He edged downward and pulled himself to his feet once more. The back of the house was some fifty yards away, and he covered the ground quickly, loping somewhat lopsidedly as he had done all the way back from the Pak Tai Temple. Odd, he thought, how your sense of balance went with one arm out of action.

By the time he reached the low wall nobody had spotted him.

He moved silently, as though walking on eggs, toward the house. When it happened it came suddenly, with no warning.

The sound echoed from the other side of the

house, the noise he had dreaded from the beginning of his journey back—a terrible, piercing scream—female, but like an animal in dreadful pain. His mind was lanced by a vivid picture of Ebbie having her mouth forced open, with Chernov wielding a scalpel for the obscene punishment. The scream seemed to go on and on, and as it rose in a high, pleading pitch, the guard came round the corner of the house to check the rear.

The man stopped, his jaw dropping open as though he was staring at a ghost. The machine pistol came up but, before the guard could fire, the Luger jumped twice—two bullets crashing into the man's chest, knocking him down like a skittle. As Bond stepped forward, he thought there was movement to his right, for a second and at the edge of his vision, but when he turned, Luger ready, there was nobody there. A trick of the early morning light.

There was a shout from the front of the garden and the sound of running feet, but before anyone could even get to the angle of the wall, Bond was on top of the man he had just killed, wrenching at the machine pistol, identifying it almost by feel alone as an Uzi—the mini, scaled-down version with the stock folded back—and wondering why the KGB were using Israeli weapons.

All this in less than two seconds. Mischa came pounding around the corner as Bond lifted the Uzi, one-handed, giving Chernov's right-hand man a squirt that almost cut him in two.

He fired on the run, and was at the front of the house almost before he knew it, yelling at Chernov, who stood undecided outside the window, unarmed except for a scalpel, his face pale and shocked.

"Drop the cutter and freeze," Bond yelled.

Chernov made one pitiful shrug, then threw the scalpel into the garden, raising his hands, shoulders drooping.

Maxim Smolin, Susanne Dietrich, and Jungle Baisley were still chained together, dumped and wide-eyed in the corner, while Ebbie lay strapped to a wide plank set astride three sawhorses.

"My God, you *really* meant it!" Chernov backed away, for Bond's voice had risen to an uncontrolled, murderous yell. "You bastard, Chernov, you must be crazy."

"Vengeance is not just the prerogative of the gods." Chernov's voice was shaky—but his eyes blazed with a commingling of fury and frustration. "One day, James Bond. One day all the ghosts of the old SMERSH will rise and crush you. That will be vengeance."

Bond rarely felt the true desire to inflict pain, but in that moment he pictured Chernov being hit by the three horrific steel darts from the pen gun in the front pocket of the overalls—one into each eye and one in the throat.

But Chernov had to be taken alive.

"We'll see about vengeance!" Bond started back. Then, nodding: "The keys, General. I want those chains undone."

Chernov hesitated for a second, then his hand moved toward the table, and Bond saw the keys lying there. "Pick them up gently"—under control now—"and unlock them."

Again, Chernov hesitated, his eyes flickering to a point behind Bond's shoulders. No, Bond thought, you don't fall for an old trick like that. "Just do as

I say, Kolya . . ." he began, then the hairs on the nape of his neck prickled and he turned.

"If I were you, Jacko, I'd simply be putting your gun down on the table very carefully." Norman Murray faced him, having come quietly in through the door, his police-issue Walther PPK steady in his right hand.

"What—?" Bond could hardly credit it.

"Kolya," Murray said calmly. "I'd leave the keys where they are. Whatever vengeance you're wanting'll have to wait, because I've a feeling we're going to get some visitors up here soon enough. I'm sorry that I'm so late, but it was a bit of a teaser, avoiding my own people and the Brits. Not an easy job."

Chernov made a tchah-ing sound.

"Well, when it comes to us getting out safely, we'll have to use your man, Bond, as collateral, will we not?"

Bond backed away. "Norman? What in God's name—?"

"Ah, Jacko, the evils of this wicked world. You recall that lovely book of Robert Louis Stevenson—*Treasure Island*? Grand book, that. You remember the bit where young Jim Hawkins meets the castaway, Benn Gunn was his name? Well, auld Benn Gunn tries to explain to Jim how he got started on his iniquitous life of piracy. He says, 'It begun with chuck-farthen on the blessed gravestones'—playing what we'd be after calling shove-ha'penny on the gravestones. Well, I suppose it was like that for me—now will you put that cannon on the table, Jacko Bond."

Bond turned his back carefully, placing the Luger near to the keys.

"Now, hands *on* your head, Jacko."

"I've got a broken arm."

"Well, *hand* on your head then. You're a pedantic divil, Jacko."

By the time Bond turned again, slowly raising his right hand, he had slipped the pen from the breast pocket of the overalls, covering it with his right palm. Two traitors, he thought, not just one but two—and the second one an officer of the Republic of Ireland's Special Branch. A man who had a special, secret relationship with the British Service over matters of intelligence, even cooperated with M himself.

"Good," Murray continued. "As I was saying, Jacko. It started by playing shove-ha'penny on the gravestones for me, after a fashion; only, my game was the horses. The auld, auld joke—slow horses and fast women. The debts and the lady who, one night in Dublin, had me compromised and trussed neat as a turkey at Christmas. I just want you to know it wasn't a political thing with me—more a matter of money."

"Money?" Bond sounded disgusted at the thought. "Money? Then why bother to rescue me from Chernov?"

"Now, that was a bit of cover. None of us ever think we'll blow our cover, do we, Jacko? And I was playing it three ways—my own people, you Brits, and these fellas. I'm a treble, really, Jacko, and I didn't know the cover had gone until I got you to Dublin airport. So, that's water under the bridge now."

"It doesn't matter, Norm—and don't tell me not

to call you Norm again, because you're Comrade Norm now."

"I suppose you're right. I don't know how I'm goin' to like it in yon country, it's goin' to be awful cold there, so it is. But, you see, Jacko, they're most of them on to me now. Your man, M's on to me for sure, so I'm getting a lift out with Kolya here." He turned toward Chernov—"And don't you think we should be getting a move on, Kolya? The porpoises must be close behind me now. Treading on my tail, so they were when I left Dublin."

Chernov nodded gravely. "We go as soon as the business is completed here."

During the momentary distraction, Bond used the first finger and thumb of his right hand to twist the two sections of the pen counterclockwise, then turn it so the weapon faced forward, his thumb moving to the back, where the push trigger was located. "Norman!" he called, swiveling his body so that he was aligned with Murray's head. He pressed the trigger twice, in quick succession. "Sorry, Norman," as the two steel darts left tiny red pinpoint holes in the Special Branch man's head, just above the eyes.

"Jacko!"

The word came as a reflex, for Murray must have been dead as he spoke, pitching forward, the gun dropping from his hand at the same moment as Bond reached out and retrieved the Luger from the table. Now it was done. Those who might cause scandal were dead. Chernov would be a coup. All that needed to be done was the tidying up, and some plausible explanations to the press.

"Now, Kolya Chernov." James Bond's voice was not as steady as it might have been, for he had liked Murray, yet his part in the business also explained many things—both past and present. "The keys. Just unlock these good people." He looked at Ebbie. "When you're free, go to the phone, darling, and dial the number I tell you. It's my own department's Resident here in Hong Kong. You'll have to cover the General here, while I do some very fast talking. We have to go official on this."

Chernov began to unlock the shackles, and Ebbie went to the telephone. The conversation took three minutes, during which the others were freed—Jungle and Smolin using their initiative and securing Chernov with the chains. He seemed cowed now, as though all the fight had gone out of him.

Bond put down the telephone, resting his good hand on the table. There was a light touch on his shoulder, the hand sliding down to lie on top of his own.

"Thank you," Ebbie said, her voice breaking. "James, I have to thank you so much."

"It was nothing," he replied.

The pain returned, the dizziness took over, and his legs buckled under him. In a far corner of his mind he welcomed the oblivion.

James Bond became conscious in a private hospital room. The Service Resident was by his bedside, and it did not take Bond long to realize that his left arm was encased in plaster.

"It's broken in two places, and there are some torn muscles." The Resident was well known to Bond.

They had worked together, once in Switzerland, and again in Berlin.

"Apart from that"—Bond smiled—"how did you enjoy the play, Mrs. Lincoln?" It was a very old joke they had shared in the past.

"M sends congratulations, together with some harsh words about you allowing that girl to travel here with you."

Bond closed his eyes, feeling very tired. "Girls like Ebbie are not easy to stop. Don't worry, it wasn't my only mistake."

"He wants you back in London. The doctors say you can leave the hospital tomorrow, but they also say you're to stay here for a couple of weeks. Reluctantly our Chief has said okay. The quacks just wish to keep an eye on the arm, if you follow me."

"The others?" Bond asked.

"Everything's tidied up. No mess. No questions. Chernov was flown to London this afternoon. You've been out for the best part of a day, incidentally."

"Open him up." Bond's mouth turned down, betraying his innate cruel streak.

"We're denying all knowledge at the moment. Our people'll put him through the mill before we go public—if we ever do. Ms. Dietrich, young Baisley, and Maxim have gone as well. Smolin's no use in the field anymore, but they'll find plenty for him to do on the Eastern Bloc desk at Headquarters. You just rest now, James. You've wrapped up the last crumbs of *Cream Cake,* and all's well with the world."

"Ebbie?"

"I have a surprise for you."

The Resident winked and left the room. A minute

later, Ebbie Heritage came in. She stood looking at him, then approached the bed.

"I put my feet down." Her face broke into a smile. "I put my feet down and said I would take care of you. My surprise was great. They told me yes, okay. We are very grand, James. We even have bodyguards until you're well enough to travel."

"I guess I might need one." He smiled and she laid the palm of her hand on his brow.

"That feels very nice." Bond's arm might be damaged, but he knew other parts of his body were in working order. "Your hand's so cool."

"There is old Chinese saying." She looked at him. Butter would not have even softened on her lips. "Woman with cool palm has fire under skirt."

"Never heard that." Bond's eyes twinkled.

"Really?"

"Never."

"It's a true saying. I know, because an elderly Japanese gentleman once told me."

In spite of the plaster cast, they spent a very active couple of weeks together, staying at The Mandarin, and eventually leaving by Cathay Pacific.

As the carpet of lights that was Hong Kong disappeared from sight, the jolly female Cathay purser came over to introduce herself. "Mr. Bond? Ms. Heritage? Welcome aboard." She had a broad grin and infectious laugh. "You have had a good time in Hong Kong?"

"Wonderful," said Ebbie.

"Full of surprises," Bond added.

"Holiday?" the purser asked.

"A sort of working holiday."

"So now you return to London." The purser gave

what was almost a guffaw of laughter. "This route has a special name in Cathay Pacific, you know."

"Really?" Ebbie sipped her champagne.

"Yes. We call this route from Hong Kong, Chinese Takeaway, ha!"

Ebbie giggled, and Bond gave a wry smile. "No doubt we'll be back," he said. "One day we'll be back."